TWO OUT OF THREE AIN'T BAD . . .

Something very large occluded the light for a moment in the next room, then the lights went out, and Diana Tregarde distinctly heard the sound of the chandelier being torn from the ceiling and thrown against the wall. She winced.

There go my Romance Writers of the World dues up again, she thought.

"I got a glimpse," Andre said. "It was very large, perhaps ten feet tall, and—*cherie*, looked like nothing so much as a rubber creature from a very bad movie. Except that I do not think it was rubber."

What shambled in through the door was nothing that Diana had ever heard of. It was, indeed, about ten feet tall. It was covered with luxuriant brown hair—all over. It was built along the lines of a powerful body-builder, taken to exaggerated lengths, and it drooled. It also stank, a combination of sulfur and musk so strong it would have brought tears to the eyes of a skunk.

Di groaned, putting two and two together and coming up with—*Valentine Vervain cast a spell for a tall, dark and handsome soul-mate, but she forgot to specify "human."* "Are you thinking what I'm thinking?"

The other writer nodded. "Tall, check. Dark, check. Long hair, check. Handsome—well, I suppose in some circles." Harrison stared at the thing in fascination.

The thing saw Valentine and lunged for her. Reflexively, Di and Harrison both shot. He emptied his cylinder and one speed loader. Di gave up after four shots. No effect. The thing backhanded Andre into a wall hard enough to put him through plasterboard. Andre was out for the count. There are some things even a vampire has a little trouble recovering from.

"Harrison, distract it, make a noise, anything!" Diana pulled the atheme from her boot sheath and began cutting Sigils in the air with it, getting the Words of Dismissal out as fast as she could without slurring the syllables.

The thing lunged toward Harrison, missing him by inches, just as Di concluded the Ritual of Dismissal.

To no effect. . . .

—from "Satanic, Versus ..."

BARDIC VOICES

The Lark & the Wren
The Robin & the Kestrel
The Eagle & the Nighingales
The Free Bards (omnibus)
Four & Twenty Blackbirds
Bardic Choices:
A Cast of Corbies
(with Josepha Sherman)

The Fire Rose
Fiddler Fair
Werehunter
The Ship Who Searched
(with Anne McCaffrey)
Wing Commander: Freedom Flight
(with Ellen Guon)
Lammas Night
(ed. by Jospeha Sherman)

URBAN FANTASIES

Bedlam's Bard (omnibus with Ellen Guon)
Beyond World's End (with Rosemary Edghill)
Spirits White as Lightning (with Rosemary Edghill)
Mad Maudlin (with Rosemary Edghill)
Music to My Sorrow (with Rosemary Edghill)
This Scepter'd Isle (with Roberta Gellis)
Ill Met by Moonlight (with Roberta Gellis)
By Slanderous Tongues (with Roberta Gellis)

THE SERRAted EDGE

Chrome Circle (with Larry Dixon)
The Chrome Borne (with Larry Dixon)
The Otherworld (omnibus with Mark Shepard & Holly Lisle)

THE BARD'S TALE NOVELS

Castle of Deception (with Josepha Sherman)
Fortress of Front & Fire (with Ru Emerson)
Prison of Souls (with Mark Shepard)

The Shadow of the Lion (with Eric Flint & Dave Freer)
This Rough Magic (with Eric Flint & Dave Freer)

The Wizard of Karres (with Eric Flint & Dave Freer)

WEREHUNTER

MERCEDES LACKEY

BAEN

WEREHUNTER

A Baen Books Original

Baen Publishing Enterprises
P.O. Box 1403
Riverdale, NY 10471
www.baen.com

ISBN: 0-671-57805-7
ISBN 13: 978-0-671-57805-3

Cover art by Bob Eggleton

First printing, April 1999
Third printing, April 2007

Distributed by Simon & Schuster
1230 Avenue of the Americas
New York, NY 10020

Typeset by Windhaven Press (www.windhaven.com)
Printed in the United States of America.

Contents

Introduction

Those of you who are more interested in the stories than in some chatty author stuff should just skip this part, since it will be mostly about the things people used to ask us about at science fiction conventions.

For those of you who have never heard of SF conventions (or "cons" as they are usually called), these are gatherings of people who are quite fanatical about their interest in one or more of the various fantasy and science fiction media. There are talks and panel discussions on such wildly disparate topics as costuming, propmaking, themes in SF/F literature, *Star Wars*, *Star Trek*, *Babylon 5*, *X-Files*, SF/F art, medieval fighting, horsetraining, dancing, and the world of fans in general. There are workshops on writing and performance arts. Guests featured in panels and question and answer sessions are often featured performers from television and movies along with various authors and the occasional professional propmaker. Larry and I no longer attend conventions for a number of reasons, not the least of which is that we have a great many responsibilities that require us to be home.

Some of those responsibilities are that we are volunteers for our local fire department. Larry is a driver and outside man; I am learning to do dispatch, and hopefully will be able to take over the night shift, since we are awake long after most of the rest of the county has gone to sleep. Our local department is strictly volunteer and works on a very tight budget. Our equipment is old and needs frequent repair, we get what we can afford, and what we can afford is generally third or fourth-hand, having passed through a large metropolitan department or the military to a small municipal department to the Forestry Service and finally to us. In summer I am a water-carrier at grass-fires, meaning that I bring drinking-water to the overheated firefighters so they don't collapse in the 100 plus degree heat.

Another duty is with the EOC (formerly called the Civil Defense Office). When we are under severe weather conditions, the firefighters are called in to wait at the station in case of emergency, so Larry is there. I go in to the EOC office to read weather-radar for the storm-watchers in the field. Eventually I hope to get my radio license so I can also join the ranks of the storm-watchers. We don't "chase" as such, although there are so few of the storm-watchers that they may move to active areas rather than staying put. Doppler radar can only give an indication of where there is rotation in the clouds; rotation may not produce a tornado. You have to have people on the ground in the area to know if there is a funnel or a tornado (technically, it isn't a tornado until it touches the ground; until then it is a funnel-cloud). Our area of Oklahoma is not quite as active as the area of the Panhandle or around Oklahoma City and Norman (which is why the National Severe Storms Laboratory is located there) but we get plenty of severe, tornado-producing storms.

In addition, we have our raptor rehabilitation duties.

Larry and I are raptor rehabilitators; this means that we are licensed by both the state and the federal government to collect, care for, and release birds of prey that are injured or ill. Occasionally we are asked to bring one of our "patients" for a talk to a group of adults or children, often under the auspices of our local game wardens.

I'm sure this sounds very exciting and glamorous, and it certainly impresses the heck out of people when we bring in a big hawk riding on a gloved hand, but there are times when I wonder how we managed to get ourselves into this.

We have three main "seasons"—baby season, stupid fledgling season, and inexpert hunter season.

Now, injuries—and victims of idiots with guns—can come at any time. We haven't had too many shooting victims in our area, thank heavens, in part because the cattle-farmers around our area know that shooting a raptor only adds field rats and mice to their property. But another rehabber gave up entirely a few years ago, completely burned out, because she got the same redtail hawk back *three times*, shot out of the sky. Injuries that we see in our area are most often the case of collision—literally—with man's environmental changes. Birds hit windows that seem to them to be sky, Great Blue Herons collide with power-lines, raptors get electrocuted by those same lines. But most often, we get birds hit by cars. Owls will chase prey across the road, oblivious to the fact that something is approaching, and get hit. Raptors are creatures of opportunity and will quite readily come down to feed on roadkill and get hit. Great Horned Owls, often called the "tigers of the sky," are top predators, known to chase even eagles off nests to claim the nest for themselves—if a Great Horned is eating roadkill and sees a car approaching, it will stand its ground, certain that it will get the better of anything daring to try to snatch its dinner! After all, they have been developing and evolving for millions of years, and swiftly moving vehicles have only been around for about seventy-five years; they haven't had nearly enough time to adapt to the situation as a species. Individuals *do* learn, though, often to take advantage of the situation.

Kestrels and redtails are known to hang around fields being harvested to snatch the field-rats running from the machinery, or suddenly exposed after the harvesters have passed. Redtails are also known to hang about railway right-of-ways, waiting for trains to spook out rabbits!

Our current education bird, a big female redtail we call Cinnamon, is one such victim; struck in the head by a CB whip-antenna, she has only one working eye and just enough brain damage to render her partially paralyzed on one side and make her accepting and calm in our presence. This makes her a great education-bird, as nothing alarms her and children can safely touch her, giving them a new connection with wild things that they had never experienced before.

But back to the three "seasons" of a raptor rehabber, and the different kinds of work they involve.

First is "baby season," which actually extends from late February through to July, beginning with Great Horned Owl babies and ending when the second round of American Kestrels (sparrowhawks, or "spawks" as falconers affectionately call them) begins to push their siblings out of nests. The first rule of baby season is—try to get the baby back into the nest, or something like the nest. Mother birds are infinitely better at taking care of their youngsters than any human, so when wind or weather send babies (eyases, is the correct term) tumbling, that is our first priority. This almost always involves climbing, which means that poor Larry puts on his climbing gear and dangles from trees. When nest and all have come down, we supply a substitute, in as close to the same place as possible; raptor mothers are far more fixated on the kids than the house, and a box filled with branches will do nicely, thank you.

Sometimes, though, it's not possible to put the eyases back. Youngsters are found with no nest in sight, or the nest is literally unreachable (a Barn Owl roost in the roof of an institution for the criminally insane, for instance), or worst of all, the parents are known to be dead.

Young raptors eat a lot. Kestrels need feeding every hour or so, bigger birds every two to three, and that's from dawn to dusk. We've taken eyases with us to doctor's appointments, on vacation, on shopping expeditions, and even to racing school! And we're not talking Gerber's here; "mom" (us) gets to take the mousie, dissect the mousie, and feed the mousie parts to baby. By hand. Yummy! Barred Owl eyases are the easiest of the lot; they'll take minnows, which are of a size to slip down their little throats easily, but not the rest. There's no use thinking you can get by with a little chicken, either—growing babies need a lot of calcium for those wonderful hollow bones that they're growing so fast, so they need the whole animal.

Fortunately, babies do grow up, and eventually they'll feed themselves. Then it's just a matter of helping them learn to fly (which involves a little game we call "Hawk Tossing") and teaching them to hunt. The instincts are there; they just need to connect instinct with practice. But this is *not* for the squeamish or the tender-hearted; for the youngsters to grow up and have the skills to make them successful, they have to learn to kill.

The second season can stretch from late April to August, and we call it "silly fledgling season." That's when the eyases, having learned to fly at last, get lost. Raptor mothers—with the exception of Barn Owls—continue to feed the youngsters and teach them to hunt after they've fledged, but sometimes wind and weather again carry the kids off beyond finding their way back to mom. Being inexperienced flyers and not hunters at all yet, they usually end up helpless on the ground, which is where we come in.

These guys are actually the easiest and most rewarding; they know the basics of flying and hunting, and all we have to do is put some meat back on their bones and give them a bit more experience. We usually have anywhere from six to two dozen kestrels at this stage every year, which is when *we* get a fair amount of exercise, catching grasshoppers for them to hunt.

Then comes the "inexpert hunter" season, and I'm not referring to the ones with guns. Some raptors are the victims of a bad winter, or the fact that they concentrated on those easy-to-kill grasshoppers while their siblings had graduated to more difficult prey. Along about December, we start to get the ones that nothing much is wrong with except starvation. Sometimes starvation has gone too far for them to make it; frustrating and disappointing for us.

We've gotten all sorts of birds over the years; our wonderful vet, Dr. Paul Welch (on whom may blessings be heaped!) treats wildlife for free, and knows that we're always suckers for a challenge, so he has gotten some of the odder things to us. We've had two Great Blue Herons, for instance. One was an adult that had collided with a powerline. It had a dreadful fracture, and we weren't certain if it would be able to fly again (it did) but since we have a pond, we figured we could support a land-bound heron. In our ignorance, we had no idea that Great Blues are terrible challenges to keep alive because they are so shy; we just waded right in, force-feeding it minnows when it refused to eat, and stuffing the minnows right back down when it tossed them up. This may not sound so difficult, but remember that a Great Blue has a two-foot sword on the end of its head, a spring-loaded neck to put some force behind the stab, and the beak-eye coordination to impale a minnow in a foot of water. It has *no* trouble targeting your eye.

We fed it wearing welding-masks.

We believe very strongly in force-feeding; our experience has been that if you force-feed a bird for two to three days, it gives up trying to die of starvation and begins eating on its own. Once again, mind you, this is not always an easy proposition; we're usually dealing with fully adult birds who want nothing whatsoever to do with us, and have the equipment to enforce their preferences. We very seldom get a bird that is so injured that it gives us no resistance. Great Horned Owls can exert pressure of 400 ft/lbs per talon, which can easily penetrate a Kevlar-lined welding glove, as I know personally and painfully.

That is yet another aspect of rehabbing that most people don't think about—injury. Yours, not the bird's. We've been "footed" (stabbed with talons), bitten, pooped on (okay, so that's not an injury, but it's not pleasant), gouged, and beak-slashed. And we have to stand there and continue doing whatever it was that earned us those injuries, because it certainly isn't the *bird's* fault that he doesn't recognize the fact that you're trying to help him.

We also have to know when we're out of our depth, or when the injury is *so* bad that the bird isn't releasable, and do the kind and responsible thing. Unless a bird is *so* endangered that it can go into a captive breeding project, or is the rare, calm, quiet case like Cinnamon who will be a perfect education bird, there is no point in keeping one that can't fly or hunt again. You learn how to let go and move on very quickly, and just put your energy into the next one.

On the other hand, we have personal experience that raptors are a great deal tougher than it might appear. We've successfully released one-eyed hawks, who learn to compensate for their lack of binocular vision very well. Birds with one "bad" leg learn to strike only with the good one. One-eyed owls are routine for us now; owls mostly hunt by sound anyway and don't actually need both eyes. But the most amazing is that another rehabber in our area has routinely gotten successful releases with owls that are minus a wingtip; evidently owls are such strong fliers that they don't need their entire wingspan to prosper, and *that* is quite amazing and heartening.

We've learned other things, too; one of the oddest is that owls by-and-large don't show gradual recovery from head-injuries. They will go on, day after day, with nothing changing—then, suddenly, one morning you have an owl fighting to get out of the box you've put him in to keep him quiet and contained! We've learned that once birds learn to hunt, they prefer fresh-caught dinner to the frozen stuff we offer; we haven't had a single freeloader keep coming back long after he should be independent. We've learned that "our" birds learn quickly not to generalize about humans feeding them—once they are free-flying (but still supplementing their hunting with handouts) they don't bother begging for food from anyone but those who give them the proper "come'n'get it" signal, and even then they are unlikely to get close to anyone they don't actually recognize.

We already knew that eyases in the "downy" stage, when their juvenile plumage hasn't come in and they look like little white puffballs, will imprint very easily, so we quickly turn potentially dangerous babies (like Great Horned Owls) over to rehabbers who have "foster moms"—non-releasable birds of the right species who will at least provide the right role-model for the youngsters. Tempting as the little things are, so fuzzy and big-eyed, none of us wants an imprinted Great Horned coming back in four or five years when sexual maturity hits, looking for love in all the wrong places! Remember those talons?

For us, though, all the work is worth the moment of release, when we take the bird that couldn't fly, or the now-grown-up and self-sufficient baby, and turn him loose. For some, we just open the cage door and step back; for others, there's a slow process called "hacking out," where the adolescent comes back for food until he's hunting completely on his own. In either case, we've performed a little surgery on the fragile ecosystem, and it's a good feeling to see the patient thriving.

Those who have caught the raptor-bug seem like

family; we associate with both rehabber and falconers. If you are interested in falconry—and bear in mind, it is an extremely labor-intensive hobby—contact your local Fish and Wildlife department for a list of local falconers, and see if you can find one willing to take you as an apprentice. If you want to get into rehab, contact Fish and Wildlife for other rehabbers who are generally quite happy to help you get started.

Here are some basic facts about birds of prey. Faloners call the young in the nest an eyas; rehabbers and falconers call the very small ones, covered only in fluff, "downies." In the downy stage, they are very susceptible to imprinting; if we have to see babies we would rather they were at least in the second stage, when the body-feathers start to come in. That is the only time that the feathers are not molted; the down feathers are actually attached to the juvenile feathers, and have to be picked off, either by the parent or the youngster. Body-feathers come in first, and when they are about half-grown, the adults can stop brooding the babies, for they can retain their body-heat on their own, and more importantly, the juvenile feathers have a limited ability to shed water, which the down will not do. If a rainstorm starts, for instance, the downies will be wet through quickly before a parent can return to the nest to cover them, they'll be hypothermic in seconds and might die; babies in juvenile plumage are safe until a parent gets back to cover them.

When eyases never fight in the nest over food this means both that their environmeent provides a wealth of prey and that their parents are excellent hunters. If they are hungry, the youngest of the eyases often dies or is pushed out of the nest to die.

Redtails can have up to four offspring; two is usual. Although it is rare, they have been known to double-clutch if a summer is exceptionally long and warm. They may also double-clutch if the first batch is infertile.

Redtails in captivity can live up to twenty-five years;

half that is usual in the wild. They can breed at four years old, though they have been known to breed as young as two. In their first year they do not have red tails and their body-plumage is more mottled than in older birds; this is called "juvenile plumage" and is a signal to older birds that these youngsters are no threat to them. Kestrels do not have juvenile plumage, nor do most owls, and eagles hold their juvenile plumage for four years. Kestrels live about five years in the wild, up to fifteen in captivity, eagles live fifty years in captivity and up to twenty-five in the wild.

Should you find an injured bird of prey, you need three things for a rescue: a heavy blanket or jacket, cohesive bandage (the kind of athletic wrap that sticks to itself), and a heavy, dark-colored sock. Throw the blanket over the victim, locate and free the head and pull the sock over it. Locate the feet, and wrap the feet together with the bandage; keep hold of the feet, remove the blanket, get the wings folded in the "resting" position and wrap the body in cohesive bandage to hold the wings in place. Make a ring of a towel in the bottom of a cardboard box just big enough to hold the bird, and put the bird in the box as if it was sitting in a nest. Take the sock off and quickly close up the box and get the victim to a rehabber, a local game warden or Fish and Wildlife official, or a vet that treats injured wildlife. Diurnal raptors are very dependent on their sight; take it away and they "shut down"—which is the reason behind the traditional falcon-hood. By putting the sock over the head, you take away the chief source of stress, the sight of enormous two-legged predators bearing down on it.

Andre Norton, who (as by now you must be aware) I have admired for ages, was doing a "Friends of the Witch World" anthology, and asked me if I would mind doing a story for her.

Would I mind? *I flashed back to when I was thirteen or fourteen years old, and I read* Witch World *and fell completely and totally into this wonderful new cosmos. I had already been a fan of Andre's since I was nine or ten and my father (who was a science fiction reader) loaned me* Beast Master *because it had a horse in it and I was horse-mad. But this was something different, science fiction that didn't involve thud and blunder and iron-thewed barbarians. I was in love.*

Oh—back in "the old days" it was all called "science fiction." There was no category for "fantasy," and as for "hard s/f," "sword and sorcery," "urban fantasy," "high fantasy," "cyberpunk," "horror," "space-opera"—none of those categories existed. You'd find Clark Ashton Smith right next to E. E. "Doc" Smith, and Andre Norton and Fritz Leiber wrote gothic horror, high fantasy, and science fiction all without anyone wondering what to call it. Readers of imaginative literature read everything, *and neither readers nor writers were compelled by marketing considerations to read or write in only a single category.*

At any rate, many years later, my idol Andre Norton asked me for a story set in one of my favorite science-fiction worlds. Somehow I managed to tell Andre that I would be very happy to write a story. This is it. In fact, this is the longer version; she asked me to cut some, not because she didn't like it the way it was, but because she was only allowed stories of 5,000 words or less; here it is as I originally wrote it.

Werehunter

It had been raining all day, a cold, dismal rain that penetrated through clothing and chilled the heart to numbness. Glenda trudged through it, sneakers soaked; beneath her cheap plastic raincoat her jeans were soggy to the knees. It was several hours past sunset now, and still raining, and the city streets were deserted by all but the most hardy, the most desperate, and the faded few with nothing to lose.

Glenda was numbered among those last. This morning she'd spent her last change getting a bus to the welfare office, only to be told that she hadn't been a resident long enough to qualify for aid. That wasn't true—but she couldn't have known that. The supercilious clerk had taken in her age and inexperience at a glance, and assumed "student." If he had begun processing her, he'd have been late for lunch. He guessed she wouldn't know enough to contradict him, and he'd been right. And years of her aunt's browbeating ("Isn't one 'no' good enough for you?") had drummed into her the lesson that there were no second chances. He'd gone off to his lunch date; she'd trudged back home in the rain. This afternoon she'd eaten the last packet of cheese and crackers and had made "soup" from the stolen packages of fast-food ketchup—there was nothing left in her larder that even resembled food. Hunger had been with her for so long now that the ache in her stomach had become as much a part of her as her hands or feet. There were three days left in the month; three days of shelter, then she'd be kicked out of her shoddy efficiency and into the street.

When her Social Security orphan's benefits had run out when she'd turned eighteen, her aunt had "suggested" she find a job and support herself—elsewhere. The suggestion had come in the form of finding her belongings in boxes on the front porch with a letter to that effect on top of them.

So she'd tried, moving across town to this place, near the university; a marginal neighborhood surrounded by bad blocks on three sides. But there were no jobs if you had no experience—but how did you get experience without a job? The only experience she'd ever had was at shoveling snow, raking leaves, mowing and gardening; the only ways she could earn money for college, since her aunt had never let her apply for a job that would have been beyond walking distance of her house. Besides that, there were at least forty university students competing with her for every job that opened up anywhere around here. Her meager savings (meant, at one time, to pay for college tuition) were soon gone.

She rubbed the ring on her left hand, a gesture she was completely unaware of. That ring was all she had of the mother her aunt would never discuss—the woman her brother had married over her own strong disapproval. It was silver, and heavy; made in the shape of a crouching cat with tiny glints of topaz for eyes. Much as she treasured it, she would gladly have sold it—but she couldn't get it off her finger, she'd worn it for so long.

She splashed through the puddles, peering listlessly out from under the hood of her raincoat. Her lank, mouse-brown hair straggled into her eyes as she squinted against the glare of headlights on rain-glazed pavement. Despair had driven her into the street; despair kept her here. It was easier to keep the tears and hysterics at bay out here, where the cold numbed mind as well as body, and the rain washed all her thoughts until they were thin and lifeless. She could see no way out of this trap—except maybe by killing herself.

But her body had other ideas. *It* wanted to survive, even if Glenda wasn't sure *she* did.

A chill of fear trickled down her backbone like a drop of icy rain, driving all thoughts of suicide from her, as behind her she recognized the sounds of footsteps.

She didn't have to turn around to know she was being followed, and by more than one. On a night like tonight, there was no one on the street but the fools and the hunters. She knew which she was.

It wasn't much of an alley—a crack between buildings, scarcely wide enough for her to pass. *They* might not know it was there—even if they did, they couldn't know what lay at the end of it. She did. She dodged inside, feeling her way along the narrow defile, until one of the two buildings gave way to a seven-foot privacy fence.

She came to the apparent dead-end, building on the right, a high board fence on the left, building in front. She listened, stretching her ears for sounds behind her, taut with fear. Nothing; they had either passed this place by, or hadn't yet reached it.

Quickly, before they could find the entrance, she ran her hand along the boards of the fence, counting them from the dead-end. Four, five—when she touched the sixth one, she gave it a shove sideways, getting a handful of splinters for her pains. But the board moved, pivoting on the one nail that held it, and she squeezed through the gap into the yard beyond, pulling the board back in place behind her.

Just in time; echoing off the stone and brick of the

alley were harsh young male voices. She leaned against the fence and shook from head to toe, clenching her teeth to keep them from chattering, as they searched the alley, found nothing, and finally (after hours, it seemed) went away.

"Well, you've got yourself in a fine mess," she said dully. "Now what? You don't dare leave, not yet—they might have left someone in the street, watching. Idiot! Home may not be much, but it's dry, and there's a bed. Fool, fool, fool! So now you get to spend the rest of the night in the back yard of a spookhouse. You'd just better hope the spook isn't home."

She peered through the dark at the shapeless bulk of the tri-story townhouse, relic of a previous century, hoping *not* to see any signs of life. The place had an uncanny reputation; even the gangs left it alone. People had vanished here—some of them important people, with good reasons to want to disappear, some who had been uninvited visitors. But the police had been over the house and grounds more than once, and never found anything. No bodies were buried in the back yard—the ground was as hard as cement under the inch-deep layer of soft sand that covered it. There was nothing at all in the yard but the sand and the rocks; the crazy woman that lived here told the police it was a "Zen garden." But when Glenda had first peeked through the boards at the back yard, it didn't look like any Zen garden *she* had ever read about. The sand wasn't groomed into wave-patterns, and the rocks looked more like something out of a mini-Stonehenge than islands or mountain-peaks.

There were four of those rocks—one like a garden bench, that stood before three that formed a primitive arch. Glenda felt her way towards them in the dark, trusting to the memory of how the place had looked by daylight to find them. She barked her shin painfully on the "bench" rock, and her legs gave out, so that she sprawled ungracefully over it. Tears of pain mingled with the rain, and she swore under her breath.

She sat huddled on the top of it in the dark, trying to remember what time it was the last time she'd seen a clock. Dawn couldn't be too far off. When dawn came, and there were more people in the street, she could probably get safely back to her apartment.

For all the good it would do her.

Her stomach cramped with hunger, and despair clamped down on her again. She shouldn't have run—she was only delaying the inevitable. In two days she'd be out on the street, and this time with nowhere to hide, easy prey for them, or those like them.

"So wouldn't you like to escape altogether?"

The soft voice out of the darkness nearly caused Glenda's heart to stop. She jumped, and clenched the side of the bench-rock as the voice laughed. Oddly enough, the laughter seemed to make her fright wash out of her. There was nothing malicious about it—it was kind-sounding, gentle. Not crazy.

"Oh, I like to make people think I'm crazy; they leave me alone that way." The speaker was a dim shape against the lighter background of the fence.

"Who—"

"I am the keeper of this house—and this place; not the first, certainly not the last. So there is nothing in this city—in this world—to hold you here anymore?"

"How—did you know *that*?" Glenda tried to see the speaker in the dim light reflected off the clouds, to see if it really was the woman that lived in the house, but there were no details to be seen, just a human-shaped outline. Her eyes blurred. Reaction to her narrow escape, the cold, hunger; all three were conspiring to make her light-headed.

"The only ones who come to me are those who have no will to live *here*, yet who still have the will to live. Tell me, if another world opened before you, would you walk into it, not knowing what it held?"

This whole conversation was so surreal, Glenda began

to think she was hallucinating the whole thing. Well, if it was a hallucination, why not go along with it?

"Sure, why not? It couldn't be any worse than here. It might be better."

"Then turn, and look behind you—and choose."

Glenda hesitated, then swung her legs over the bench-stone. The sky was lighter in that direction—dawn was breaking. Before her loomed the stone arch—

Now she *knew* she was hallucinating—for framed within the arch was no shadowy glimpse of board fence and rain-soaked sand, but a patch of reddening sky, and another dawn—

A dawn that broke over rolling hills covered with waving grass, grass stirred by a breeze that carried the scent of flowers, not the exhaust-tainted air of the city.

Glenda stood, unaware that she had done so. She reached forward with one hand, yearningly. The place seemed to call to something buried deep in her heart—and she wanted to answer.

"Here—or there? Choose now, child."

With an inarticulate cry, she stumbled toward the stones—

And found herself standing alone on a grassy hill.

After several hours of walking in wet, soggy tennis shoes, growing more spacey by the minute from hunger, she was beginning to think she'd made a mistake. Somewhere back behind her she'd lost her raincoat; she couldn't remember when she'd taken it off. There was no sign of people anywhere—there were animals; even sheep, once, but nothing like "civilization." It was frustrating, maddening; there was food all around her, on four feet, on wings—surely even some of the plants were edible—but it was totally inaccessible to a city-bred girl who'd never gotten food from anywhere but a grocery or restaurant. She might just as well be on the moon.

Just as she thought that, she topped another rise to find herself looking at a strange, weatherbeaten man standing beside a rough pounded-dirt road.

She blinked in dumb amazement. He looked like something out of a movie, a peasant from a King Arthur epic. He was stocky, blond-haired; he wore a shabby brown tunic and patched, shapeless trousers tucked into equally patched boots. He was also holding a strung bow, with an arrow nocked to it, and frowning—a most unfriendly expression.

He gabbled something at her. She blinked again. She knew a little Spanish (you had to, in her neighborhood); she'd taken German and French in high school. This didn't sound like any of those.

He repeated himself, a distinct edge to his voice. To emphasize his words, he jerked the point of the arrow off back the way she had come. It was pretty obvious he was telling her to be on her way.

"No, wait—please—" she stepped toward him, her hands outstretched pleadingly. The only reaction she got was that he raised the arrow to point at her chest, and drew it back.

"Look—I haven't got any weapons! I'm lost, I'm *hungry*—"

He drew the arrow a bit farther.

Suddenly it was all too much. She'd spent all her life being pushed and pushed—first her aunt, then at school, then out on the streets. This was the last time *anybody* was going to back her into a corner—this time she was going to fight!

A white-hot rage like nothing she'd ever experienced before in her life took over.

"Damn you!" she was so angry she could hardly think. "You stupid clod! I *need help*!" she screamed at him, as red flashes interfered with her vision, her ears began to buzz, and her hands crooked into involuntary claws, "*Damn you and everybody that looks like you!*"

He backed up a pace, his blue eyes wide with surprise at her rage.

She was so filled with fury that grew past controlling—she couldn't see, couldn't think; it was like being possessed. Suddenly she gasped as pain lanced from the top of her head to her toes, pain like a bolt of lightning—

—her vision blacked out; she fell to her hands and knees on the grass, her legs unable to hold her, convulsing with surges of pain in her arms and legs. Her feet, her hands felt like she'd shoved them in a fire—her face felt as if someone were stretching it out of shape. And the ring finger of her left hand—it burned with more agony than both hands and feet put together! She shook her head, trying to clear it, but it spun around in dizzying circles. Her ears rang, hard to hear over the ringing, but there was a sound of cloth tearing—

Her sight cleared and returned, but distorted. She looked up at the man, who had dropped his bow, and was backing away from her, slowly, his face white with terror. She started to say something to him—

—and it came out a snarl.

With that, the man screeched, turned his back on her, and ran.

And she caught sight of her hand. It wasn't a hand anymore. It was a paw. Judging by the spotted pelt of the leg, a leopard's paw. Scattered around her were the ragged scraps of cloth that had once been her clothing.

Glenda lay in the sun on top of a rock, warm and drowsy with full-bellied content. Idly she washed one paw with her tongue, cleaning the last taint of blood from it. Before she'd had a chance to panic or go crazy back there when she'd realized what had happened to her, a rabbit-like creature had broken cover practically beneath her nose. Semi-starvation and confusion had kept her dazed long enough for leopard-instincts to take over. She'd caught and killed the thing and had half eaten it before the reality of what she'd done and become broke through her shock. Raw rabbit-thing tasted *fine* to leopard-Glenda; when she realized that, she finished it, nose to tail. Now for the first time in weeks she was warm and content. And for the first time in years *she* was something to be afraid of. She gazed about her from her vantage-point on the warm boulder, taking in the grassy hills and breathing in the warm, hay-scented air with a growing contentment.

Becoming a leopard might not be a bad transformation.

Ears keener than a human's picked up the sound of dogs in the distance; she became aware that the man she'd frightened might have gone back home for help. They just *might* be hunting her.

Time to go.

She leapt down from her rock, setting off at a right angle to the direction the sound of the baying was coming from. Her sense of smell, so heightened now that it might have been a new sense altogether, had picked up the coolth of running water off this way, dimmed by the green odor of the grass. And running water was a good way to break a trail; she knew that from reading.

Reveling in the power of the muscles beneath her sleek coat, she ran lightly over the slopes, moving through the grass that had been such a waist-high tangle to girl-Glenda with no impediment whatsoever. In almost no time at all, it seemed, she was pacing the side of the stream that she had scented.

It was quite wide, twenty feet or so, and seemed fairly deep in the middle. Sunlight danced on the surface, giving her a hint that the current might be stiffish beneath the surface. She waded into it, up to her stomach, hissing a little at the cold and the feel of the water on her fur. She trotted upstream a bit until she found a place where the course had narrowed a little. It was still over her head, but she found she could swim it with nothing other than discomfort. The stream wound between the grassy hills, the banks never getting very high, but there rarely being any more cover along them than a few scattered bushes. Something told her that she would be no match for the endurance of the hunting pack if she tried to escape across the grasslands. She stayed in the watercourse until she came to a wider valley than anything she had yet encountered. There were trees here; she waded onward until she found one leaning well over the streambed. Gathering herself and eying the broad branch that arced at least six feet above the watercourse, she leaped for it, landing awkwardly, and having to scrabble with her claws fully extended to keep her balance.

She sprawled over it for a moment, panting, hearing the dogs nearing—belling in triumph as they caught her trail, then yelping in confusion when they lost it at the stream.

Time to move again. She climbed the tree up into the higher branches, finding a wide perch at least fifty or sixty feet off the ground. It was high enough that it was unlikely that anyone would spot her dappled hide among the dappled leaf-shadows, wide enough that she could recline, balanced, at her ease, yet it afforded to leopard-eyes a good view of the ground and the stream.

As she'd expected, the humans with the dogs had figured out her scent-breaking ploy, and had split the pack, taking half along each side of the stream to try and pick up where she'd exited. She spotted the man who had stopped her easily, and filed his scent away in her memory for the future. The others with him were dressed much the same as he, and carried nothing more sophisticated than bows. They looked angry, confused; their voices held notes of fear. They looked into and under the trees with noticeable apprehension, evidently fearing what might dwell under their shade. Finally they gave up, and pulled the hounds off the fruitless quest, leaving her smiling catwise, invisible above them in her tree, purring.

Several weeks later Glenda had found a place to lair up; a cave amid a tumble of boulders in the heart of the forest at the streamside. She had also discovered why the hunters hadn't wanted to pursue her into the forest itself. There was a—thing—an evil presence, malicious, but invisible, that lurked in a circle of standing stones that glowed at night with a sickly yellow color. Fortunately it seemed unable to go beyond the bounds of the stones themselves. Glenda had been chasing a half-grown deer-beast that had run straight into the middle of the circle, forgetting the danger before it because of the danger pursuing it. She had nearly been caught there herself, and only the thing's preoccupation with the first prey had saved her. She had hidden in her lair, nearly paralyzed with fear, for a day and a night until hunger and thirst had driven her out again.

Other than that peril, easily avoided, the forest seemed safe enough. She'd found the village the man had come from by following the dirt road; she'd spent long hours when she wasn't hunting lurking within range of sight and hearing of the place. Aided by some new sense she wasn't sure that she understood—the one that had alerted her to the danger of the stone circle as she'd blundered in—she was beginning to make some sense of their language. She understood at least two-thirds of what was being said now, and could usually guess the rest.

These people seemed to be stuck at some kind of feudal level—had been overrun by some higher-tech invaders the generation before, and were only now recovering from that. The hereditary rulers had mostly been killed in that war, and the population decimated; the memories of that time were still strong. The man who'd stopped her had been on guard-duty and had mistrusted her appearance out of what they called "the Waste" and her strange clothing. When she'd transformed in front of his eyes, he must have decided she was some kind of witch.

Glenda had soon hunted the more easily-caught game out; now when hunger drove her, she supplemented her diet with raids on the villager's livestock. She was getting better at hunting, but she still was far from being an expert, and letting leopard-instincts take over involved surrendering herself to those instincts. She was beginning to have the uneasy feeling that every time she did that she lost a little more of her humanity. Life as leopard-Glenda was much easier than as girl-Glenda, but it might be getting to be time to think about trying to regain her former shape—before she was lost to the leopard entirely.

She'd never been one for horror or fantasy stories, so her only guide was vague recollections of fairy-tales and late-night werewolf movies. She didn't think the latter would be much help here—after all, she'd transformed into a leopard, not a wolf, and by the light of day, not the full moon.

But—maybe the light of the full moon would help.

She waited until full dark before setting off for her goal, a still pond in the far edge of the forest, well away from the stone circle, in a clearing that never seemed to become overgrown. It held a stone, too; a single pillar of some kind of blueish rock. That pillar had never "glowed" at night before, at least not while Glenda had been there, but the pond and the clearing seemed to form a little pocket of peace. Whatever evil might lurk in the rest of the forest, she was somehow sure it would find no place there.

The moon was well up by the time she reached it. White flowers had opened to the light of it, and a faint, crisp scent came from them. Glenda paced to the poolside, and looked down into the dark, still water. She could see her leopard form reflected clearly, and over her right shoulder, the full moon.

Well, anger had gotten her into this shape, maybe anger would get her out. She closed her eyes for a moment, then began summoning all the force of that emotion she could—*willing* herself back into the form she'd always worn. She stared at her reflection in the water, forcing it, angrily, to be *her*. Whatever power was playing games with her was *not* going to find her clay to be molded at will!

As nothing happened, her frustration mounted; soon she was at the boiling point. Damn everything! She—would—not—be—played—with—

The same incoherent fury that had seized her when she first changed washed over her a second time—and the same agonizing pain sent blackness in front of her eyes and flung her to lie twitching helplessly beside the pool. Her left forepaw felt like it was afire—

In moments it was over, and she found herself sprawling beside the pond, shivering with cold and reaction, and totally naked. Naked, that is, except for the silver cat-ring, whose topaz eyes glowed hotly at her for a long moment before the light left them.

The second time she transformed to leopard was much easier; the pain was less, the amount of time less. She decided against being human—after finding herself without a stitch on, in a perilously vulnerable and helpless form, leopard-Glenda seemed a much more viable alternative.

But the ability to switch back and forth proved to be very handy. The villagers had taken note of her raids on their stock; they began mounting a series of systematic hunts for her, even penetrating into the forest so long as it was by daylight. She learned or remembered from reading countless tricks to throw the hunters off, and being able to change from human to leopard and back again made more than one of those possible. There *were* places girl-Glenda could climb and hide that leopard-Glenda couldn't, and the switch in scents when she changed confused and frightened the dog-pack. She began feeling an amused sort of contempt for the villagers, often leading individual hunters on wild-goose chases for the fun of it when she became bored.

But on the whole, it was better to be leopard; leopard-Glenda was comfortable and content sleeping on rocks or on the dried leaves of her lair—girl-Glenda shivered and ached and wished for her roach-infested efficiency. Leopard-Glenda was perfectly happy on a diet of raw fish, flesh and fowl—girl-Glenda wanted to throw up when she thought about it. Leopard-Glenda was content with nothing to do but tease the villagers and sleep in the sun when she wasn't hunting—girl-Glenda fretted, and longed for a book, and wondered if what she was doing was right . . .

So matters stood until Midsummer.

Glenda woke, shivering, with a mouth gone dry with panic. The dream—

It wasn't just a nightmare. This dream had been so real she'd expected to wake with an arrow in her ribs. She was still panting with fright even now.

There had been a man—he hadn't looked much like any of the villagers; they were mostly blond or brown-haired, and of the kind of hefty build her aunt used to call "peasant-stock" in a tone of contempt. No, he had resembled her in a way—as if she were a kind of washed-out copy of the template from which his kind had been cut. Where her hair was a dark mousy-brown, his was just as dark, but the color was more intense. They had the same general build: thin, tall, with prominent cheekbones. His eyes—

Her aunt had called her "cat-eyed," for she didn't have eyes of a normal brown, but more of a vague yellow, as washed-out as her hair. But *his* had been truly and intensely gold, with a greenish back-reflection like the eyes of a wild animal at night.

And those eyes had been filled with hunter-awareness; the eyes of a predator. And *she* had been his quarry!

The dream came back to her with extraordinary vividness; it had begun as she'd reached the edge of the forest, with him hot on her trail. She had a vague recollection of having begun the chase in human form, and having switched to leopard as she reached the trees. He had no dogs, no aid but his own senses—yet nothing she'd done had confused him for more than a second. She'd even laid a false trail into the stone circle, something she'd never done to another hunter, but she was beginning to panic—he'd avoided the trap neatly. The hunt had begun near mid-morning; by false dawn he'd brought her to bay and trapped her—

And that was when she'd awakened.

She spent the early hours of the morning pacing beside the pond; feeling almost impelled to go into the village, yet afraid to do so. Finally the need to *see* grew too great; she crept to the edge of the village past the guards, and slipped into the maze of whole and half-ruined buildings that was the village-proper.

There was a larger than usual market-crowd today; the usual market stalls had been augmented by strangers with more luxurious goods, foodstuffs, and even a couple of ragged entertainers. Evidently this was some sort of fair. With so many strangers about, Glenda was able to remain unseen. Her courage came back as she skirted the edge of the marketplace, keeping to shadows and sheltering within half-tumbled walls, and the terror of the night seemed to become just one more shadow.

Finally she found an ideal perch—hiding in the shadow just under the eaves of a half-ruined building that had evidently once belonged to the local lordling, and in whose courtyard the market was usually held. From here she could see the entire court and yet remain unseen by humans and unscented by any of the livestock.

She had begun to think her fears were entirely

groundless—when she caught sight of a stranger coming out of the door of what passed for an inn here, speaking earnestly with the village headman. Her blood chilled, for the man was tall, dark-haired, and lean, and dressed entirely in dark leathers just like the man in her dream.

He was too far away for her to see his face clearly, and she froze in place, following him intently without moving a muscle. The headman left him with a satisfied air, and the man gazed about him, as if looking for something—

He finally turned in her direction, and Glenda nearly died of fright—for the face was that of the man in her dream, and he was staring directly at her hiding place as though he knew exactly where and what she was!

She broke every rule she'd ever made for herself—broke cover, in full sight of the entire village. In the panicked, screaming mob, the hunter could only curse—for the milling, terror-struck villagers were only interested in fleeing in the opposite direction from where Glenda stood, tail lashing and snarling with fear.

She took advantage of the confusion to leap the wall of the courtyard and sprint for the safety of the forest. Halfway there she changed into human for a short run—there was no one to see her, and it might throw him off the track. Then at forest edge, once on the springy moss that would hold no tracks, she changed back to leopard. She paused in the shade for a moment, to get a quick drink from the stream, and to rest, for the full-out run from the village had tired her badly—only to look up, to see him standing directly across the stream from her. He was shading his eyes with one hand against the sun that beat down on him, and it seemed to her that he was smiling in triumph.

She choked on the water, and fled.

She called upon every trick she'd ever learned, laying false trails by the dozen; fording the stream as it threaded through the forest not once but several times; breaking her trail entirely by taking to the treetops on an area where she could cross several hundred feet without once having to set foot to the ground. She even drove a chance-met herd of deer-creatures across her back-trail, muddling the tracks past following. She didn't remember doing any of this in her dream—in her dream she had only run, too fearful to do much that was complicated—or so she remembered. At last, panting with weariness, she doubled back to lair-up in the crotch of a huge tree, looking back down the way she had passed, certain that she would see him give up in frustration.

He walked so softly that even *her* keen ears couldn't detect his tread; she was only aware that he was there when she saw him. She froze in place—she hadn't really expected he'd get *this* far! But surely, surely when he came to the place she'd taken to the branches, he would be baffled, for she'd first climbed as girl-Glenda, and there wasn't any place where the claw-marks of the leopard scored the trunks within sight of the ground.

He came to the place where her tracks ended—and closed his eyes, a frown-line between his brows. Late afternoon sun filtered through the branches and touched his face; Glenda thought with growing confidence that he had been totally fooled by her trick. He carried a strung bow, black as his clothing and highly polished, and wore a sword and dagger, which none of the villagers ever did. As her fear ebbed, she had time to think (with a tiny twinge) that he couldn't have been much older than she—and was very, very attractive.

As if that thought had touched something that signaled him, his eyes snapped open—and he looked straight through the branches that concealed her to rivet his own gaze on *her* eyes.

With a mew of terror she leapt out of the tree and ran in mindless panic as fast as she could set paw to ground.

The sun was reddening everything; she cringed and thought of blood. Then she thought of her dream, and the dweller-in-the-circle. If, instead of a false trail, she laid a *true* one—waiting for him at the end of it—

If she rushed him suddenly, she could probably startle him into the power of the thing that lived within the shelter of those stones. Once in the throes of its mental grip, she doubted he'd be able to escape.

It seemed a heaven-sent plan; relief made her light-headed as she ran, leaving a clear trail behind her, to the place of the circle. By the time she reached its vicinity it was full dark—and she knew the power of the dweller was at its height in darkness. Yet, the closer she drew to those glowing stones, the slower her paws moved; and a building reluctance to do this thing weighed heavily on her. Soon she could see the stones shining ahead of her; in her mind she pictured the man's capture—his terror—his inevitable end.

Leopard-Glenda urged—kill!

Girl-Glenda wailed in fear of him, but stubbornly refused to put him in the power of *that*.

The two sides of her struggled, nearly tearing her physically in two as she half-shifted from one to the other, her outward form paralleling the struggle within.

At last, with a pathetic cry, the leopard turned in her tracks and ran from the circle. The will of girl-Glenda had won.

Whenever she paused to rest, she could hear him coming long before she'd even caught her breath. The stamina of a leopard is no match for that of a human; they are built for the short chase, not the long. And the stamina of girl-Glenda was no match for that of he who hunted her; in either form now, she was exhausted. He had driven her through the moon-lit clearings of the forest she knew out beyond the territory she had ranged before. This forest must extend deep into the Waste, and this was the direction he had driven her. Now she stumbled as she ran, no longer capable of clever tricks, just fear-prodded running. Her eyes were glazed with weariness; her mind numb with terror. Her sides heaved as she panted, and her mouth was dry, her thirst a raging fire inside her.

She fled from bush to tangled stand of undergrowth, at all times avoiding the patches of moonlight, but it seemed as if her foe knew this section of the wilderness as well or better than she knew her own territory. She could not rid herself of the feeling that she was being driven to some goal only he knew.

Suddenly, as rock-cliff loomed before her, she realized that her worst fears were correct. He had herded her into a dead-end ravine, and there was no escape for her, at least not in leopard-form.

The rock before her was sheer; to either side it slanted inward. The stone itself was brittle shale; almost impassable—yet she began shifting into her human form to make that attempt. Then a sound from behind her told her that she had misjudged his nearness—and it was too late.

She whirled at bay, half-human, half-leopard, flanks heaving as she sucked in pain-filled gasps of air. He blocked the way out; dark and grim on the path, nocked bow in hand. She thought she saw his eyes shine with fierce joy even in the darkness of the ravine. She had no doubts that he could see her as easily as she saw him. There was nowhere to hide on either side of her.

Again leopard-instinct urged—kill!

Her claws extended, and she growled deep in her throat, half in fear, half in warning. He paced one step closer.

She could—she could fight him. She could dodge the arrow—at this range he could never get off the second. If she closed with him, she could kill him! His blood would run hot between her teeth—

Kill!

No! Never, never had she harmed another human being, not even the man who had denied her succor. No!

Kill!

She fought the leopard within, knowing that if it won, there would never be a girl-Glenda again; only the predator, the beast. And that would be the death of her—a death as real as that which any arrow could bring her.

And he watched from the shadows; terrible, dark, and menacing, his bow half-drawn. And yet—he did not move, not so much as a single muscle. If he had, perhaps the leopard would have won; fear triumphing over will. But he stirred not, and it was the human side of her that conquered.

And she waited, eyes fixed on his, for death.

:Gentle, lady.:

She started as the voice spoke in her head—then shook it wildly, certain that she had been driven mad at last.

:Be easy—do not fear me.:

Again that voice! She stared at him, wild-eyed—was he some kind of magician, to speak in her very thoughts?

And as if that were not startlement enough, she watched, dumbfounded, as he knelt, slowly—slowly eased the arrow off the string of his bow—and just as slowly laid them to one side. He held out hands now empty, his face fully in the moonlight—and *smiled.*

And rose—and—

At first she thought it was the moonlight that made him seem to writhe and blur. Then she thought that certainly her senses were deceiving her as her mind had—for his body *was* blurring, shifting, changing before her eyes, like a figure made of clay softening and blurring and becoming another shape altogether—

Until, where the hunter had stood, was a black leopard, half-again her size.

Glenda stared into the flames of the campfire, sipping at the warm wine, wrapped in a fur cloak, and held by a drowsy contentment. The wine, the cloak and the campfire were all Harwin's.

For that was the name of the hunter—Harwin. He had coaxed her into her following him; then, once his camp had been reached, coaxed her into human form again. He had given her no time to be shamed by her nakedness, for he had shrouded her in the cloak almost before the transformation was complete. Then he had built this warming fire from the banked coals of the old, and fed her the first cooked meal she'd had in months, then pressed the wine on her. And all with slow, reassuring movements, as if he was quite well aware how readily she could be startled into transforming back again, and fleeing into the forest. And all without speaking much besides telling her his name; his silence not unfriendly, not in the least, but as if he were waiting with patient courtesy for her to speak first.

She cleared her throat, and tentatively spoke her first words in this alien tongue, her own voice sounding strange in her ears.

"Who—are you? *What* are you?"

He cocked his head to one side, his eyes narrowing in concentration, as he listened to her halting words.

"You speak the speech of the Dales as one who knows it only indifferently, lady," he replied, his words measured, slow, and pronounced with care, as if he guessed she needed slow speech to understand clearly. "Yet you do not have the accent of Arvon—and I do not think you are one of the Old Ones. If I tell you who and what I am, will you do me like courtesy?"

"I—my name is Glenda. I couldn't do—this—at home. Wherever home is. I—I'm not sure what I am."

"Then your home is not of this world?"

"There was—" it all seemed so vague, like a dream now, "A city. I—lived there, but not well. I was hunted—I found a place—a woman. I thought she was crazy, but—she said something, and I saw this place—and I had to come—"

"A Gate, I think, and a Gate-Keeper," he nodded,

as if to himself. "That explains much. So you found yourself here?"

"In the Waste. Though I didn't know that was what it was. I met a man—I was tired, starving, and he tried to drive me away. I got mad."

"The rest I know," he said. "For Elvath himself told me of how you went *were* before his eyes. Poor lady—how bewildered you must have been, with no one to tell you what was happening to you! And then?"

Haltingly, with much encouragement, she told him of her life in the forest; her learning to control her changes—and her side of the night's hunt.

"And the woman won over the beast," he finished. "And well for you that it did." His gold eyes were very somber, and he spoke with emphasis heavy in his words. "Had you turned on me, I doubt that you would ever have been able to find your human self again."

She shuddered. "What am I?" she asked at last, her eyes fixed pleadingly on his. "And where am I? And why has all this been happening to me?"

"I cannot answer the last for you, save only that I think you are here because your spirit never fit truly in that strange world from which you came. As for where—you are in the Dale lands of High Hal-leck, on the edge of the Waste—which tells you nothing, I know. And what you are—like me, you are plainly of some far-off strain of Wereblood. Well, perhaps not quite like me; among my kind the females are not known for being able to shape-change, and I myself am of half-blood only. My mother is Kildas of the Dales; my father Harl of the Wereriders. And I—I am Harwin," he smiled, rue-fully, "of no place in particular."

"Why—why did you hunt me?" she asked. "Why did they want *you* to hunt me?"

"Because they had no notion of my Wereblood," he replied frankly. "They only know of my reputation as a hunter—shall I begin at the beginning? Perhaps it will give you some understanding of this world you have fallen into."

She nodded eagerly.

"Well—you may have learned that in my father's time the Dales were overrun by the Hounds of Alizon?" At her nod, he continued. "They had strange weapons at their disposal, and came very close to destroying all who opposed them. At that time my father and his brother-kin lived in the Waste, in exile for certain actions in the past from the land of Arvon, which lies to the north of the Waste. They—as I, as you—have the power of shape-change, and other powers as well. It came to the defenders of the Dales that one must battle strangeness with strangeness, and power with power; they made a pact with the Wereriders. In exchange for aid, they would send to them at the end of the war in the Year of the Unicorn twelve brides and one. You see, if all went well, the Wererider's exile was to end then—but if all was not well, they would have remained in exile, and they did not wish their kind to die away. The war ended, the brides came—the exile ended. But one of the bridegrooms was—like me—of half-blood. And one of the brides was a maiden of Power. There was much trouble for them; when the trouble was at an end they left Arvon together, and I know nothing more of their tale. Now we come to my part of the tale. My mother Kildas has gifted my father with three children, of which two are a pleasure to his heart and of like mind with him. I am the third."

"The misfit? The rebel?" she guessed shrewdly.

"If by that you mean the one who seems destined always to anger his kin with all he says and does—aye. We cannot agree, my father and I. One day in his anger, he swore that I was another such as Herrel. Well, that was the first that *I* had ever heard of one of Wereblood who was like-minded with me—I plagued my mother and father both until they gave me the tale of Herrel Half-blood and his Witch-bride. And from that moment,

I had no peace until I set out to find them. For surely, I thought, I would find true kin-feeling with them, the which I lacked with those truly of my blood."

"And did you find them?"

"Not yet," he admitted. "At my mother's request I came here first, to give word to her kin that she was well, and happy, and greatly honored by her lord. Which is the entire truth. My father—loves her dearly; grants her every wish before she has a chance to voice it. I could wish to find a lady with whom—well, that was one of the reasons that I sought Herrel and his lady."

He was silent for so long, staring broodingly into the flames, that Glenda ventured to prompt him.

"So—you came here?"

"Eh? Oh, aye. And understandably enough, earned no small reputation among my mother-kin for hunting, though they little guessed in what form I did my tracking!" He grinned at her, and she found herself grinning back. "So when there were rumors of another Were here at the edge of the Waste—and a Were that thoughtlessly preyed on the beasts of these people as well as its rightful game—understandably enough, I came to hear of it. I thought at first that it must be Herrel, or a son. Imagine my surprise on coming here to learn that the Were was female! My reputation preceded me—the headman begged me to rid the village of their 'monster'—" He spread his hands wide. "The rest, you know."

"What—what will you do with me now?" she asked in a small, fearful voice.

"Do with you?" he seemed surprised. "Nothing—nothing not of your own will, lady. I am not going to harm you—and I am not like my father and brother, to force a one in my hand into anything against her wishes. I—I go forward as I had intended—to find Herrel. You, now that you know what your actions should *not* be, lest you arouse the anger of ordinary folk against you, may remain here—"

"And?"

"And I shall tell them I have killed the monster. You shall be safe enough—only remember that you must *never* let the leopard control you, or you are lost. Truly, you should have someone to guide and teach you, though—"

"I—know that, now," she replied, very much aware of how attractive he was, gold eyes fixed on the fire, a lock of dark hair falling over his forehead. But no man had ever found her to be company to be sought-after. There was no reason to think that he might be hinting—

No reason, that is, until he looked full into her eyes, and she saw the wistful loneliness there, and a touch of pleading.

"I would be glad to teach you, lady," he said softly. "Forgive me if I am over-forward, and clumsy in my speech. But—I think you and I could companion well together on this quest of mine—and—I—" he dropped his eyes to the flames again, and blushed hotly "—I think you very fair."

"Me?" she squeaked, more startled than she had been since he transformed before her.

"Can you doubt it?" he replied softly, looking up eagerly. He held out one hand to her. "Can I hope—you *will* come with me?"

She touched his fingers with the hesitation of one who fears to break something. "You mean you really want me with you?"

"Since I touched your mind—lady, more than you could dream! Not only are you kin-kind, but—mind-kin, I think."

She smiled suddenly, feeling almost light-headed with the revelations of the past few hours—then giggled, as an irrelevant though came to her. "Harwin—what happens to your clothes?"

"My *what*?" he stared at her for a moment as if she had broken into a foreign tongue—then looked at her, and back at himself—and blushed, then grinned.

"Well? I mean, I left bits of jeans and t-shirt all over the Waste when *I* changed—"

"What happens to your ring, lady?"

"It—" her forehead furrowed in thought. "I don't know, really. It's gone when I change, it's back when I change back." She regarded the tiny beast thoughtfully, and it seemed as if one of its topaz eyes closed in a slow wink. But—no. That could only have been a trick of the firelight.

"Were-magic, lady. And magic I think I shall let you avail yourself of, seeing as I can hardly let you take a chill if you are to accompany me—" He rummaged briefly in his pack and came up with a shirt and breeches, both far too large for her, but that was soon remedied with a belt and much rolling of sleeves and cuffs. She changed quickly under the shelter of his cloak.

"They'll really change with me?" she looked down at herself doubtfully.

"Why not try them?" He stood, and held out his hand—then blurred in that disconcerting way. The black leopard looked across the fire at her with eyes that glowed with warmth and approval.

:The night still has time to run, Glenda-my-lady. Will you not run with it, and me?:

The eyes of the cat-ring glowed with equal warmth, and Glenda found herself filled with a feeling of joy and freedom—and of *belonging*—that she tossed back her head and laughed aloud as she had never in her life done before. She stretched her own arms to the stars, and called on the power within her for the first time with joy instead of anger—

And there was no pain—only peace—as she transformed into a slim, lithe she-leopard, whose eyes met that of the he with a happiness that was heart-filling.

:Oh yes, *Harwin-my-lord! Let us run the night to dawn!:*

The four SKitty stories appeared in Cat Fantastic *Anthologies edited by Andre Norton. I'm very, very fond of SKitty; it might seem odd for a bird person to be fond of cats, but I am, so there it is. I was actually a cat-person before I was a bird-mother, and I do have two cats, both Siamese-mix, both rather old and very slow. Just, if the other local cats poach too often at my bird feeders, they can expect to get a surprise from the garden-hose.*

SKitty

:Nasty,: SKitty complained in Dick's head. She wrapped herself a little closer around his shoulders and licked drops of oily fog from her fur with a faint mew of distaste. *:Smelly.:*

Dick White had to agree. The portside district of Lacu'un was pretty unsavory; the dismal, foggy weather made it look even worse. Shabby, cheap, and ill-used.

Every building here—all twenty of them!—was offworld design; shoddy prefab, mostly painted in shades of peeling grey and industrial green, with garish neon-bright holosigns that were (thank the Spirits of Space!) mostly tuned down to faintly colored ghosts in the daytime. There were six bars, two gambling-joints, one chapel run by the neo-Jesuits, one flophouse run by the Reformed Salvation Army, five government buildings, four stores, and once place better left unnamed. They had all sprung up, like diseased fungus, in the year since the planet and people of Lacu'un had been declared Open for trade. There was nothing native here; for that you had to go outside the Fence—

And to go outside the Fence, Dick reminded himself, *you have to get permits signed by everybody and his dog.*

:Cat,: corrected SKitty.

Okay, okay, he thought back with wry amusement. *Everybody and his cat. Except they don't have cats here, except on the ships.*

SKitty sniffed disdainfully. *:Fools,:* she replied, smoothing down an errant bit of damp fur with her tongue, thus dismissing an entire culture that currently had most of the Companies on their collective knees begging for trading concessions.

Well, we've seen about everything there is to see, Dick thought back at SKitty, reaching up to scratch her ears as she purred in contentment. *Are you quite satisfied?*

:Hunt now?: she countered hopefully.

No, you can't hunt. You know that very well. This is a Class Four world; you have to have permission from the local sapients to hunt, and they haven't given us permission to even sneeze outside the Fence. And inside the Fence you are valuable merchandise subject to catnapping, as you very well know. I played shining knight for you once, furball, and I don't want to repeat the experience.

SKitty sniffed again. *:Not love me.:*

Love you too much, pest. Don't want you ending up in the hold of some tramp freighter.

SKitty turned up the volume on her purr, and rearranged her coil on Dick's shoulders until she resembled a lumpy black fur collar on his gray shipsuit. When she left the ship—and often when she was in the ship—that was SKitty's perch of choice. Dick had finally prevailed on the purser to put shoulderpads on all his shipsuits—sometimes SKitty got a little careless with her claws.

When man had gone to space, cats had followed; they were quickly proven to be a necessity. For not only did man's old pests, rats and mice, accompany his trade—there seemed to be equivalent pests on every new world. But the shipscats were considerably different from their Earth-bound ancestors. The cold reality was that a spacer couldn't afford a pet that had to be cared for—he needed something closer to a partner.

Hence SKitty and her kind; gene-tailored into something more than animals. SKitty was BioTech Type F-021; forepaws like that of a raccoon, more like stubby little hands than paws. Smooth, short hair with no undercoat to shed and clog up airfilters. Hunter second to none. Middle-ear tuning so that she not only was not bothered by hyperspace shifts and freefall, she actually enjoyed them. And last, but by no means least, the enlarged head showing the boosting of her intelligence.

BioTech released the shipscats for adoption when they reached about six months old; when they'd not only been weaned, but trained. Training included maneuvering in freefall, use of the same sanitary facilities as the crew, and emergency procedures. SKitty had her vacuum suit, just like any other crew member; a transparent hard plex ball rather like a tiny lifeslip, with a simple panel of controls inside to seal and pressurize it. She was positively paranoid about having it *with* her; she'd haul it along on its tether, if need be, so that it was always in the same compartment that she was. Dick respected her paranoia; any good spacer would.

Officially she was "Lady Sundancer of Greenfields"; Greenfields being BioTech Station NA-73. In actuality, she was SKitty to the entire crew, and only Dick remembered her real name.

Dick had signed on to the CatsEye Company ship *Brightwing* just after they'd retired their last shipscat to spend his final days with other creaky retirees from the spacetrade in the Tau Epsilon Old Spacers Station. As junior officer Dick had been sent off to pick up the replacement. SOP was for a BioTech technician to give you two or three candidates to choose among—in actuality, Dick hadn't had any choice. "Lady Sundancer" had taken one look at him and launched herself like a little black rocket from the arms of the tech straight for him; she'd landed on his shoulders, purring at the top of her lungs. When they couldn't pry her off, not without injuring her, the "choice" became moot. And Dick was elevated to the position of Designated Handler.

For the first few days she was "Dick White's Kitty"—the rest of his fellow crewmembers being vastly amused that she had so thoroughly attached herself to him. After a time that was shortened first to "Dick's Kitty" and then to "SKitty," which name finally stuck.

Since telepathy was *not* one of the traits BioTech was supposedly breeding and genesplicing for, Dick had been more than a little startled when she'd started speaking to him. And since none of the others ever mentioned hearing her, he had long ago come to the conclusion that he was the only one who could. He kept that a secret; at the least, should BioTech come to hear of it, it would mean losing her. BioTech would want to know where *that* particular mutation came from, for fair.

"Pretty gamy," he told Erica Makumba, Legal and Security Officer, who was the current on-watch at the airlock. The dusky woman lounged in her jumpseat with deceptive casualness, both hands behind her curly head—but there was a stun-bracelet on one wrist, and Erica just happened to be the *Brightwing*'s current karate champ.

"Eyeah," she replied with a grimace. "Had a look out there last night. Talk about your low-class dives! I'm not real surprised the Lacu'un threw the Fence up around it. Damn if *I'd* want that for neighbors! Hey, we may be getting a break, though; invitation's gone out to about three cap'ns to come make trade-talk. Seems the Lacu'un got themselves a lawyer—"

"So much for the 'unsophisticated primitives,'" Dick laughed. "I thought TriStar was riding for a fall, taking that line."

Erica grinned; a former TriStar employee, she had no great love for her previous employer. "Eyeah. So, lawyer goes and calls up the records on every Company making bids, goes over 'em with a fine-tooth. Seems only three of us came up clean; us, SolarQuest, and UVN. We got invites, rest got bye-byes. Be hearing a buncha ships clearing for space in the next few hours."

"My heart bleeds," Dick replied. "Any chance they can fight it?"

"Ha! Didn't tell you *who* they got for their mouthpiece. Lan Ventris."

Dick whistled. "*Somebody's* been looking out for them!"

"Terran Consul; she was the scout that made first contact. They wouldn't have anybody else, adopted her into the ruling sept, keep her at the Palace. Nice lady, shared a beer or three with her. She likes these people, obviously, takes their welfare real personal. Now—you want the quick low-down on the invites?"

Dick leaned up against the bulkhead, arms folded, taking care not to disturb SKitty. "Say on."

"One—" she held up a solemn finger. "Vena—that's the Consul—says that these folk have a long martial tradition; they're warriors, and admire warriors—but they admire honor and honesty even more. The trappings of primitivism are there, but it's a veneer for considerable sophistication. So whoever goes needs to walk a line between pride and honorable behavior that will be a *lot* like the old Japanese courts of Terra. Two, they are very serious about religion—they give us a certain amount of leeway for being ignorant outlanders, but if you transgress too far, Vena's not sure what the penalties may be. So you want to watch for signals, body-language from the priest-caste; that could warn you that you're on dangerous ground. Three—and this is what may give us an edge over the other two—they are very big on their totem animals; the sept totems are actually an important part of sept pride and the religion. So the Cap'n intends to make you and Her Highness there part of the delegation. Vena says that the Lacu'un intend to issue three contracts, so we're all gonna get one, but the folks that impress them the most will be getting first choice."

If Dick hadn't been leaning against the metal of the bulkhead he might well have staggered. As most junior on the crew, the likelihood that he was going to even go beyond the Fence had been staggeringly low—but that he would be included in the first trade delegation was mind-melting!

SKitty caroled her own excitement all the way back to his cabin, launching herself from his shoulder to land in her own little shock-bunk, bolted to the wall above his.

Dick began digging through his catch-all bin for his dress-insignia; the half-lidded topaz eye for CatsEye Company, the gold wings of the ship's insignia that went beneath it, the three tiny stars signifying the three missions he'd been on so far. . . .

He caught flickers of SKitty's private thoughts then; thoughts of pleasure, thoughts of nesting—

Nesting!

Oh *no!*

He spun around to meet her wide yellow eyes, to see her treading out her shock-bunk.

SKitty, he pled, *Please don't tell me you're pregnant—*

:Kittens,: she affirmed, very pleased with herself.

You swore to me that you weren't in heat when I let you out to hunt!

She gave the equivalent of a mental shrug. *:I lie.:*

He sat heavily down on his own bunk, all his earlier excitement evaporated. BioTech shipscats were supposed to be sterile—about one in a hundred weren't.

And you had to sign an agreement with BioTech that you wouldn't neuter yours if it proved out fertile; they wanted the kittens, wanted the results that came from outbreeding. Or you could sell the kittens to other ships yourself, or keep them; provided a BioTech station wasn't within your ship's current itinerary. But of course, only BioTech would take them before they were six months old and trained. . . .

That was the rub. Dick sighed. SKitty had already had one litter on him—only two, but it had seemed like twenty-two. There was this problem with kittens in a spaceship; there was a period of time between when they were mobile and when they were about four months old that they had exactly two neurons in those cute, fluffy little heads. One neuron to keep the body moving at warp speed, and one neuron to pick out the situation guaranteed to cause the most trouble.

Everyone in the crew was willing to play with them—but no one was willing to keep them out of trouble. And since SKitty was Dick's responsibility, it was *Dick* who got to clean up the messes, and *Dick* who got to fish the little fluffbrains out of the bridge console, and *Dick* who got to have the anachronistic litter pan in his cabin until SKitty got her babies properly toilet trained.

Securing a litter pan for freefall was not something he had wanted to have to do again. Ever.

"How could you *do* this to me?" he asked SKitty reproachfully. She just curled her head over the edge of her bunk and trilled prettily.

He sighed. Too late to do anything about it now.

" . . . and you can see the carvings adorn every flat surface," Vena Ferducci, the small, darkhaired woman who was the Terran Consul, said, waving her hand gracefully at the walls. Dick wanted to stand and gawk; this was *incredible!*

The Fence was actually an opaque forcefield, and only *one* of the reasons the Companies wanted to trade with the Lacu'un.Though they did not have spaceflight, there were certain applications of forcefield technologies they *did* have that seemed to be beyond the Terran's abilities. On the other side of the Fence was literally another world.

These people built to last, in limestone, alabaster, and marble, in the wealthy district, and in cast stone in the outer city. The streets were carefully poured sections of concrete, cleverly given stress-joints to avoid temperature-cracking, and kept clean enough to eat from by a small army of street-sweepers. No animals were allowed on the streets themselves, except for house-trained pets. The only vehicles permitted were single or double-being electric carts, that could move no faster than a man could walk. The Lacu'un dressed either in filmy, silken robes, or in more practical, shorter versions of the same garments. They were a handsome race, upright bipeds, skin tones in varying shades of browns and dark golds, faces vaguely avian, with a frill like an iguana's running from the base of the neck to a point between and just above the eyes.

As Vena had pointed out, every wall within sight was heavily carved, the carvings all having to do with the Lacu'un religion.

Most of the carvings were depictions of various processions or ceremonies, and no two were exactly alike.

"That's the Harvest-Gladness," Vena said, pointing, as they walked, to one elaborate wall that ran for yards. "It's particularly appropriate for Kla'dera; he made all his money in agriculture. Most Lacu'un try to have something carved that reflects on their gratitude for 'favors granted.' "

"I think I can guess that one," the Captain, Reginald Singh, said with a smile that showed startlingly white teeth in his dark face. The carving he nodded to was a series of panels; first a celebration involving a veritable kindergarten full of children, then those children—now sex-differentiated and seen to be all female—worshiping at the alter of a very fecund-looking Lacu'un female, and finally the now-maidens looking sweet and demure, each holding various religious objects.

Vena laughed, her brown eyes sparkling with amusement. "No, that one isn't hard. There's a saying, 'as fertile as Gel'vadera's wife.' Every child was a female, too, that made it even better. Between the bride-prices he got for the ones that wanted to wed, and the officer's price he got for the ones that went into the armed services, Gel'vadera was a rich man. His First Daughter owns the house now."

"Ah—that brings up a question," Captain Singh replied. "Would you explain exactly who and what we'll be meeting? I read the briefing, but I still don't quite understand who fits in where with the government."

"It will help if you think of it as a kind of unholy mating of the British Parliamentary system and the medieval Japanese Shogunates," Vena replied. "You'll be meeting with the 'king'—that's the Lacu'ara—his consort, who has equal powers and represents the priesthood—that's the Lacu'teveras—and his three advisors, who are elected. The advisors represent the military, the bureaucracy, and the economic sector. The military advisor is always female; all officers in the military are female, because the Lacu'un believe that females will not seek glory for themselves, and so will not issue reckless orders. The other two can be either sex. 'Advisor' is not altogether an accurate term to use for them; the Lacu'ara and Lacu'teveras rarely act counter to their advice."

Dick was paying scant attention to this monologue; he'd already picked all this up from the faxes he'd called out of the local library after he'd read the briefing. He was more interested in the carvings, for there was something about them that puzzled him.

All of them featured strange little six-legged creatures scampering about under the feet of the carved Lacu'un. They were about the size of a large mouse, and seemed to Dick to be wearing very smug expressions . . . though of course, he was surely misinterpreting.

"Excuse me Consul," he said, when Vena had finished explaining the intricacies of Lacu'un government to Captain Singh's satisfaction. "I can't help wondering what those little lizard-like things are."

"Kreshta," she said, "*I* would call them pests; you don't see them out on the streets much, but they are the reason the streets are kept so clean. You'll see them soon enough once we get inside. They're like mice, only worse; fast as lightning—they'll steal food right off your plate. The Lacu'un either can't or won't get rid of them, I can't tell you which. When I asked about them once, my host just rolled his eyes heavenward and said what translates to 'it's the will of the gods.'"

"Insh'allah?" Captain Singh asked.

"Very like that, yes. I can't tell if they tolerate the pests because it is the gods' will that they must, or if they tolerate them because the gods favor the little monsters. Inside the Fence we have to close the government buildings down once a month, seal them up, and fumigate. We're just lucky they don't breed very fast."

:Hunt?: SKitty asked hopefully from her perch on Dick's shoulders.

No! Dick replied hastily. *Just look, don't hunt!*

The cat was gaining startled—and Dick thought, appreciative—looks from passersby.

"Just what is the status value of a totemic animal?" Erica asked curiously.

"It's the fact that the animal can be tamed at all. Aside from a handful of domestic herbivores, most animal life on Lacu'un has never been tamed. To be able to take a carnivore and train it to the hand implies that the gods are with you in a very powerful way." Vena dimpled. "I'll let you in on a big secret; frankly, Lan and I preferred the record of the *Brightwing* over the other two ships; you seemed to be more sympathetic to the Lacu'un. That's why we told you about the totemic animals, and why we left you until last."

"It wouldn't have worked without Dick," Captain Singh told her. "SKitty has really bonded to him in a remarkable way; I don't think this presentation would come off half so impressively if he had to keep her on a lead."

"It wouldn't," Vena replied, directing them around a corner. At the end of a short street was a fifteen foot wall—carved, of course—pierced by an arching entranceway.

"The palace," she said, rather needlessly.

Vena had been right. The kreshta were *everywhere.*

Dick could feel SKitty trembling with the eagerness to hunt, but she was managing to keep herself under control. Only the lashing of her tail betrayed her agitation.

He waited at parade rest, trying not to give in to the temptation to stare, as the Captain and the Negotiator, Grace Vixen, were presented to the five rulers of the Lacu'un in an elaborate ceremony that resembled a stately dance. Behind the low platform holding the five dignitaries in their iridescent robes were five soberly clad retainers, each with one of the "totemic animals." Dick could see now what Vena had meant; the handlers had their creatures under control, but only barely. There was something like a bird, something resembling a small crocodile, something like a snake, but with six very tiny legs, a creature vaguely catlike, but with a feathery coat, and a beast resembling a teddybear with scales. None of the handlers was actually holding his beast, except the bird-handler. All of the animals were on short chains, and all of them punctuated the ceremony with soft growls and hisses.

So SKitty, perched freely on Dick's shoulders, had drawn no few murmurs of awe from the crowd of Lacu'un in the Audience Hall.

The presentation glided to a conclusion, and the Lacu'teveras whispered something to Vena behind her fan.

"With your permission, Captain, the Lacu'teveras would like to know if your totemic beast is actually as tame as she appears?"

"She is," the Captain replied, speaking directly to the consort, and bowing, exhibiting a charm that had crossed species barriers many times before this.

It worked its magic again. The Lacu'teveras fluttered her fan and trilled something else at Vena. The audience of courtiers gasped.

"Would it be possible, she asks, for her to touch it?"

SKitty? Dick asked quickly, knowing that she was getting the sense of what was going on from his thoughts.

:Nice,: the cat replied, her attention momentarily distracted from the scurrying hints of movement that were all that could be seen of the kreshta. *:Nice lady. Feels good in head, like Dick.:*

Feels good in head? he thought, startled.

"I don't think that there will be any problem, Captain," Dirk murmured to Singh, deciding that he could worry about it later. "SKitty seems to like the Lacu'un. Maybe they smell right."

SKitty flowed down off his shoulder and into his arms as he stepped forward to present the cat to the Lacu'teveras. He showed the Lacu'un the cat's favorite spot to be scratched, under the chin. The long talons sported by all Lacu'un were admirably suited to the job of cat-scratching.

The Lacu'teveras reached forward with one lilac-tipped finger, and hesitantly followed Dick's example. The Audience Hall was utterly silent as she did so, as if the entire assemblage was holding its breath, waiting for disaster to strike. The courtiers gasped at her temerity when the cat stretched out her neck—then gasped again, this time with delight, as SKitty's rumbling purr became audible.

SKitty's eyes were almost completely closed in sensual

delight; Dick glanced up to see that the Lacu'teveras' amber, slit-pupiled eyes were widened with what he judged was an equal delight. She let her other six fingers join the first, tentative one beneath the cat's chin.

"Such soft—" she said shyly, in musically-accented Standard. "—such nice!"

"Thank you, High Lady," Dick replied with a smile. "We think so."

:Verrry nice,: SKitty seconded. *:Not head-talk like Dick, but feel good in head, like Dick. Nice lady have kitten soon, too.:*

The Lacu'teveras took her hand away with some reluctance, and signed that Dick should return to his place. SKitty slid back up onto his shoulders and started to settle herself.

It was then that everything fell apart.

The next stage in the ceremony called for the rulers to take their seats in their five thrones, and the Captain, Vena, and Grace to assume theirs on stools before the thrones so that each party could present what it wanted out of a possible relationship.

But the Lacu'teveras, her eyes still wistfully on SKitty, was not looking where she placed her hand. And on the armrest of the throne was a kreshta, frozen into an atypical immobility.

The Lacu'teveras put her hand—with all of her weight on it—right on top of the kreshta. The evil-looking thing squealed, squirmed, and bit her as hard as it could.

The Lacu'teveras cried out in pain—the courtiers gasped, the Advisors made warding gestures—and SKitty, roused to sudden and protective rage at this attack by *vermin* on the nice lady who was *with kitten*—leapt.

The kreshta saw her coming, and blurred with speed—but it was not fast enough to evade SKitty, gene-tailored product of one of BioTech's finest labs. Before it could cover even half of the distance between it and safety, SKitty had it. There was a crunch audible all over the Audience Chamber, and the ugly little thing was hanging limp from SKitty's jaws.

Tail high, in a silence that could have been cut up into bricks and used to build a wall, she carried her prize to the feet of the injured one Lacu'un and laid it there.

:Fix him!: Dick heard in his mind. *:Not hurt nice-one-with-kitten!:*

The Lacu'ara stepped forward, face rigid, every muscle tense.

Spirits of Space! Dick thought, steeling himself for the worst, *that's bloody well torn it—*

But the Lacu'ara, instead of ordering the guards to seize the Terrans, went to one knee and picked up the broken-backed kreshta as if it were a fine jewel.

Then he brandished it over his head while the entire assemblage of Lacu'un burst into cheers—and the Terrans looked at one another in bewilderment.

SKitty preened, accepting the caresses of every Lacu'un that could reach her with the air of one to whom adulation is long due. Whenever an unfortunate kreshta happened to attempt to skitter by, she would turn into a bolt of black lightning, reenacting her kill to the redoubled applause of the Lacu'un.

Vena was translating as fast as she could, with the three Advisors all speaking at once. The Lacu'ara was tenderly bandaging the hand of his consort, but occasionally one or the other of them would put in a word too.

"Apparently they've never been able to exterminate the kreshta; the natural predators on them *can't* be domesticated and generally take pieces out of anyone trying, traps and poisoned baits don't work because the kreshta won't take them. The only thing they've *ever* been able to do is what we were doing behind the Fence: close up the building and fumigate periodically. And even that has problems—the Lacu'teveras, for instance, is violently allergic to the residue left when the fumigation is done."

Vena paused for breath.

"I take it they'd like to have SKitty around on a permanent basis?" the Captain said, with heavy irony.

"Spirits of Space, Captain—they think SKitty is a sign from the gods, incarnate! I'm not sure they'll let her leave!"

Dick heard that with alarm—in a lot of ways, SKitty was the best friend he had—

To leave her—the thought wasn't bearable!

SKitty whipped about with alarm when she picked up what he was thinking. With an anguished yowl, she scampered across the slippery stone floor and flung herself through the air to land on Dick's shoulders. There she clung, howling her objections at the idea of being separated at top of her lungs.

"What in—" Captain Singh exclaimed, turning to see what could be screaming like a damned soul.

"She doesn't want to leave me, Captain," Dick said defiantly. "And I don't think you're going to be able to get her off my shoulder without breaking her legs or tranking her."

Captain Singh looked stormy. "Damn it then, get a trank—"

"I'm afraid I'll have to veto that one, Captain," Erica interrupted apologetically. "The contract with BioTech clearly states that only the designated handler—and that's Dick—or a BioTech representative can treat a shipscat. And furthermore—" she continued, halting the Captain before he could interrupt, "it also states that to leave a shipscat without its designated handler will force BioTech to refuse anymore shipscats to *Brightwing* for as long as you are the Captain. Now I don't want to sound like a troublemaker, Captain, but I for one will flatly refuse to serve on a ship with no cat. Periodic vacuum purges to kill the vermin do *not* appeal to me."

"Well then, I'll order the boy to—"

"Sir, I *am* the *Brightwing*'s legal advisor—I hate to say this, but to order Dick to ground is a clear violation of *his* contract. He hasn't got enough hours spacing yet to qualify him for a ground position."

The Lacu'teveras had taken Vena aside, Dick saw, and was chattering at her at top speed, waving her bandaged hand in the air.

"Captain Singh," she said, turning away from the Lacu'un and tugging at his sleeve, "the Lacu'teveras has figured out that something you said or did is upsetting the cat, and she's not very happy with that—"

Captain Singh looked just about ready to swallow a bucket of heated nails. "Spacer, *will* you get that feline calmed down before they throw me in the local brig?"

"I'll—try sir—"

Come on, old girl—they won't take you away. Erica and the nice lady won't let them, he coaxed. *You're making the nice lady unhappy, and that might hurt her kitten—*

SKitty subsided, slowly, but continued to cling to Dick's shoulder as if he was the only rock in a flood. *:Not take Dick.:*

Erica won't let them.

:Nice Erica.:

A sudden thought occurred to him. *SKitty-love, how long would it take before you had your new kittens trained to hunt?*

She pondered the question. *:From wean? Three heats,:* she said finally.

About a year, then, from birth to full hunter. "Captain, I may have a solution for you—"

"I would be overjoyed to hear one," the Captain replied dryly.

"SKitty's pregnant again—I'm sorry, sir, I just found out today and I didn't have time to report it—but sir, this is going to be to our advantage! If the Lacu'un insisted, *we* could handle the whole trade deal, couldn't we, Erica? And it should take something like a year to get everything negotiated and set up, shouldn't it?"

"Up to a year and a half, standard, yes," she confirmed. "And basically, whatever the Lacu'un want, they get, so far as the Company is concerned."

"Once the kittens are a year old, they'll be hunters just as good as SKitty is—so if you could see your way clear to doing all the set up—and sort-of wait around for us to get done rearing the kittens—"

Captain Singh burst into laughter. "Boy, do you have any notion just how *many* credits handling the entire trade negotiations would put in *Brightwing*'s account? Do you have any idea what that would do for *my* status?"

"No sir," he admitted.

"Suffice it to say I *could* retire if I chose. And—Spirits of Space—kittens? Kittens we *could* legally sell to the Lacu'un? I don't suppose you have any notion of how many kittens we can expect this time?"

He sent an inquiring tendril of thought to SKitty. "Uh—I think four, sir."

"Four! And they were offering us *what* for just her?" the Captain asked Vena.

"A more-than-considerable amount," she said dryly. "Exclusive contract on the forcefield applications."

"How would they feel about bargaining for four to be turned over in about a year?"

Vena turned to the rulers and translated. The excited answer she got left no doubts in anyone's mind that the Lacu'un were overjoyed at the prospect.

"Basically, Captain, you've just convinced the Lacu'un that you hung the moon."

"Well—why don't we settle down to a little serious negotiation, hmm?" the Captain said, nobly refraining from rubbing his hands together with glee. "I think that all our problems for the future are about to be solved in one fell swoop! Get over here, spacer. You and that cat have just received a promotion to Junior Negotiator."

:Okay?: SKitty asked anxiously.

Yes, love, Dick replied, taking Erica's place on a negotiator's stool. *Very okay!*

A Tail of Two SKittys

The howls coming from inside the special animal shipping crate sounded impatient, and had been enough to seriously alarm the cargo handlers. Dick White, Spaceman First Class, Supercargo on the CatsEye Company ship *Brightwing*, put his hand on the outside of the plastile crate, just above the word "Property." From within the crate the muffled voice continued to yowl general unhappiness with the world.

Tell her that it's all right, SKitty, he thought at the black form that lay over his shoulders like a living fur collar. *Tell her I'll have her out in a minute. I don't want her to come bolting out of there and hide the minute I crack the crate.*

SKitty raised her head. Yellow eyes blinked once, sleepily. Abruptly, the yowling stopped.

:She fine,: SKitty said, and yawned, showing a full mouth of needle-pointed teeth. *:Only young, scared. I think she make good mate for Furrball.:*

Dick shook his head; the kittens were not even a year old, and already their mother was matchmaking. Then again, that *was* the tendency of mothers the universe over.

At least now he'd be able to uncrate this would-be "mate" with a minimum of fuss.

The full legend imprinted on the crate read "Female Shipscat Astra Stardancer of Englewood, Property of BioTech Interstellar, leased to CatsEye Company. Do not open under penalty of law." Theoretically, Astra was, like SKitty, a bio-engineered shipscat, fully capable of handling freefall, alien vermin, conditions that would poison, paralyze, or terrify her remote Terran ancestors, and all without turning a hair. In actuality, Astra, like the nineteen other shipscats Dick had uncrated, was a failure. The genetic engineering of her middle-ear and other balancing organs had failed. She could not tolerate freefall, and while most ships operated under grav-generators, there were always equipment malfunctions and accidents.

That made her and her fellows failures by BioTech standards. A shipscat that could not handle freefall was not a shipscat.

Normally, kittens that washed out in training were adopted out to carefully selected planet- or station-bound families of BioTech employees. However, this was not a "normal" circumstance by any stretch of the imagination.

The world of the Lacu'un, graceful, bipedal humanoids with a remarkably sophisticated, if planet-bound, civilization, was infested with a pest called a "kreshta." Erica Makumba, the Legal Advisor and Security Chief of Dick's ship described them as "six-legged crosses between cockroaches and mice." SKitty described them only as "nasty," but she hunted them gleefully anyway. The Lacu'un opened their world to trade just over a year ago, and some of their artifacts and technologies made them a desirable trade-ally indeed. The *Brightwing* had been one of the three ships invited to negotiate, in part because of SKitty, for the Lacu'un valued totemic animals highly.

And that was what had led to Captain Singh of the

Brightwing conducting the entire trade negotiations with the Lacu'un—and had kept *Brightwing* ground-bound for the past year. SKitty had done the—to the Lacu'un—impossible. She had killed kreshta. She had already been assumed to be *Brightwing*'s totemic animal; that act elevated her to the status of "god-touched miracle," and had given the captain and crew of her ship unprecedented control and access to the rulers here.

SKitty had been newly-pregnant at the time; part of the price for the power Captain Singh now wielded had been her kittens. But Dick had gotten another idea, and had used his own share of the profits *Brightwing* was taking in to purchase the leases of twenty more "failed" cats to supplement SKitty's four kittens. BioTech cats released for leases were generally sterile, SKitty being a rare exception. If these twenty worked out, the Lacu'un would be very grateful, and more importantly, so would Vena Ferducci, the attractive, petite Terran Consul assigned to the new embassy here. In the past few months, Dick had gotten to know Vena very well—and he hoped to get to know her better. Vena had originally been a Survey Scout, and she was getting rather restless in her ground-based position as Consul. And in truth, the Lacu'un lawyer, Lan Ventris, was much better suited to such a job than Vena. She had hinted that as soon as the Lacu'un felt they could trust Ventris, she would like to resign and go back to space. Dick rather hoped she might be persuaded to take a position with the *Brightwing*. It was too soon to call this little dance a "romance," but he had hopes. . . .

Hopes which could be solidified by this experiment. If the twenty young cats he had imported worked out as well as SKitty's four half-grown kittens, the Lacu'un would be able to import their intelligent pest-killers at a fraction of what the lease on a shipscat would be. This would make Vena happy; anything that benefited her Lacu'un made her happy. And if Dick was the cause of that happiness. . . .

:Dick go courting?: SKitty asked innocently, salting her query with decidedly *not*-innocent images of her own "courting."

Dick blushed. *No courting,* he thought firmly. *Not yet, anyway.*

:Silly,: SKitty replied scornfully. The overtones of her thoughts were—why waste such a golden opportunity? Dick did not answer her.

Instead, he thumbed the lock on the crate, a lock keyed to his DNA only. A tiny prickle was the only indication that the lock had taken a sample of his skin for comparison, but a moment later a hairline-thin crack appeared around the front end of the crate, and Dick carefully opened the door and looked inside.

A pair of big green eyes in a pointed gray face looked out at him from the shadows. "Meowrrrr?" said a tentative voice.

Tell her it's all right, SKitty, he thought, extending a hand for Astra to sniff. It was too bad that his telepathic connection with SKitty did not extend to these other cats, but she seemed to be able to relay everything he needed to tell them.

Astra sniffed his fingers daintily, and oozed out of the crate, belly to the floor. After a moment though, a moment during which SKitty stared at her so hard that Dick was fairly certain his little friend was communicating any number of things to the newcomer, Astra stood up and looked around, her ears coming up and her muscles relaxing. Finally she looked up at Dick and blinked.

"Prrow," she said. He didn't need SKitty's translation to read that. He held out his arms and the young cat leapt into them, to be carried in regal dignity out of the Quarantine area.

As he turned away from the crate, he thought he caught a hint of movement in the shadows at the back. But when he turned to look, there was nothing there, and he dismissed it as nothing more than his imagination. If there *had* been anything else in Astra's crate, the manifest would have listed it—and Astra was definitely sterile, so it could not have been an unlicensed kitten.

Erica Makumba and Vena were waiting for him in the corridor outside. Vena offered her fingers to the newcomer; much more secure now, Astra sniffed them and purred. "She's lovely," Vena said in admiration. Dick had to agree; Astra was a velvety blue-gray from head to tail, and her slim, clean lines clearly showed her descent from Russian Blue ancestors.

:She for Furrball,: SKitty insisted, gently nipping at his neck.

Is this your idea or hers? Dick retorted.

:Sees Furrball in head; likes Furrball.: That seemed to finish it as far as SKitty was concerned. *:Good hunter, too.:* Dick gave in to the inevitable.

"Didn't we promise one of these new cats to the Lacu'teveras?" Dick asked. "This one seems very gentle; she'd probably do very well as a companion for Furrball." SKitty's kittens all had names as fancy as Astra's—or as SKitty's official name, for that matter. Furrball was "Andreas Widefarer of Lacu'un," Nuisance was "Misty Snowspirit of Lacu'un," Rags was "Lady Flamebringer of Lacu'un" and Trey was "Garrison Starshadow of Lacu'un." But they had, as cats always do, acquired their own nicknames that had nothing to do with the registered names. Astra would without a doubt do the same.

Each of the most prominent families of the Lacu'un had been granted one cat, but the Royal Family had three. Two of SKitty's original kittens, and one of the newcomers. Astra would bring that number up to four, a sacred number to the Lacu'un and very propitious.

"We did," Vena replied absently, scratching a pleased Astra beneath her chin. "And I agree with you; I think this one would please the Lacu'teveras very much." She laughed a little. "I'm beginning to think you're psychic or something, Dick; you haven't been wrong with your selections yet."

"Me?" he said ingenuously. "Psychic? Spirits of Space, Vena, the way these people are treating the cats, it doesn't matter anyway. Any 'match' I made would be a good one, so far as the cat is concerned. They couldn't be pampered more if they were Lacu'un girl-babies!"

"True," she agreed, and reluctantly took her hand away. "Well, four cats should be just about right to keep the Palace vermin-free. It's really kind of funny how they've divided the place up among them with no bickering. They almost act as if they were humans dividing up patrols!" Erica shot him an unreadable glance; did she remember how he had sat down with the original three and SKitty—and a floor-plan of the place—when he first brought them all to the Palace?

"They are bred for high intelligence," he reminded both of them hastily. "No one really knows how bright they are. They're bright enough to use their life-support pods in an emergency, and bright enough to learn how to use the human facilities in the ships. They seem to have ways of communicating with each other, or so the people at BioTech tell me, so maybe they did establish patrols."

"Well, maybe they did," Erica said after a long moment. He heaved a mental sigh of relief. The last thing he needed was to have someone suspect SKitty's telepathic link with him. BioTech was not breeding for telepathy, but if such a useful trait ever showed up in a *fertile* female, they would surely cancel *Brightwing*'s lease and haul SKitty back to their nearest cattery to become a breeding queen. SKitty was his best friend; to lose her like that would be terrible.

:No breeding,: SKitty said firmly. *:Love Dick, love ship. No breeding; breeding dull, kittens a pain. Not leave ship ever.:*

Well, at least SKitty agreed.

For now, anyway, now that her kittens were weaned.

Whenever she came into season, she seemed to change her mind, at least about the part that resulted in breeding, if not the breeding itself.

The Lacu'teveras, the Ruling Consort of her people, accepted Astra into the household with soft cries of welcome and gladness. Erica was right, the Lacu'un could not possibly have pampered their cats more. Whenever a cat wanted a lap or a scratch, one was immediately provided, whether or not the object of feline affection was in the middle of negotiations or a session of Council or not. Whenever one wished to play—although with the number of kreshta about, there was very little energy left over for playing—everything else was set aside for that moment. And when one brought in a trophy kreshta, tail and ears held high with pride, the entire court applauded. Astra was introduced to Furrball at SKitty's insistence. Noses were sniffed, and the two rubbed cheeks. It appeared that Mama's matchmaking was going to work.

The three humans and the pleased feline headed back across the city to the spaceport and the Fence around it. The city of the Lacu'un was incredibly attractive, much more so than any other similar city Dick had ever visited. Because of the rapidity with which the kreshta multiplied given any food and shelter, the streets were kept absolutely spotless, and the buildings clean and in repair. Most had walls about them, giving the inhabitants little islands of privacy. The walls of the wealthy were of carved stone; those of the poor of cast concrete. In all cases, ornamentation was the rule, not the exception.

The Lacu'un themselves walked the streets of their city garbed in delicate, flowing robes, or shorter more practical versions of the same garments. Graceful and handsome, they resembled avians rather than reptiles; their skin varied in shade from a dark brown to a golden tan, and their heads bore a kind of frill like an iguana's, that ran from the base of the neck to a point just above and between the eyes.

Their faces were capable of something like a smile, and the expression meant the same for them as it did for humans. Most of them smiled when they saw Dick and SKitty; although the kreshta-destroying abilities of the cat were not something any of them would personally feel the impact of for many years, perhaps generations, they still appreciated what the cats Dick had introduced could do. The kreshta had been a plague upon them for as long as their history recorded, even being so bold as to steal the food from plates and injure unguarded infants. For as long as that history, it had seemed that there would never be a solution to the depredations of the little beasts. But now—the most pious claimed the advent of the cats was a sign of the gods' direct intervention and blessing, and even the skeptics were thrilled at the thought that an end to the plague was in sight. It was unlikely that, even with a cat in every household, the kreshta would ever be destroyed—but such things as setting a guard on sleeping babies and locking meals in metal containers set into the tables could probably be eliminated.

When they crossed the Fence into Terran territory, however, the surroundings dropped in quality by a magnitude or two. Dick felt obscurely ashamed of his world whenever he looked at the shabby, garish spaceport "facilities" that comprised most of the Terran spaceport area. At least the headquarters that Captain Singh and CatsEye had established were handsome; adaptations of the natives' own architecture, in cast concrete with walls decorated with stylized stars, spaceships, and suggestions of slit-pupiled eyes. SolarQuest and UVN, the other two Companies that had been given Trade permits, were following CatsEye's lead, and had hired the same local architects and contractors to build their own headquarters. It looked from the half-finished buildings as if SolarQuest was going with a motif taken from their own logo of a stylized sunburst; UVN was going for geometrics in their wall-decor.

There were four ships here at the moment rather than the authorized three; for some reason, the independent freighter that had brought in the twenty shipscats was still here on the landing field. Dick wondered about that for a moment, then shrugged mentally. Independents often ran on shoestring budgets; probably they had only loaded enough fuel to get them here, and refueling was taking more time than they had thought it would.

Suddenly, just as they passed through the doors of the building, SKitty howled, hissed, and leapt from Dick's shoulders, vanishing through the rapidly-closing door.

He uttered a muffled curse and turned to run after her. What had gotten into her, anyway?

He found himself looking into the muzzle of a weapon held by a large man in the nondescript coveralls favored by the crew of that independent freighter. The man was as nondescript as his clothing, with ash-blond hair cut short and his very ordinary face—with the exception of that weapon, and the cold, calculating look in his iron-gray eyes. Dick put up his hands, slowly. He had the feeling this was a very bad time to play hero.

"Where's the damn cat?" snapped the one Dick was coming to think of as "the Gray Man." One of his underlings shrugged.

"Gone," the man replied shortly. "She got away when we rounded up these three, and she just vanished somewhere. Forget the cat. How much damage could a cat do?"

The Gray Man shrugged. "The natives might get suspicious if they don't see her with our man."

"She probably wouldn't have cooperated with our man," the underling pointed out. "Not like she did with this one. It doesn't matter—White got the new cats installed, and we don't need an animal that was likely to be a handful anyway."

The Gray Man nodded after a while and went back to securing the latest of his prisoners. The offices in the new CatsEye building had been turned into impromptu cells; Dick had gotten a glimpse of Captain Singh in one of them as he had been frog-marched past. He didn't know what these people had done with the rest of the crew or with Vena and Erica, since Vena had been taken off somewhere separately and Erica had been stunned and dragged away without waiting for her surrender.

The Gray Man watched him with his weapon trained on him as two more underlings installed a tangle-field generator across the doorway. With no windows, these little offices made perfect holding-pens. Most of them didn't have furniture yet, those that did didn't really contain anything that could be used as a weapon. The desks were simple slabs of native wood on metal supports, the chairs molded plastile, and both were bolted to the floor. There was nothing in Dick's little cubicle that could even be thrown.

Dick was still trying to figure out who and what these people were, when something finally clicked. He looked up at the Gray Man. "You're from TriStar, aren't you?" he asked.

If the Gray Man was startled by this, he didn't show it. "Yes," the man replied, gun-muzzle never wavering. "How did you figure that out?"

"BioTech never ships with anyone other than TriStar if they can help it," Dick said flatly. "I wondered why they had hired a tramp-freighter to bring out their cats; it didn't seem like them, but then I thought maybe that was all they could get."

"You're clever, White," the Gray Man replied, expressionlessly. "Too clever for your own good, maybe. We might just have to make you disappear. You and the Makumba woman; she'll probably know some of us as soon as she wakes up, and we don't have the time or the equipment to brain-wipe you."

Dick felt a chill going down his back, as the men at the door finished installing the field and left, quickly. "BioTech is going to wonder if one of their designated handlers just vanishes. And without me, you're never going to get SKitty back; BioTech isn't going to care for that, either. They might start asking questions that you can't answer."

The Gray Man stared at him for a long moment; his expression did not vary in the least, but at least he didn't make any move to shoot. "I'll think about it," he said finally. He might have said more, but there was a shout from the corridor outside.

"The cat!" someone yelled, and the Gray Man was out of the door before Dick could blink. Unfortunately, he paused long enough to trigger the tangle-field before he ran off in pursuit of what could only have been SKitty.

Dick slumped down into the chair, and buried his face in his hands, but not in despair. He was thinking furiously.

TriStar didn't like getting cut out of the negotiations; what they can't get legally, they'll get any way they can. Probably they intend to use us as hostages against Vena's good behavior, getting her to put them up as the new negotiators. I solved the problem of getting the cats for them; now there's no reason they couldn't just step in. But that can't go on forever, sooner or later Vena is going to get to a com unit or send some kind of message offworld. So what would these people do then?

TriStar had a reputation as being ruthless, and he'd heard from Erica that it was justified. So how do you get rid of an entire crew of a spaceship *and* the Terran Consul? And maybe the crews of the other two ships into the bargain?

Well, there was always one answer to that, especially on a newly-opened world. Plague.

The chill threaded his backbone again as he realized just what a good answer that was. These TriStar goons could use sickness as the excuse for why the CatsEye people weren't in evidence. A rumor of plague might well drive the other two ships offworld before *they* came down with it. The TriStar people could even claim to be taking care of the *Brightwing*'s crew.

Then, after a couple of weeks, they all succumb to the disease, the Terran Consul with them. . . .

It was a story that would work, not only with the Terran authorities, but with the Lacu'un. The Fence was a very effective barrier to help from the natives; the Lacu'un would not cross it to find out the truth, even if they were suspicious.

I have to get to a com set, he thought desperately. His own usefulness would last only so long as it took them to trap SKitty and find some way of caging her. No one else, so far as he knew, could hear her thoughts. All they needed to do would be to catch her and ship her back to BioTech, with the message that the designated handler was dead of plague and the cat had become unmanageable. It wouldn't have been the first time.

A soft hiss made him look up, and he strangled a cry of mingled joy and apprehension. It was SKitty! She was right outside the door, and she seemed to be trying to do something with the tangle-field generator.

SKitty! he thought at her as hard as he could. *SKitty, you have to get away from here, they're trying to catch you—* There was no way SKitty was going to be able to deal with those controls; they were deliberately made difficult to handle, just precisely because shipscats were known to be curious. And how could she know what complicated series of things to do to take down the field anyway?

But SKitty ignored him, using her stubby raccoon-like hands on the controls of the generator and hissing in frustration when the controls would not cooperate.

Finally, with a muffled yowl of triumph, she managed to twist the dial into the "off" position and the field went down. Dick was out the door in a moment, but SKitty was uncharacteristically running off ahead of him instead of waiting for him. Not that he minded! She was safer on the ground in case someone spotted him and stunned him; she was small and quick, and if they caught him again, she would still have a chance to hide and get away. But there was something odd about her bounding run; as if her body was a little longer than usual. And her tail seemed to be a lot longer than he remembered—

Never mind that, get moving! he scolded himself, trying to recall where they'd set up all the coms and if any of them were translight. SKitty whisked ahead of him, around a corner; when he caught up with her, she was already at work on the tangle-field generator in front of another door.

Practice must have made perfect; she got the field down just before he reached the doorway, and shot down the hall like a streak of black lightning. Dick stopped; inside was someone lying down on a cot, arm over her dark mahogany head. Erica!

"Erica!" he hissed at her. She sat bolt upright, wincing as she did so, and he felt a twinge of sympathy. A stun-migraine was no picnic.

She saw who was at the door, saw at the same moment that there was no tangle-field shimmer between them, and was on her feet and out in a fraction of a second. "How?" she demanded, scanning the corridor and finding it as curiously empty as Dick had.

"SKitty took the generator offline," he said. "She got yours, too, and she headed off that way—" He pointed towards the heart of the building. "Do you remember where the translight coms are?"

"Eyeah," she said. "In the basement, if we can get there. That's the emergency unit and I don't think they know we've got it."

She cocked her head to one side, as if she had suddenly heard something. He strained his ears—and there was a clamor, off in the distance beyond the walls of the building. It sounded as if several people were chasing something. But it couldn't have been SKitty; she was still in the building.

"It sounds like they're busy," Erica said, and grinned. "Let's go while we have the chance!"

But before they reached the basement com room, they were joined by most of the crew of the *Brightwing*, some of whom had armed themselves with whatever might serve as a weapon. All of them told the same story, about how the shipscat had taken down their tangle-fields and fled. Once in the basement of the building—after scattering the multiple nests of kreshta that had moved right in—the Com Officer took over while the rest of them found whatever they could to make a barricade and Dick related what he had learned and what his surmises were. Power controls were all down here; there would be no way short of blowing the building up for the TriStar goons to cut power to the com. Now all they needed was time—time to get their message out, and wait for the Patrol to answer.

But time just might be in very short supply, Dick told himself as he grabbed a sheet of reflective insulation to use as a crude stun-shield. And as if in answer to that, just as the Com Officer got the link warmed up and began to send, Erica called out from the staircase.

"Front and center—here they come!"

Dick slumped down so that the tiny medic could reach his head to bandage it. He knew he looked like he'd been through a war, but either the feeling of elated triumph or the medic's drugs or both prevented him from really feeling any of his injuries. In the end, it had come down to the crudest of hand-to-hand combat on the staircase, as the Com Officer resent the message as many times as he could and the rest of them held off the TriStar bullies. He could only thank the Spirits of Space that they had no weapons stronger than stunners—or at least, they hadn't wanted to use them down in the basement where so many circuits lay bare. Eventually, of course, they had been overwhelmed, but by then it was too late. The Com Officer had gotten a reply from the Patrol. Help was on the way. Faced with the collapse of their plan, the TriStar people had done the only wise thing. They had retreated.

With them, they had taken all evidence that they *were* from TriStar; there was no way of proving who and what they were, unless the Patrol corvette now on the way in could intercept them and capture them. Contrary to what the Gray Man had thought, Erica had recognized none of her captors.

But right now, none of that mattered. What did matter was that *they* had come through this—and that SKitty had finally reappeared as soon as the TriStar ship blasted out, to take her accustomed place on Dick's shoulders, purring for all she was worth and interfering with the medic's work.

"Dick—" Vena called from the door to the medic's office, "I found your—"

Dick looked up. Vena was cradling SKitty in her arms.

But SKitty was already on his shoulders.

She must have looked just as stunned as he did, but he recovered first, doing a double-take. *His* SKitty was the one on her usual perch—Vena's SKitty was a little thinner, a little taller—

And most *definitely* had a lot longer tail!

:Is Prrreet,: SKitty said with satisfaction. *:Handsome, no? Is bred for being Patrol-cat, war-cat.:*

"Vena, what's the tattoo inside that cat's ear?" he asked, urgently. She checked.

"FX-003," she said, "and a serial number. But the X designation is for experimental, isn't it?"

"Uh—yeah." He got up, ignoring the medic, and came to look at the new cat. Vena's stranger also had much more human-like hands than his SKitty; suddenly the mystery of how the cat had managed to manipulate the tangle-field controls was solved.

Shoot, he might even have been trained *to do that!*

:Yes,: SKitty said simply. *:I go play catch-me-stupid, he open human-cages. He hear of me on station, come to see me, be mate. I think I keep him.:*

Dick closed his eyes for a moment. Somewhere, there was a frantic BioTech station trying to figure out where one of their experimentals had gone. He *should* turn the cat over to them!

:No,: SKitty said positively. *:No look. Is deaf one ear; is pet. Run away, find me.:*

"He uh—must have come in as an extra with that shipment," Dick improvised quickly. "I found an extra invoice, I just thought they'd made a mistake. He's deaf in one ear, that's why they washed him out. I uh—I suppose *Brightwing* could keep him."

"I was kind of hoping I could—" Vena began, and flushed, lowering her eyes. "I suppose I still could . . . after this, the embassy is going to have to have a full staff with Patrol guards and a real Consul. They won't need me anymore."

Dick began to grin, as he realized what Vena was saying. "Well, he will need a handler. And I have all I can do to take care of *this* SKitty."

:Courting?: SKitty asked slyly, reaching out to lick one of Prrreet's ears.

This time Dick did not bother to deny it.

SCat

"NoooOOOWOWOWOW!"

The metal walls of Dick's tiny cabin vibrated with the howl. Dick White ignored it, as he injected the last of the four contraception-beads into SKitty's left hind leg. The black-coated shipscat did not move, but she did continue her vocal and mental protest. *:Mean,:* she complained, as Dick held the scanner over the right spot to make certain that he *had* gotten the bead placed where it was supposed to go. *:Mean, mean Dick.:*

Indignation showing in every line of her, she sat up on his fold-down desk and licked the injection site. It hadn't hurt; he *knew* it hadn't hurt, for he'd tried it on himself with a neutral bead before he injected her.

Nice, nice Dick, you should be saying, he chided her. *One more unauthorized litter and BioTech would be coming to take you away for their breeding program. You're too fertile for your own good.*

SKitty's token whine turned into a real yowl of protest, and her mate, now dubbed "SCat," joined her in the wail from his seat on Dick's bunk. *:Not leave Dick!:* SKitty shrilled in his head. *:Not leave ship!:*

Then no more kittens—at least not for a while! he

responded. *No more kittens means SKitty and SCat stay with Dick.*

SKitty leapt to join her mate on the bunk, where both of them began washing each other to demonstrate their distress over the idea of leaving Dick. SKitty's real name was "Lady Sundancer of Greenfields," and she was the proud product of BioTech's masterful genesplicing. Shipscats, those sturdy, valiant hunters of vermin of every species, betrayed their differences from Terran felines in a number of ways. BioTech had given them the "hands" of a raccoon, the speed of a mongoose, the ability to adjust to rapid changes in gravity or no gravity at all, and greatly enhanced mental capacity. What they did not know was that "Lady Sundancer"—aka "Dick White's Kitty," or "SKitty" for short—had another, invisible enhancement. She was telepathic—at least with Dick.

Thanks to SKitty and to her last litter, the CatsEye Company trading ship *Brightwing* was one of the most prosperous in this end of the Galaxy. That was due entirely to SKitty's hunting ability; she had taken swift vengeance when a persistent pest native to the newly-opened world of Lacu'un had bitten the consort of the ruler, killing with a single blow a creature the natives had *never* been able to exterminate. That, and her own charming personality, had made her kittens-to-be *most* desirable acquisitions, so precious that not even the leaders of Lacu'un "owned" them; they were held in trust for the world. Thanks to the existence of that litter and the need to get them appropriately pedigreed BioTech mates, SKitty's own mate—called "Prrreet" by SKitty and unsurprisingly dubbed "SCat" by the crew, for his ability to vanish—had made his own way to SKitty, stowing aboard with the crates containing more BioTech kittens for Lacu'un.

Where *he* came from, only he knew, although he was definitely a shipscat. His tattoo didn't match anything in the BioTech register. Too dignified to be called a "kitty," this handsome male was "Dick White's Cat."

And thanks to SCat's timely arrival and intervention, an attempt to kill the entire crew of the *Brightwing* and the Terran Consul to Lacu'un in order to take over the trading concession had been unsuccessful. SCat had disabled critical equipment holding them all imprisoned, so that they were able to get to a com station to call for help from the Patrol, while SKitty had distracted the guards.

SCat had never demonstrated telepathic powers with Dick, for which Dick was grateful, but he certainly possessed something of the sort with SKitty, and he was odd in other ways. Dick would have been willing to take an oath that SCat's forepaws were even more handlike than SKitty's, and that his tail showed some signs of being prehensile. There were other secrets locked in that wide black-furred skull, and Dick only wished he had access to them.

Dick was worried, for the *Brightwing* was in space again and heading towards one of the major stations with the results of their year-long trading endeavor with the beings of Lacu'un in their hold. Shipscats simply did not come out of nowhere; BioTech kept very tight control over them, denying them to ships or captains with a record of even the slightest abuse or neglect, and keeping track of where every one of them was, from birth to death. They were expensive—traders running on the edge could not afford them, and had to rid themselves of vermin with periodic vacuum-purges. SKitty claimed that her mate had "heard about her" and had come specifically to find her—but she would not say from where. SCat had to come from *somewhere*, and wherever that was, someone from there was probably looking for him. They would very likely take a dim view of their four-legged Romeo heading off on his own in search of his Juliet.

Any attempt to question the tom through SKitty was

useless. SCat would simply stare at him with those luminous yellow eyes, then yawn, and SKitty would soon grow bored with the proceedings. After all, to her, the important thing was that SCat was *here*, not where he had come from.

Behind Dick, in the open door of the cabin, someone coughed. He turned to find Captain Singh regarding Dick and cats with a jaundiced eye. Dick saluted hastily.

"Sir—contraceptive devices in place and verified sir!" he affirmed, holding up the injector to prove it.

The Captain, a darkly handsome gentleman as popular with the females of his own species as SCat undoubtably was with felines, merely nodded. "We have a problem, White," he pointed out. "The *Brightwing*'s manifest shows *one* shipscat, not two. And we still don't know where number two came from. I know what will happen if we try to take SKitty's mate away from her, but I also know what will happen if anyone finds out we have a second cat, origin unknown. BioTech will take a dim view of this."

Dick had been thinking at least part of this through. "We *can* hide him, sir," he offered. "At least until I can find out where he came from."

"Oh?" Captain Singh's eyebrows rose. "Just how do you propose to hide him, and where?"

Dick grinned. "In plain sight, sir. Look at them—unless you have them side-by-side, you wouldn't be able to tell which one you had in front of you. They're both black with yellow eyes, and it's only when you can see the size difference and the longer tail on SCat that you can tell them apart."

"So we simply make sure they're never in the same compartment while strangers are aboard?" the Captain hazarded. "That actually has some merit; the Spirits of Space know that people are always claiming shipscats can teleport. No one will even notice the difference if we don't say anything, and they'll just think she's getting around by way of the access tubes. How do you intend to find out where this one came from without making people wonder why you're asking about a stray cat?"

Dick was rather pleased with himself, for he had actually thought of this solution first. "SKitty is fertile—unlike nine-tenths of the shipscats. That is why we had kittens to offer the Lacu'un in the first place, and was why we have the profit we do, even after buying the contracts of the other young cats for groundside duty as the kittens' mates."

The Captain made a faint grimace. "You're stating the obvious."

"Humor me, sir. Did you know that BioTech routinely offers their breeding cats free choice in mates? That otherwise, they don't breed well?" As the Captain shook his head, Dick pulled out his trump card. "I am—ostensibly—going to do the same for SKitty. As long as we 'find' her a BioTech mate that she approves of, BioTech will be happy. And we need more kittens for the Lacu'un; we have no reason to *buy* them when we have a potential breeder of our own."

"But we got mates for her kittens," the Captain protested. "Won't BioTech think there's something odd going on?"

Dick shook his head. "You're thinking of house-cats. Shipscats aren't fertile until they're four or five. At that rate, the kittens won't be old enough to breed for four years, and the Lacu'un are going to want more cats before then. So I'll be searching the BioTech breeding records for a tom of the right age and appearance. Solid black is recessive—there can't be *that* many black toms of the right age."

"And once you've found your group of candidates—?" Singh asked, both eyebrows arching. "You look for the one that's missing?" He did not ask how Dick was supposed to have found out that SKitty "preferred" a black tom; shipscats were more than intelligent enough to choose a color from a set of holos.

Dick shrugged. "The information may be in the

records. Once I know where SCat's from, we can open negotiations to add him to our manifest with BioTech's backing. *They* won't pass up a chance to make SKitty half of a breeding pair, and I don't think there's a captain willing to go on BioTech's record as opposing a shipscat's choice of mate."

"I won't ask how you intend to make that particular project work," Singh said hastily. "Just remember, no more kittens in freefall."

Dick held up the now-empty injector as a silent promise.

"I'll brief the crew to refer to both cats as 'SKitty'—most of the time they do anyway," the Captain said. "Carry on, White. You seem to have the situation well in hand."

Dick was nowhere near that certain, but he put on a confident expression for the Captain. He saluted Singh's retreating back, then sat down on the bunk beside the pair of purring cats. As usual, they were wound around each other in a knot of happiness.

I wish my love-life was going that well. He'd hit it off with the Terran Consul well enough, but she had elected to remain in her ground-bound position, and his life was with the ship. Once again, romance took a second place to careers. Which in his case, meant no romance. There wasn't a single female in this crew that had shown anything other than strictly platonic interest in him.

If he *wanted* a career in space, he had to be very careful about what he did and said. As most junior officer on the *Brightwing,* he was the one usually chosen for whatever unpleasant duty no one else wanted to handle. And although he could actually *retire,* thanks to the prosperity that the Lacu'un contract had brought the whole crew, he didn't want to. That would mean leaving space, leaving the ship—and leaving SKitty and SCat.

He could also transfer within the company, but why change from a crew full of people he liked and respected, with a good Captain like Singh, to one about which he knew nothing? That would be stupid. And he couldn't leave SKitty, no matter what. She was his best friend, even if she did get him into trouble sometimes.

He also didn't have the experience to be anything other than the most junior officer in any ship, so transferring wouldn't have any benefits.

Unless, of course, he parlayed his profit-share into a small fortune and bought his own ship. Then he could be Captain, and he might even be able to buy SKitty's contract—but he lacked the experience that made the difference between prosperity and bankruptcy in the shaky world of the Free Traders. He was wise enough to know this.

As for the breeding project—he had some ideas. The *Brightwing* would be visiting Lacu'un for a minimum of three weeks on every round of their trading-route. Surely something could be worked out. Things didn't get chancy until after the kittens were mobile and before SKitty potty-trained them to use crew facilities. Before they were able to leave the nest-box, SKitty took care of the unpleasant details. If they could arrange things so that the period of mobility-to-weaning took place while they were on Lacu'un. . . .

Well, he'd make that Jump when the coordinates came up. Right now, he had to keep outsiders from discovering that there was feline contraband on board, and find out where that contraband came from.

:Dick smart,: SKitty purred proudly. *:Dick fix everything.:*

Well, he thought wryly, *at least I have* her *confidence, if no-one else's!*

It had been a long time since the *Brightwing* had been docked at a major port, and predictably, everyone wanted shore leave. Everyone except Dick, that is. He had no intentions of leaving the console in Cargo where he was doing his "mate-hunting" unless and until he found his match. The fact that there was nothing but a skeleton crew aboard, once the inspectors left, only made it easier for Dick to run his searches through the BioTech database available through the station. This database was part of the public records kept on every station, and updated weekly by BioTech. Dick had a notion that he'd get his "hit" within a few hours of initiating his search.

He was pleasantly surprised to discover that there were portraits available for every entry. It might even be possible to identify SCat just from the portraits, once he had all of the black males of the appropriate age sorted out. That would give him even more rationale for the claim that SKitty had "chosen" her mate herself.

With an interested feline perching on each arm of the chair, he logged into the station's databases, identified himself and gave the station his billing information, then began his run.

There was nothing to do at that point but sit back and wait.

"I hope you realize all of the difficulties I'm going through for you," he told the tom, who was grooming his face thoughtfully. "I'm doing without shore-leave to help you here. I wouldn't do this for a fellow human!"

SCat paused in his grooming long enough to rasp Dick's hand with his damp-sandpaper tongue.

The computer *beeped* just at that moment to let him know it was done. He was running all this through the Cargo dumb-set; he could have used the *Brightwing*'s Expert-System AI, but he didn't want the AI to get curious, and he didn't want someone wondering why he was using a Mega-Brain to access feline family-trees. What he *did* want was the appearance that this was a brainstorm of his own, an attempt to boost his standing with his Captain by providing further negotiable items for the Lacu'un contract. There was something odd about all of this, something that he couldn't put his finger on, but something that just felt wrong and made him want to be extra-cautious. Why, he didn't know. He only knew that he didn't want to set off any tell-tales by acting as if this mate-search was a priority item.

The computer asked if he wanted to use the holo-table, a tiny square platform built into the upper right hand corner of the desk. He cleared off a stack of hard-copy manifests, and told it "yes." Then the first of his feline biographies came in.

He'd made a guess that SCat was between five and ten years old; shipscats lived to be fifty or more, but their useful lifespan was about twenty or thirty years. All too often their job was hazardous; alien vermin had poisonous fangs or stings, sharp claws and teeth. Cats suffered disabling injuries more often than their human crewmates, and would be retired with honors to the homes of retired spacers, or to the big "assisted living" stations holding the very aged and those with disabling injuries of their own. Shipscats were always welcome, anywhere in space.

And I can think of worse fates than spending my old age watching the stars with SKitty on my lap. He gazed down fondly at his furred friend, and rubbed her ears.

SKitty purred and butted her head into his hand. She paid very little attention to the holos as they passed slowly in review. SCat was right up on the desk, however, not only staring intently at the holos, but splitting his attention between the holos and the screen.

You don't suppose he can read . . . ?

Suddenly, SCat let out a yowl, and swatted the holoplate. Dick froze the image and the screen-biography that accompanied it.

He looked first at the holo—and it certainly looked more like SCat than any of the others had. But SCat's attention was on the screen, not the holo, and he stared fixedly at the modest insignia in the bottom right corner.

Patrol?

He looked down at SCat, dumbfounded. "You were with the Patrol?" He whispered it; you did not invoke the Patrol's name aloud unless you wanted a visit from them.

Yellow eyes met his for a moment, then the paw tapped the screen. He read further.

Type MF-025, designation Lightfoot of Sun Meadow. Patrol ID FX-003. Standard Military genotype, standard Military training. Well, that explained how he had known how to shut down the "pirate" equipment. Now Dick wondered how much else the cat had done, outside of his sight. And a military genotype? He hadn't even known there *was* such a thing.

Assigned to Patrol ship DIA-9502, out of Oklahoma Station, designated handler Major Logan Greene.

Oklahoma Station—that was *this* station. Drug Interdiction? He whistled softly.

Then a date, followed by the ominous words, *Ship missing, all aboard presumed dead.*

All aboard—except the shipscat.

The cat himself gave a mournful yowl, and SKitty jumped up on the desk to press herself against him comfortingly. He looked back down at SCat. "Did you jump ship before they went missing?"

He wasn't certain he would get an answer, but he had lived with SKitty for too long to underestimate shipscat intelligence. The cat shook his head, slowly and deliberately—in the negative.

His mouth went dry. "Are you saying—you got away?"

A definite nod.

"Your ship was boarded, and you got away?" He was astonished. "But how?"

For an answer, the cat jumped down off the desk and walked over to the little escape pod that neither he nor SKitty ever forgot to drag with them. He seized the tether in his teeth and dragged it over to an access tube. It barely fit; he wedged it down out of sight, then pawed open the door, and dropped down, hidden, and now completely protected from what must have happened.

He popped back out again, and walked to Dick's feet.

Dick was thinking furiously. There had been rumors that drug-smugglers were using captured Patrol ships; this more-or-less confirmed those rumors. *Disable the ship, take the exterior airlock and blow it. Whoever wasn't suited up would die. Then they board and finish off whoever* was *suited up. They patch the lock, restore the air, and weld enough junk to the outside of the ship to disguise it completely. Then they can bring it in to any port they care to—even the ship's home port.*

This station. Which is where SCat escaped.

"Can you identify the attackers?" he asked SCat. The cat slowly nodded.

:They know he gone. He run, they chase. He try get home, they stop. He hear of me on dock, go hide in ship bringing mates. They kill he, get chance,: SKitty put in helpfully.

He could picture it easily enough; SCat being pursued, cut off from the Patrol section of the station—hiding out on the docks—catching the scent of the mates being shipped for SKitty's kittens and deciding to seek safety offworld. Cats, even shipscats, did not tend to grasp the concept of "duty"; he knew from dealing with SKitty that she took her bonds of personal affection seriously, but little else. So once "his" people were dead, SCat's personal allegiance to the Patrol was nonexistent, and his primary drive would be self-preservation. *Wonderful. I wonder if they—whoever they are—figured out he got away on another ship.* Another, more alarming thought occurred to him. *I wonder if my fishing about in the BioTech database touched off any tell-tales!*

No matter. There was only one place to go now—straight to Erica Makumba, the Legal and Security Officer.

He dumped a copy of the pertinent datafile to a memory cube, then scooped up both cats and pried their life-support ball out of its hiding place. Then he *ran* for Erica's cabin, praying that she had not gone off on shore-leave.

The Spirits of Space were with him; the indicator outside her cabin door indicated that she was in there, but did not want to be disturbed. He pounded on the door anyway. Erica *might* kill him—but there were people after SCat who had murdered an entire Patrol DIA squad.

After a moment, the door cracked open a centimeter.

"White." Erica's flat, expressionless voice boded extreme violence. "This had better be an emergency."

He said the one word that would guarantee her attention. "Hijackers."

The door snapped open; she grabbed him and pulled him inside, cats, support-ball and all, and slammed the door shut behind him. She was wearing a short robe, tying it hastily around herself, and she wasn't alone. But the man watching them both alertly from the disheveled bed wasn't one of the *Brightwing*'s crew, so Dick flushed, but tried to ignore him.

"I found out where SCat's from," he babbled, dropping one cat to hand the memory-cube to her. "Read that—quick!"

She punched up the console at her elbow and dropped the cube in the receiver. The BioTech file, minus the holo, scrolled up on the screen. The man in the bed leaned forward to read it too, and whistled.

Erica swiveled to glare at him. "You keep this to yourself, Jay!" she snapped. Then she turned back to Dick. "Spill it!" she ordered.

"SCat's ship was hijacked, probably by smugglers," he said quickly. "He hid his support-ball in an access tube, and he was in it when they blew the lock. They missed him in the sweep, and when they brought their prize in here, he got away. But they know he's gone, and they know he can ID them."

"And they'll be giving the hairy eyeball to every ship with a black cat on it." She bit her knuckle—and Jay added his own two credits' worth.

"I hate to say this, but they've probably got a telltale on the BioTech data files, so they know whenever anyone accesses them. It's not restricted data, so anyone could leave a tell-tale." The man's face was pale beneath his normally dusky skin-tone. "If they don't know you've gone looking by now, they will shortly."

They all looked at each other. "Who's still on board?" Dick asked, and gulped.

Erica's mouth formed a tight, thin line. "You, me, Jay and the cats. The cargo's offloaded, and regs say you don't need more than two crew on board in-station. *Theoretically* no one can get past the security at the lock."

Jay barked a laugh, and tossed long, dark hair out of his eyes. "Honey, I'm a comptech. Trust me, you can get past the security. You just hack into the system, tell it the ship in the bay is bigger than it really is, and upload whoever you want as additional personnel."

Erica swore—but Jay stood up, wrapping the sheet around himself like a toga, and pushed her gently aside. "What can be hacked can be unhacked—or at least I can make it a lot more difficult for them to get in and make those alterations stick. Give me your code to the AI."

Erica hesitated. He turned to stare into her eyes. "I need the AI's help. *You* two and the cats are going to get out of here—get over to the Patrol side of the station. I'm going to hold them off as long as I can, and play stupid when they do get in, but I need the speed of the AI to help me lay traps. You've known me for three years. You trusted me enough to bring me here, didn't you?"

She swore again, then reached past him to key in her code. He sat down, ignoring them and plunging straight into a trance of concentration.

"Come on!" Erica grabbed Dick's arm, and put the support-ball on the floor. SKitty and SCat must have been reading *her* mind, for they both squirmed into the ball, which was big enough for more than one cat. They'd upgraded the ball after SKitty had proved to be so—fertile. Erica shoved the ball at Dick, and kept hold of his arm, pulling him out into the corridor.

"Where are we going?" he asked.

"To get our suits, then to the emergency lock," she replied crisply. "If we try to go out the main lock into the station, they'll get us for certain. So we're going outside for a little walk."

A little walk? All the way around the station? Outside?

He could only hope that "they" hadn't thought of that as well. They reached the suiting-up room in seconds flat.

He averted his eyes and climbed into his own suit as Erica shed her robe and squirmed into hers. "How far is it to the Patrol section?" he asked.

"Not as far as you think," she told him. "And there's a maintenance lock just this side of it. What I want to know is how *you* got all this detailed information about the hijacking."

He turned, and saw that she was suited up, with her faceplate still open, staring at him with a calculating expression.

This is probably not the time to hold out on her.

He swallowed, and sealed his suit up, leaving his own faceplate open. Inside the ball, the cats were watching both of them, heads swiveling to look from one face to the other, as if they were watching a tennis-match.

"SKitty's telepathic with me," he admitted. "I think SCat's telepathic with her. She seems to be able to talk with him, anyway."

He waited for Erica to react, either with disbelief or with revulsion. Telepaths of any species were not always popular among humankind. . . .

But Erica just pursed her lips and nodded. "Eyeah. I thought she might be. And telepathy's one of the traits BioTech doesn't talk about, but security people have know for a while that the MF type cats are bred for it. Maybe SKitty's momma did a little wandering over on the miltech side of the cattery, hmm?"

SKitty made a "silent" meow, and he just shrugged, relieved that Erica wasn't phobic about it. And equally relieved to learn that telepathy was already a trait that BioTech had established in their shipscat lines. *So they won't be coming to take SKitty away from me when they find out that she's a 'path. . . .*

But right now, he'd better be worrying about making a successful escape. He pulled his faceplate down and sealed it, fastening the tether-line of the ball to a snaplink on his waistband. He warmed up his suit-radio, and she did the same. "I hope you know what you're getting us into," he said, as Erica sealed her own plate shut and led the way to the emergency lock.

She looked back over her shoulder at him.

"So do I," she replied soberly.

The trip was a nightmare.

Dick had never done a spacewalk on the exterior of a station before. It wasn't at all like going out on the hull of a ship. There were hundreds of obstacles to avoid—windows, antenna, instrument-packages, maintenance robots. Any time an inspection drone came along, they had to hide to avoid being picked up on camera. It was work, hard work, to inch their way along the station in this way, and Dick was sweating freely before a half an hour was up.

It seemed like longer. Every time he glanced up at the chronometer in his faceplate HUD, he was shocked to see how little time had passed. The suit-fans whined in his ears, as the life-support system alternately fought to warm him up when they hid in the shade, or cool him down when they paused in full sunlight. Stars burned down on them, silent points of light in a depth of darkness that made him dizzy whenever he glanced out at it. The knowledge that he could be lost forever out there if he just made one small mistake chilled his heart.

Finally, Erica pointed, and he saw the outline of a maintenance lock just ahead. The two of them pulled themselves hand-over-hand toward it, reaching it at the same instant. But it was Erica who opened it, while Dick reeled the cats in on their tether.

With all four of them inside, Erica sealed the lock from the inside and initiated pressurization. Within moments, they were both able to pop their faceplates and breathe station-air again.

Something prompted Dick to release the cats from their ball before Erica unsealed the inner hatch. He unsnapped the tether and was actually straightening up, empty ball in both hands, when Erica opened the door to a hallway—

—and dropped to the floor, as the shrill squeal of a stun-gun pierced the quiet of the lock.

"Erica!" Without thinking, he ran forward, and found himself facing the business-end of a powerful stunner, held by a nondescript man who held it as if he was quite used to employing it. He was *not* wearing a station-uniform.

The man looked startled to see him, and Dick did the only thing he could think of. He threw the support-ball at the man, as hard as he could.

It hit cleanly, knocking the man to the floor as it impacted with his chest. He clearly was not aware that the support-balls were as massy as they were. The two cats flashed past him, heading for freedom, and Dick tried to follow their example. But the man was quick to recover, and as Dick tried to jump over his prone body, the fellow grabbed his ankle and tripped him up.

Then it turned into a brawl, with Dick the definite underdog. Even in the suit, the stranger still outweighed him.

Within a few seconds, Dick was on his back on the floor, and the stranger held him down, easily. The stun-gun was no longer in his hands, but it didn't look to Dick as if he really needed it.

In fact, as the man's heavy fist pounded into Dick's face, he was quickly convinced that he didn't need it. Pain lanced through his jaw as the man's fist smashed into it; his vision filled with stars and red and white flashes of light. More agony burst into his skull as the blows continued. He flailed his arms and legs, but there was nothing he could do—he was trapped in the suit, and he couldn't even get enough leverage to defend himself. He tasted blood in his mouth—he couldn't see—

:BAD MAN!:

There was a terrible battle-screech from somewhere out in the corridor, and the blows stopped. Then the weight lifted from his body, as the man howled in pain.

Dick managed to roll to one side, and stagger blindly to his feet with the aid of the corridor bulkhead—he still couldn't see. He dashed blood out of his eyes with one hand, and shook his head to clear it, staring blindly in the direction of the unholy row.

"*Get it off! Get it off me!*" Human screams mixed with feline battle-cries, telling him that whichever of the cats had attacked, they were giving a good accounting of themselves.

But there were other sounds—the sounds of running feet approaching, and Dick tried frantically to get his vision to clear. A heavy body crashed into him, knocking him into the bulkhead with enough force to drive all the breath from his body, as the *zing* of an illegal neurogun went off somewhere near him.

SKitty!

But whoever was firing swore, and the cat-wail faded into the distance.

"It got away!" said one voice, over the sobbing of another.

A third swore, as Dick fought for air. "You. Go after it," the third man said, and there was the sound of running feet. Meanwhile, footsteps neared where Dick lay curled in a fetal bundle on the floor.

"What about this?" the second voice asked.

The third voice, cold and unemotional, wrote Dick's death warrant. "Get rid of it, and the woman, too."

And Dick could not even move. He heard someone breathing heavily just above him; sensed the man taking aim—

Then—

"Patrol! Freeze! Drop your weapons now!"

Something clattered to the deck beside him, as more running feet approached; and with a sob of relief, Dick finally drew a full breath. There was a scuffle just beside him, then someone helped him to stand, and he heard the hiss of a hypospray and felt the tell-tale sting against the side of his neck. A moment later, his eyes cleared—just in time for him to catch SKitty as she launched herself from the arms of a uniformed DIA officer into his embrace.

"So, the bottom line is, you'll let us take SCat's contract?" Captain Singh sat back in his chair while Dick rubbed SKitty's ears. She and SCat both burdened Dick's lap, as they had since SCat, the Captain, the DIA negotiator, and Erica had all walked into the sickbay where Dick was still recovering. Erica was clearly nursing a stun-headache; the Captain looked a little frazzled. The DIA man, as most of his ilk, looked as unemotional as an android. The DIA had spent many hours with a human-feline telepathic specialist debriefing SCat. Apparently SCat was naturally only a receptive telepath; it took a human who was also a telepath to "talk" to him.

"There's no reason why not," the DIA agent said. "You civilians have helped materially in this case; both you and he are entitled to certain compensation, and if that's what you all want, then he's yours with our blessing—the fact that he is only a receptive telepath makes him less than optimal for further Patrol duties." The agent shrugged. "We can always get other shipscats with full abilities. According to the records, the only reason we kept him was because Major Logan selected him."

SKitty bristled, and Dick sent soothing thoughts at her.

Then the agent smiled, making his face look more human. "Major Logan was a good agent, but he didn't particularly care for having a cat talking to him. I gather that Lightfoot and he got along all right, but there wasn't the strong bond between them that we would have preferred. It would have been just a matter of time before that squad and ship got a new cat-agent team. Besides, we aren't completely inhuman. If your SKitty and this boy here are happily mated, who and what in the Patrol can possibly want to separate them?"

"Judging by the furrows SKitty left in that 'jacker's face and scalp, it isn't a good idea to get between her and someone she loves," Captain Singh said dryly. "He's lucky she left him one eye."

The agent's gaze dropped briefly to the swath of black fur draped over Dick's lap. "Believe me," he said fervently. "That *is* a consideration we had taken into account. Your little lady there is a warrior for fair, and we have no intention of denying her anything her heart is set on. If she wants Lightfoot, and he wants her, then she's got him. We'll see his contract is transferred over to *Brightwing* within the hour." His eyes rose to meet Dick's. "You're a lucky man to have a friend like her, young man. She put herself between you and certain death. Don't you ever forget it."

SKitty's purr deepened, and SCat's joined with hers as Dick's hands dropped protectively on their backs. "I know that, sir," he replied, through swollen lips. "I knew it before any of this happened."

SKitty turned her head, and he gazed into amused yellow eyes. *:Smart Dick,:* she purred, then lowered her head to her paws. *:Smart man. Mate happy here, mate stay. Everything good. Love you.:*

And that, as far as SKitty was concerned, was the end of it. The rest were simply "minor human matters."

He chuckled, and turned his own attention to dealing with those "minor human matters," while his best friend and her mate drifted into well-earned sleep.

A Better Mousetrap

If there was one thing that Dick White had learned in all his time as SuperCargo of the CatsEye Company Free Trader *Brightwing*, it was that having a cat purring in your ear practically forced you to relax. The extremely comfortable form-molding chair he sat in made it impossible to feel anything but comfortable, and warm black fur muffled both of Dick White's ears, a steady vibration massaging his neck. "Build a better mousetrap, and the world will beat a path to your door," Dick said idly, as SCat poured himself like a second fluid, black rug over the blue-grey of his lap. It was SKitty who was curled up around his shoulders, vibrating contentedly in what Dick called her "subsonic purr-mode," while her mate took it as his responsibility to make sure there was plenty of shed hair on the legs of his grey shipsuit uniform.

"What?" asked Terran Ambassador Vena Ferducci, looking up from the list of Lacu'un nobles petitioning for one of SKitty's latest litter. The petite, dark-haired woman sat in a less comfortable, metal chair behind a stone desk, which stood next to a metal rack stuffed with archaic rolled paper documents. The Lacu'un had not yet devised the science of filing paperwork in multiples yet, which made them ultra-civilised in Vena's opinion. This, her office in the Palace of the Lacu'ara and Lacu'teveras, was not often used for that very reason. When she dealt with *Terran* bureaucracy, she needed every electronic helper she could get.

The list she perused was very long, and made rather cumbersome due to the Lacu'un custom of presenting all official court-documents in the form of a massively ornamented yellow-parchment scroll, with case and end caps of engraved bronze and illuminated capital-initials. Dick had a notion that somewhere in the universe there probably was a collector of handwritten documents who would pay a small fortune for it, but when every petitioner on the list had been satisfied, it would probably be sent to the under-clerks, scraped clean, and reused.

"It's an old Terran folk-saying," Dick elaborated, and gestured to the list by way of explanation. "One which certainly seems to be borne out by our present situation."

"Yes, well, given the length of this list we're doubly fortunate that SKitty and SCat are so—ah—*fertile*, and that BioTech is willing to send us their shipscat washouts." Vena stretched out her hand towards SCat's head, and the huge black tom cooperated by craning his neck towards her. Even before her fingers contacted his fur, SCat was purring loudly, giving Dick an uncannily similar sensation to being strapped in while the ship he served was under full power.

Dick White could well be one of the wealthiest supercargoes in the history of space-trade—his share of the profits from CatsEye Company's lucrative trade with the Lacu'un amounted to quite a tidy sum. It wasn't enough to buy and outfit his own ship—yet—but if trade progressed as it had begun, there was the promise that one day it would be.

Not that I want my own ship yet! he told himself. *Not until I know as much as Captain Singh. There are easier ways to commit suicide than pretending I know enough to command a starship when all I really know is how to run the cargo hold!*

Not that Captain Singh would *let* him take his profit-share and do something so stupid. Dick grinned to himself, imagining the Captain's face if he showed up in the office with *that* kind of harebrained proposal. Captain Singh's expression would be one to behold—following which, Dick would probably find himself stunned unconscious and wake under the solicitous attentions of a concerned head-shrinker!

The Captain *had* been willing, even more than willing, to let Dick stay on-planet for few Terran-months though, after SKitty and SCat announced the advent of a litter-to-be. One of her last litter was co-opted to serve as shipscat pro tem, while Dick and his two charges waited out the delivery, maturation, and weaning of eight little black furballs who were, if that was possible, even cuter than the last batch. It was a good thing that they all *were* on-planet, too, because the Octet managed to get themselves into a hundred times more mischief than the previous lot.

The trouble is, they have a lot of energy, absolutely no sense, and no fear at all at this age. Brainless kitten antics rapidly begin to pall when you've fished a wailing fuzz-mote out of the comconsole for the fifteenth time in a single shift.

But every Lacu'un in the palace, from the Lacu'teveras down to the lowliest scullery-lad, was thrilled to the toes—or rather, claws—to play with, rescue, and cuddle the Bratlings. If SKitty and SCat had not taken their duties as parents, palace-guardians, and role-models so seriously, they wouldn't have had to do anything but lie about and wait for the kittens to be carried in to them for feeding.

Fortunately for all concerned, their parents had powerful senses of responsibility towards their offspring. Both cats were born and bred—literally—for duty. Yes, they were cats, with a cat's sense of independence and contrariness, but they took duty very, very seriously. And their duty was Vermin Control.

This was a duty that went back centuries to the very beginnings of the association of man and cat, but until BioTech developed shipscats, never had a feline been better suited to or more cooperative in the execution of that duty. Furthermore, Dick now knew what few others did—that the shipscats so necessary to the safety of traders and their ships were actually a highly profitable byproduct of other research, secret research, designed to give the men and women of the Patrol uniquely clever comrades-in-arms.

These genetically altered cats were not just clever, it was not just that they had forepaws modeled after the forepaws of raccoons—oh no. That was not enough. Patrol cats were telepaths.

SCat had been a patrol cat—but although he could understand the thoughts of humans, he couldn't speak to them. This was a flaw, so far as the Patrol was concerned, though not an insurmountable flaw. However, when criminals took over the ship he served on and killed all of those aboard, SCat was the only survivor and the only witness—unable to call for help or relate what he had witnessed, he had sought for help from his own kind and found it in SKitty. When the same criminals learned SCat was still alive and tried to eliminate him and the crew of the Free Trader ship *Brightwing*, for good measure, it had been Dick's research and deductive reasoning that had learned the truth in time, and with SCat's and SKitty's help he had foiled the plot.

As for SKitty, she was something of an aberration herself—ordinary shipscats were not supposed to be telepathic *or* fertile; she was both.

As far as Dick could tell, she was telepathic only with him—though, given that she was all cat, with a cat's puckish sense of humor, she might well choose not to let him know she could "speak" to others. Everyone on the ship knew she was fertile, though—when they had first come to the world of the Lacu'un, she'd already had one litter and was pregnant with another. That first litter—born and raised in the ship—had shown just what kind of a nightmare two loose kittens could be within the close confines of a spaceship. Dick had not been looking forward to telling Captain Singh of the second litter, when SKitty had solved the problem for them.

The Lacu'un, a race of golden-skinned, vaguely reptilian anthropoids, suffered from the depredations of a particularly voracious, fast, and apparently indestructible pest called *kreshta.* The only way to keep them from taking over completely was to lock anything edible (and the creature could eat practically anything) in airtight containers of metal, glass, ceramic, or stone, and build only in materials the pest couldn't eat. The pests did keep the streets so clean that they sparkled and there was no such thing as a trash problem, but those were the only benefits to the plague.

The Lacu'un had just opened their planet to trade from outside, and the *Brightwing* was one of several ships that had arrived to represent either themselves or one of the large Companies. Only Captain Singh had the foresight to include SKitty in their delegation, however, for only he had bothered to research the Lacu'un thoroughly enough to learn that they placed great value on totemic animals and had virtually *nothing* in the way of domesticated predators themselves. He reckoned that a tame predator would be very impressive to them, and he was right.

SKitty had been on her best behavior, charming them all, and taking to this alien race immediately. The Lacu'teveras, the female co-ruler, had been particularly charmed, so much so that she had missed the presence of one of the little pests, which had bitten her. Enraged at this attack on someone she favored, SKitty had killed the creature.

For the Lacu'un, this was nothing short of a miracle, the end of a scourge that had been with them since the beginning of their civilization. After that moment, there was no question of anyone else getting most-favored trading status with the Lacu'un, ever.

CatsEye got the plum contract, SKitty's kittens-to-be got immediate homes, and Dick White's life became incredibly complicated.

Since then, he was no longer just an apprentice supercargo and Designated Shipscat Handler on a small Free Trader ship. He'd been imprisoned by Company goons, stalked and beaten within an inch of his life by cold-blooded murderous hijackers, and had to face the Patrol itself to bargain for SCat's freedom. He'd had enough adventure in two short Standard-years to last most people for the rest of their lives.

But all that was in the past. Or so he hoped.

For a while, anyway, it would be nice if the most difficult decision I had to make would be which of the Lacu'un nobles get SKitty-babies and which have to make do with shipscat washouts.

Those "washouts" were mature cats that for one reason or another couldn't adapt to ship life. Gengineering wasn't perfect, even now; there were cats that couldn't handle freefall, cats that were claustrophobes, cats that were shy or anti-social. Those had the opportunity to come here, to join the vermin-hunting crew. Thus far, thirty had made the trip, some to become mates for the first litter, others to take up solitary residence with a noble family. There were other washouts, who didn't pass the intelligence tests, but those were never offered to the Lacu'un—they already filled a steady need for companions in children's hospitals and retirement homes, where the high shipscat intelligence wasn't needed, just a loving friend smart enough to understand what not to do around someone sick or in pain.

There were still far more Lacu'un who urgently craved the boon of a cat than there were cats to fill the need. Thus far, none of SKitty's female offspring had carried that rare gene for fertility—when one did, that one would go back to BioTech, to be treated like the precious object she was, pampered and amused, asked to breed only so often as *she* chose. There was always a trade-off in any gengineering effort; lack of fertility was a small price to pay in a species as notoriously prolific as cats.

Meanwhile, the proud parents were in the last stages of educating their current offspring. There was a pile of the dead vermin just in front of Vena's desk; every so often, one of the half-grown kittens would bring another to add to the pile, then sit politely and wait for his parents to approve. Sometimes, when the pest was particularly large, SCat would descend from Dick's lap with immense dignity, inspect the kill, and bestow a rough lick by way of special reward.

Dick couldn't keep track of how many pests each of the kittens had destroyed, but from the size of the pile so far, the parents had reason to be proud of their offspring.

The kittens certainly inherited their parents' telepathic skills as well as their hunting skills, for just as it occurred to Dick that it was about time for them to be fed, they scampered in from all available doorways. In a moment, they were neatly lined up, eight identical pairs of yellow eyes staring avidly from eight little black faces beneath sixteen enormous ears. At this age, they seemed to consist mainly of eyes, ears, paws and tails.

The Lacu'un servant whose proud duty it was to feed the weanlings arrived with a bowl heaping with their imported food. She was clothed in the simple, silky draped tunic in the deep gold of the royal household. The frilled crest running from the back of her neck to just above her eye-ridge stood totally erect and was flushed to a deep salmon-color with pleasure and pride. She started to put the bowl on the floor, and the kittens leapt to their feet and ran for the food—

But suddenly SCat sprang from Dick's lap, every hair on end, spitting and yowling. He landed at the startled servant's feet and did a complete flip over, so that he faced his kittens. As they skidded on the slick stone, he growled and batted at them, sending them flying.

"*SCat!*" Vena shouted, as she jumped to her feet, horrified and angry. "What are you doing? Bad cat!"

"No he's not!" Dick replied, making a leap of his own for the food bowl and jerking it from the frightened servant's hands. He had already heard SKitty's frantic mental screech of *:Bad food!:* as she followed her mate off Dick's shoulders to keep the kittens from the deadly bowl.

"The food's poisoned," Dick added, sniffing the puffy brown nodules suspiciously, as the servant backed away, the slits in her golden-brown eyes so wide he could scarcely see the iris. "SCat must have scented it—that's probably one of the things Patrol cats are trained in. *I* can't tell the difference, but—" as SKitty held the kittens at bay, he held the bowl down to SCat, who took a delicate sniff and backed away, growling. "See?"

Vena's expression darkened, and she turned to the servant. "The food has been poisoned," she said flatly. "Who had access to it?" They both knew that Shivari, the servant, was trustworthy; she would sooner have thrown herself between the kittens and a ravening monster than see any hurt come to them. She proved that now by her behavior; her crest-frill flattened, she turned bright yellow—the Lacu'un equivalent of turning pale—and replied instantly.

"I do not know—I got the bowl from the kitchen—"

She grabbed Vena's hand and the two of them ran off, with Dick closely behind, still carrying the bowl. When they arrived at the kitchen, Vena and Shivari cornered all the staff while Dick blocked the exit. He had a fair grasp of Lacu'un by now, but Vena and Shivari were talking much too fast for him to get more than two words in four.

Soon enough, though, Vena turned away with anger and dissatisfaction on her face, while Shivari began a blistering harangue worthy of Captain Singh. "There was a new servant that no one recognized on staff this morning," Vena said in disgust. "Obviously they were smart enough to keep him away from the food meant for people, but no one thought anything of letting him open up the cat food into a bowl."

"Well, they know better now," Dick replied grimly.

"I'll put the Embassy on alert—and give me that—" Vena took the bowl from him. "I'll have the Marines run it through an analyzer."

Embassy guards by long tradition were called "Marines," although they were merely another branch of the Patrol. Dick readily surrendered the poisoned food to Vena, knowing that if SCat could smell a poison, the forensic analyzer every Embassy possessed—just in case—would easily be able to find it. Relations with the Lacu'un were important enough that Vena had gone from being merely a trade advisor and titular Consul to a full-scale Ambassador, with the attendant staff and amenities. It was that promotion that had persuaded her to remain here instead of returning to her former position in the Scouts.

Dick himself went to the storage vault that held the imported cat-food, got a highly-compressed cube out, and opened it over a freshly washed bowl. The stuff puffed up to ten times its compressed size once it came into contact with air and humidity; it would be impossible to tamper with the packages without a resulting "explosion" of food. The entire feline family flowed into the kitchen as soon as his fingers touched the package; the kittens swarmed around his legs, mewling piteously, but he offered the bowl for SCat's inspection before allowing them to engulf it.

His mind buzzed with questions, but two were uppermost—who would have tried to poison the kittens, and why?

✧ ✧ ✧

SCat and SKitty herded their kittens along like a pair of attentive sheepdogs when they'd finished eating, following behind Dick as he left the palace, heading for the Embassy. The Marine at the entrance gave him a brisk nod of recognition, saving her grin for the moving black-furred flock behind him.

A second Marine at a desk just inside, skilled in the Lacu'un tongue, served double-duty as a receptionist. "The Ambassador is expecting you, sir," he said. "She left orders for you to go straight in."

Dick led his parade past the desk—a desk of cast marble reinforced with plastile, which would serve very nicely as a blast-and-projectile-proof bunker at need. The door to Vena's office (a cleverly concealed blast-door) was slightly ajar; it sensed his approach and opened fully for him after a retinal scan.

"Have you ever wondered why our peaceful hosts happen to field a battle-ready army?" Vena asked him, without even a preliminary greeting.

"Ah, no, I hadn't—but now that you mention it, it does seem odd." Dick took a seat, cats pooling around his ankles, as Vena tossed her compuslate aside.

"Our hosts aren't the sole representatives of their race on this dirtball," Vena replied, with no expression that Dick could see. "And *now* they finally get around to telling me this. It seems that there is another nation entirely on this continent—we thought that it was just another fief of the Lacu'ara, and they never disabused us of that impression."

"Let me guess—the other side doesn't like Terrans?" Dick hazarded.

"I wish it was that simple. Unfortunately, the other side worships the *kreshta* as children of their prime deity." Vena couldn't quite repress a snarl. "Kill one, and you've got a holy war on your hands—we've been slaughtering hundreds for better than two years. The attempt on the Octet was just the opening salvo for us heretics. The Chief Minister has been here, telling me all about it and falling all over himself in apology. Here—" She pulled a micro reader out of a drawer in her desk and tossed it to him. "My head of security advises that you commit this to memory."

"What is it?" Dick asked, thumbing it on, and seeing (with some puzzlement) the line drawing of a nude Lacu'un appear on the plate.

"How to kill or disable a Lacu'un in five easy lessons, as written by the Patrol Marines." Her face had gone back to that deadpan expression again. "Lieutenant Reynard thinks you might need it."

The prickling of claws set carefully into his clothing alerted him that one of the cats was swarming up to drape itself over his shoulders, but somewhat to his surprise, it wasn't SKitty, it was SCat. The tom peered at the screen in his hand with every evidence of fascinated concentration, too.

He was Patrol, after all. . . . was his second thought, after the initial surprise. And on the heels of that thought, he decided to hold the reader up so that SCat could use the touch screen too.

It was easier to disable a Lacu'un than to kill one, at least in hand to hand combat. Their throats were armored with bone plates, their heads with amazingly thick skulls. But there were vulnerable major nerve-points at all joints; concentrated pinpoint pressure would paralyze everything from the joint down when applied there. When Dick figured he had the scanty contents by heart, he tossed the reader back to Vena, though what he was supposed to do with the information was beyond him at the moment. He wasn't exactly trained in anything but the most basic of self-defense—that was more in Erica Makumba's line, and she was several light-years away at the moment.

"The Lacu'un Army has been alerted, the Palace has been put under tight security, and the caretakers of the other cats have been warned about the poisoning attempt. However, the mysterious kitchen-helper got clean away, so we can assume he'll make another attempt. My advisors and I would like to take him alive if we can—we've got some plans that may abort this mess before it gets worse than it already is."

SCat's deep-voiced growl showed what he thought of that idea, and Vena lowered her smoldering, dark eyes from Dick's to the tom's, and smiled grimly.

"I'd like to put a Marine guard on the cats—but I know that's hardly possible," Vena continued, as SCat and SKitty voiced identical snorts of disdain. "But let's walk back over to the Palace and talk about what we *can* do on the way."

SCat looked up at him and made an odd noise, easy enough to interpret. "SCat thinks he and SKitty can guard the kittens well enough," Dick replied, as Vena waved him through the door, a torrent of cats washing around his ankles.

"I'm sure he does," Vena retorted. "But let's remember that he's only a cat, however much his genes have been tweaked. I hardly think he's capable of understanding the danger of the current situation."

"He isn't just a cat, he was a *Patrol* cat," Dick pointed out, but Vena just shook her head at that.

"Dick, we don't even know exactly what we're into—all we know is that there was an attempt to poison the cats by an assassin that got away. We don't know if it was a lone fanatic, someone sent by our hosts' enemies, if there's only one or more than one—" She sighed as they reached the street. "We're doing all the intelligence gathering we can, but it's difficult to manage when you don't look anything like the dominant species on the planet."

The street was empty, which was fairly normal at this time of day when most Lacu'un were inside at their evening meal. The sky of this world seemed a bit greenish to him, but he'd gotten used to it—today, there were some clouds that might mean rain. Or might not, he didn't know very much about planet-side weather.

SCat's squall was all the warning Dick got to throw himself out of the way as something dark and fast whizzed through the place where he'd been standing. SKitty and the kittens fairly flew back to the safety of the Embassy, SCat whisked out of sight altogether; a larger, cloaked shape sprang from the shadows of a doorway, and before Dick managed to get halfway to his feet, the grey-cloaked, pale-skinned Lacu'un seized Vena and enveloped her, holding a knife to her throat.

"Be still, blasphemous she-demon!" it grated, holding both Vena's arms pinned behind her back in a way that had to be excruciatingly painful. She grimaced but said nothing. "And you, father of demons, be still also!" it snapped at Dick. "I am the righteous hand of Kresh'kali, the all-devouring, the purifier! I am the bringer of cleansing, the anointed of God! In His name, and by His mercy, I give you this choice—remove yourselves from our soil, take yourselves back into the sky forever, or you will die, first you and your she-demon and your god killing pests, then all of those who brought you." Its voice rose, taking on the tones of a hellfire-and-brimstone preacher. "Kresh'kali is the One, the true God, whose word is the only law, and whose minions cleanse the world in His image; His will shall not be flouted, and His servants not denied—"

It sounded like a well-rehearsed speech, and probably would have gone on for some time had it not been interrupted by the speaker's own scream of agony.

And small wonder, for SCat had crept up unseen even by Dick, until the instant he leapt for the assassin's knife-wielding wrist, and fastened his teeth unerringly into those sensitive nerves at the joining of hand and wrist.

The knife clattered to the street, Vena twisted away, and Dick charged, all at the same moment; his shoulder hit the assassin and they both went down on the hard stone paving. But not in a disorderly heap, no; by the time the Marines came piling out of the Embassy, alerted by the frantic herd of cats, Dick had the miscreant face-down on the ground with both arms paralyzed from the shoulders down. And, miracle of miracles, this time *he* wasn't the one battered and bruised—in fact, he was intact beyond a few scrapes!

He wasn't taking any chances though; he waited until the Marines had all four limbs of the assassin in stasis-cuffs before he got off his captive and surrendered him.

"Do we turn him over to the locals?" one of the Marines asked Vena diffidently.

"Not a chance," she growled. "Hustle him into the Embassy before anyone asks any questions."

"What are you going to do?" Dick asked *sotto voce,* following the Marines and their cursing burden.

"I told you, we've got some ideas—and a couple of experiments I'd rather try on this dirt-bag rather than any Lacu'un volunteers," was all she said, leaving him singularly unsatisfied. All he could be certain of was that she didn't plan to execute the assassin out-of-hand. "*We* caught him, and we've got a chance to try those ideas out."

He continued to follow, and was not prevented, as Vena led the way up the stairs to the Embassy med-lab. The entire entourage of cats followed, and Vena not only *let* them, she waved them all inside before shutting and locking the door. The prisoner was strapped into a dental chair and gagged, which at least put an end to the curses, though not to the glares he cast at them.

But Vena dropped down onto one knee and looked into SKitty's eyes. "I know you're a telepath, SKitty," she said, in Terran. "Can you project to anyone but Dick? Could you project into our prisoner's mind? Put your voice in his head?"

SKitty turned her head to look up at Dick. *:Walls,:* she complained. *:Dick has no walls for SKitty.:*

"She says he's got barriers," Dick interpreted. "I

understand that most nontelepathic people have and it's just an accident that the two of us are compatible."

"I may be able to change that," Vena replied, with a tight smile, as she got to her feet. "SKitty, I'm going to do some things to this prisoner, and I want you to tell me when the barriers are gone." She turned to a cabinet and unlocked it; inside were hypospray vials, and she selected one. "We've been cooperating with the Lacu'un Healers; putting together drugs we've been developing for the Lacu'un," she continued, "There are hypnotics that are proven to lower telepathic barriers in humans, and I have a few that may do the same for the Lacu'un. If they don't kill him, that is." She raised an eyebrow at Dick. "You can see why we didn't want to test them even on volunteers."

"But if the drugs kill him—" Dick gulped.

"Then we save the Lacu'ara the cost of an execution, and we apologize that the prisoner expired from fear," she replied smoothly. Dick gulped again; this was a ruthless side of Vena he'd had no notion existed!

She placed the first hypo against the side of the prisoner's neck; the device hissed as it discharged its contents, and the prisoner's eyes widened with fear.

An hour later, there were only two vials left in the cabinet; Vena had administered all the rest, and their antidotes, with sublime disregard for the strain this was probably putting on the prisoner's body. The effects of each had been duly noted, but none of them produced the desired effect of lowering the barriers nontelepaths had against telepathic intrusion.

Vena picked up the first of the last two, and sighed. "If one of these doesn't work, I'll have to make a decision about giving him to the locals," she said with what sounded like disappointment. "I'd really rather not do that."

Dick didn't ask why, but one of the two Marines in the room with them must have seen the question in his eyes. "If the Ambassador turns this fellow over to them, they'll execute him, and that might be enough to send cold war hostilities into a real blaze," the young lieutenant muttered as Vena administered the hypo. "And the word from the Palace is that the other side is as advanced in atomic physics as our lot is. In other words, these are religious fanatics with a nuclear arsenal."

Dick winced; the Terrans would be safe enough in a nuclear exchange, and so would the bulk of city-dwellers, for the Lacu'un had mastered force-shield technology. But in a nuclear exchange there were always accidents and as yet it wasn't possible to encase anything bigger than a city in a shield; he'd seen enough blasted lands never to wish a nuc-war on anyone, and *certainly* not on the decent folk here.

SKitty watched the prisoner as she would a mouse; his eyes unfocused when the drug took hold, and *this* time, she meowed with pleasure. It didn't take Dick's translation for Vena to know that the prisoner's telepathic barriers to SKitty's probing thoughts were gone.

"Excellent!" she exclaimed with relief. "All right, little one—we're going to leave the room until you send one of the kittens to come get us. Let him think we've lost interest in him for the moment, *then* get into his head and convince him that *he* is a very, very bad kitten and *you* are his mother and you're going to punish him unless he says he's sorry and he won't do it again. Make him think that you are so angry that you might kill him if he can't understand how bad he's been. In fact, any of you cats that can get into his head should do that. Then make him promise that he'll always obey everything you tell him to, and don't let up the pressure until he does."

SKitty looked at Vena as if she thought the human had gone crazy, then sighed. *:Stupid,:* she told Dick privately. *:But okay. I do.:*

Dick was as baffled as SKitty was, as he followed Vena out into the hall, leaving the cats with the prisoner. "Just what is that going to accomplish?" he demanded.

She chuckled. "I rather doubt he's ever heard anyone speak in his mind before," she pointed out. "Not even his god."

Now Dick saw exactly what she'd had in mind—and stifled his bark of laughter. "He's going to be certain SKitty's more powerful than *his* god if she can do that—and if she treats him like a naughty child rather than an enemy to be destroyed—"

"Exactly," Vena said with satisfaction. "This is what Lieutenant Reynard wanted me to try, though we thought we'd have to add halucinogens and a VR headset, rather than getting right directly into his head. My problem was finding a way to tell her to act like an all-powerful, rebuking god in a way she'd understand. In the drugged state he's in now, he'll accept whatever happens as the truth."

"So *he* won't threaten the cats anymore—but then what?" Dick asked.

"According to Reynard, the worst that will happen is that he'll be convinced that this new god of his enemies is a lot more powerful and real than his own, and that's the story he'll take back home."

"And the best?" Dick inquired.

She shrugged. "He converts."

"Just what will that accomplish?"

She paused, and licked her lips unconsciously. "We ran some simulations, based on what we've learned about Lacu'un psychology and projecting the rest from history. Historically, the most fanatic followers of a new religion are the converts who were just as fanatical in their former religion. In either case, imagine the reaction when he returns home, which he will, and miraculously, because we'll take a stealthed flitter and drop him over the border while he's drugged and unconscious. He'll probably figure out that we brought him, but there won't be any sign of how. Imagine what his superiors will think?"

The Marine lieutenant standing diffidently at her

elbow cleared his throat. "Actually, you don't have to guess," he said respectfully. "As the Ambassador mentioned, we've been running a psych-profiles for possible contingencies, and they agree with her educated assessment. No matter what, the fanatics will be too frightened of the power of this new 'god' to hazard either a war or another assassination attempt. And if we send back a convert—there's a seventy-four point three percent chance he'll end up starting his own crusade, or even a holy war *within* their culture. No matter what, they cease to be a problem."

"Now *that*," Dick replied with feeling, "Is really a better mousetrap!"

This is a very old story, dating back at least ten years. Published in a short-lived magazine called American Fantasy, *I doubt that many people had a chance to see it. It was old enough that I felt it needed a bit of rewriting, so although the general plot is the same, it's undergone a pretty extensive change.*

The Last of the Season

They said on TV that her name was Molly, but Jim already knew that. They also said that she was eight years old, but she didn't look eight, more like six; didn't look old enough to be in school, even. She didn't look anything like the picture they'd put up on the screen, either. The picture was at least a year old, and done by some cut-rate outfit for her school. Her hair was shorter, her face rounder, her expression so stiff she looked like a kid-dummy. There was nothing like the lively spark in her eyes, or the naughty smile she'd worn this afternoon. The kid in the picture was so clean she squeaked; where was the sticky popsicle residue on her face and hands, the dirt-smudges on her knees?

Jim lost interest as soon as the station cut away to the national news, and turned the set off.

The remote-controlled TV was the one luxury in his beige box of an apartment. His carpet was the cheapest possible brown industrial crap, the curtains on the picture-window a drab, stiff, cheap polyester stuff, backed with even cheaper vinyl that was seamed with cracks after less than a year. He had one chair (Salvation Army, brown corduroy), one lamp (imitation brass, from K-mart), one vinyl sofa (bright orange, St. Vincent de Paul) that was hard and uncomfortable, and one coffee-table (imitation Spanish, Goodwill) where the fancy color TV sat, like a king on a peasant's crude bench.

In the bedroom, just beyond the closed door, was his bedroom, no better furnished than the living-room. He stored his clothing in odd chests of folded cardboard, with a clamp-lamp attached to the cardboard table by the king-sized bed. Like the TV, the bed was top-of-the-line, with a satin bedspread. On that bed, sprawled over the royal blue satin, was Molly.

Jim rose, slowly and silently, and tiptoed across the carpet to the bedroom door, cracking it open just an inch or so, peering inside. She looked like a Norman Rockwell picture, lying on her side, so pale against the dark, vivid fabric, her red corduroy jumper rumpled across her stomach where she clutched her teddy bear with one arm. She was still out of it, sleeping off the little knock on the skull he'd given her. Either that, or she was still under the whiff of ether that had followed. When he was close to her, he could still smell the banana-scent of her popsicle, and see a sticky trace of syrup around her lips. The light from the door caught in the eyes of her teddy bear, and made them shine with a feral, red gleam.

She'd been easy, easy—so trusting, especially after all the contact he'd had with her for the past three weeks. He'd had his eye on two or three of the kids at Kennedy Grade School, but she'd been the one he'd really wanted; like the big TV, she was top-of-the-line, and any of the others would have been a disappointment. She was perfect, prime material, best of the season. Those big, chocolate-brown eyes, the golden-brown hair cut in a sweet page-boy, the round dolly-face—she couldn't have been any better.

He savored the moment, watching her at a distance, greedily studying her at his leisure, knowing that he had her all to himself and no one could interfere.

She'd been one of the last kids to leave the school on this warm, golden afternoon—the rest had scattered on down the streets, chasing the fallen leaves by the time she came out. He'd been loitering, waiting to see if he'd missed her, if someone had picked her up after school, or if she'd had a dentist appointment or something—but no one would ever give a second look at the ice-cream man loitering outside a grade school. He looked like what everybody expected, a man obviously trying to squeeze every last dime out of the rug-rats that he could.

The pattern while he'd had this area staked out was that Molly only had ice-cream money about a third of the time. He'd set her up so carefully—if she came out of the school alone, and started to pass the truck with a wistful look in her eyes, he'd made a big production out of looking around for other kids, then signalling her to come over. The first couple of times, she'd shaken her head and run off, but after she'd bought cones from him a time or two, *he* wasn't a stranger, and to her mind, was no longer in the catagory of people she shouldn't talk to. Then she responded, and he had given her a broken popsicle in her favorite flavor of banana. "Do me a favor and eat this, all right?" he'd said, in his kindest voice. "I can't sell a broken popsicle, and I'd hate for it to go to waste." Then he'd lowered his voice to a whisper and bent over her. "But don't tell the other kids, okay? Let's just keep it a secret."

She nodded, gleefully, and ran off. After that he had no trouble getting her to come over to the truck; after all, why should she be afraid of the friend who gave her ice cream for free, and only asked that she keep it a secret?

Today she'd had money, though, and from the sly gleam in her eyes he would bet she'd filched it from her momma's purse this morning. He'd laid out choices for her like a servant laying out feast-choices for a princess, and she'd sparkled at him, loving the attention as much as the treat.

She'd dawdled over her choice, her teddy bear clutched under one arm, a toy so much a part of her that it could have been another limb. That indecision bought time for the other kids to clear out of the way, and all the teachers to get to their cars and putt out of the parking-lot. His play-acting paid off handsomely, especially after he'd nodded at the truck and winked. She'd wolfed down her cone, and he gave her another broken popsicle; she lingered on, sucking on the yellow ice in a way that made his groin tighten with anticipation. He'd asked her ingenuous questions about her school and her teacher, and she chattered amiably with him between slurps.

Then she'd turned to go at the perfect moment, with not a child, a car, or a teacher in sight. He reached for the sock full of sand inside the freezer-door, and in one, smooth move, gave her a little tap in just the right place.

He caught her before she hit the ground. Then it was into the special side of the ice-cream truck with her; the side not hooked up to the freezer-unit, with ventilation holes bored through the walls in places where no one would find them. He gave her a whiff of ether on a rag, just in case, to make sure she stayed under, then he slid her limp body into the cardboard carton he kept on that side, just in case somebody wanted to look inside. He closed and latched the door, and was back in the driver's seat before two minutes were up, with still no sign of man nor beast. Luck, luck, all the way.

Luck, or pure genius. He couldn't lose; he was invulnerable.

Funny how she'd kept a grip on that toy, though. But that was luck, too; if she'd left it there—

Well, he might have forgotten she'd had it. Then somebody would have found it, and someone might have remembered her standing at the ice-cream truck with it beside her.

But it had all gone smoothly, perfectly planned, perfectly executed, ending with a drive through the warm September afternoon, bells tinkling slightly out-of-tune, no different from any other ice-cream man out for the last scores of the season. He'd felt supremely calm and in control of everything the moment he was in his seat; no one would ever suspect him, he'd been a fixture since the beginning of school. Who ever *sees* the ice-cream man? He was as much a part of the landscape as the fire-hydrant he generally stopped beside.

They'd ask the kids of course, now that Molly was officially missing—and they'd say the same stupid thing they always did. "Did you see any strangers?" they'd ask. "Any strange cars hanging around? Anyone you didn't recognize?"

Stupid; they were just stupid. *He* was the smart one. The kids would answer just like they always did, they'd say no, they hadn't seen any strangers.

No, *he* wasn't a stranger, he was the ice-cream man. The kids saw him today, and they'd see him tomorrow, he'd make sure of that. He'd be on his route for the next week at least, unless there was a cold snap. He knew how cops thought, and if he disappeared, they might look for him. No way was he going to break his pattern. Eventually the cops would question him—not tomorrow, but probably the day after that. He'd tell them he *had* seen the little girl, that she'd bought a cone from him. He'd cover his tracks there, since the other kids would probably remember that she'd been at the truck. But he'd shrug helplessly, and say that she hadn't been on the street when he drove off. He'd keep strictly to the truth, just not all the truth.

Now Molly was all his, and no one would take her away from him until he was done with her.

He drove home, stopping to sell cones when kids flagged him down, taking his time. It wouldn't do to break his pattern. He took out the box that held Molly and brought it upstairs, then made two more trips, for the leftover frozen treats, all in boxes just like the one that held Molly. The neighbors were used to this; it was another part of his routine. He was the invisible man; old Jim always brings in the leftovers and puts 'em in his freezer overnight, it's cheaper than running the truck-freezer overnight.

He knew what they said about him. That Jim was a good guy—kept to himself mostly, but when it was really hot or he had too much left over to fit in his freezer, he'd pass out freebies. A free ice-cream bar was appreciated in this neighborhood, where there wasn't a lot of money to spare for treats. Yeah, Jim was real quiet, but okay, never gave any trouble to anybody.

If the cops went so far as to look into his background, they wouldn't find anything. He ran a freelance ice-cream route in the summer and took odd jobs in the winter; there was no record of his ever getting into trouble.

Of course there was no record. He was smart. Nobody had ever caught him, not when he set fires as a kid, not when he prowled the back alleys looking for stray dogs and cats, and not later, when he went on to the targets he really wanted. He was careful. When he first started on kids, he picked the ones nobody would miss. And he kept up with the literature; he knew everything the cops would look for.

Jim's apartment was a corner-unit, under the roof. There was nobody above him, the old man under him was stone-deaf, the guy on one side was a stoner on the night-shift, and the couple on the other side kept their music blasting so loud it was a wonder that *they* weren't deaf. Nobody would ever hear a thing.

Meanwhile, Jim waited, as darkness fell outside, for Molly to sleep off her ether and her bump; it wasn't any fun for him when his trophies were out of it. Jim liked them awake; he liked to see their eyes when they realized that no one was coming to rescue them.

He changed into a pair of old jeans and a tee-shirt in the living-room, hanging his white uniform in the closet, then looked in on her again.

She still had a hold on that teddy bear. It was a really unusual toy; it was one of the many things that had marked her when he'd first looked for targets. Jim was really glad she'd kept such a tight grip on it; it was so different that there was little doubt it would have been spotted as hers if she'd dropped it. The plush was a thick, black fur, extremely realistic; in fact, he wasn't entirely certain that it *was* fake fur. There was no sign of the wear that kids usually put on that kind of beloved plaything. The mouth was half-open, lined with red felt, with white felt teeth and a red felt tongue. Instead of a ribbon bow, this bear had a real leather collar with an odd tag hanging from it; pottery or glass, maybe, or enameled metal, it certainly wasn't plastic. There was a faint, raised pattern on the back, and the word "Tedi" on the front in a childishly printed scrawl. The eyes were oddest of all—whoever had made this toy must have used the same eyes that taxidermists used; they looked real, alive.

It was going to prove a little bit of problem dealing with that bear, after. He was so careful not to leave any fiber or hair evidence; he always washed them when he was through with them, dressing them in fancy party clothing he took straight out of the packages, then wrapping them in plastic once they were dressed, to keep from contaminating them. Once he was through with her and dressed her in that frilly blue party-dress he'd bought, he'd cut up her old clothing into tiny pieces and flush them down the john, a few at a time, to keep from clogging the line. That could be fatal.

He'd do the part with the knife in the bathtub, of course, so there wouldn't be any bloodstains. He knew exactly how to get blood-evidence scrubbed out of the bathroom, what chemicals to use and everything. They'd have to swab out the pipes to find anything.

But the bear was a problem. He'd have to figure out a smart way to get rid of it, because it was bound to collect all kinds of evidence.

Maybe give it to a kid? Maybe not; there was a chance the kid would remember him. By now it had probably collected fibers. . . .

He had it; the Salvation Army box, the one on Colby, all the way across town. They'd let that thing get stuffed full before they ever emptied it, and by then the bear would have collected so much fiber and hair they'd never get it all sorted out. Then he could take her to MacArthur Park; it was far enough away from the collection box. He'd leave her there like he always did, propped up on a bench like an oversized doll, a bench off in an out-of-the-way spot. He'd used MacArthur Park before, but not recently, and at this time of year it might be days before anyone found her.

But the bear—better get it away from her now, before it collected something more than hair. For one thing, it would be harder to handle her if she kept clinging to it. Something about those eyes bothered him, too, and he wasn't in a mood to be bothered.

He cracked the door open, slipped inside, pried the bear out of her loose grip. He threw it into the bathroom, but Molly didn't stir; he was vaguely disappointed. He'd hoped she show *some* sign of coming around when he took the toy.

Well, he had all night, all weekend, as long as she lasted. He'd have to make the most of this one; she was the last of the season.

Might as well get the stuff out.

He went into the kitchenette and dragged out the plastic step-stool. Standing it in the closet in the living-room, he opened up the hatch into the crawl-space. It wasn't tall enough for him to see what was up there, but what he wanted was right by the hatch anyway. He felt across the fiberglass battings; the paper over the insulation crackled under his fingers. He groped until his hand encountered the cardboard box he'd stored up there. Getting both hands around it, straining on tiptoe to do so, he lowered it carfully down through the hatch. He had to bring it through the opening catty-cornered to make it fit. It wasn't heavy, but it was an awkward shape.

He carried it to the center of the living-room and placed it on the carpet, kneeling beside it with his stomach tight with anticipation. Slowly, with movements ritualized over time, he undid the twine holding it closed, just so. He coiled up the twine and laid it to the side, exactly five inches from the side of the box. He reached for the lid.

But as he started to open it, he thought he heard a faint sound, as if something moved in the bedroom. Was Molly finally awake?

He got to his feet, and moved softly to the door. But when he applied his eye to the crack, he was disappointed to see that she hadn't moved at all. She lay exactly as he'd left her, head pillowed on one arm, hair scattered across his pillow, lips pursed, breathing softly but regularly. Her red corduroy jumper was still in the same folds it had been when he'd put her down on the bed, rucked up over her hip so that her little pink panties showed the tiniest bit.

Then he saw the bear.

It was back right where it had been before, sitting up in the curve of her stomach. Looking at him.

He shook his head, frowning. Of course it wasn't looking at him, it was his imagination; it was just a toy. He must have been so wrapped up in anticipation that he'd flaked—and *hadn't* thrown it in the bathroom as he'd intended, or else he'd absent-mindedly put it back on the bed.

Easily fixed. He took the few steps into the room,

grabbed the bear by one ear, and threw it into the bedroom closet, closing the door on it. Molly didn't stir, and he retired to the living room and his treasure chest.

On the top layer of the box lay a tangle of leather and rubber. He sorted out the straps carefully, laying out all the restraints in their proper order, with the rubber ball for her mouth and the gag to hold it in there first in line. That was one of the most important parts. Whatever sound got past the gag wouldn't get past the neighbors' various deficiencies.

Something was definitely moving in the next room. He heard the closet door opening, then the sounds of shuffling.

He sprinted to the door—

Only to see that Molly was lying in exactly the same position, and the bear was with her.

He shook his head. Damn! He couldn't be going crazy—

Then he chuckled at a sudden memory. The third kid he'd done had pulled something like this—the kid was a sleepwalker, with a knack for lying back down in precisely the same position as before, and it wasn't until he'd stayed in the bedroom instead of going through his collection that he'd proved it to himself. Molly had obviously missed her bear, gotten up, searched blindly for her toy, found it, then lay back down again. Yeah, come to think of it, her jumper was a bit higher on her hip, and she was more on her back than her side, now.

But that bear had to go.

He marched in, grabbed the bear again, and looked around. Now where?

The bathroom, the cabinet under the sink. There was nothing in there but a pair of dead roaches, and it had a child-proof latch on it.

The eyes flashed at him as he flipped on the bathroom light and whipped the cabinet open. For one moment he almost thought the eyes glared at him with a red light of their own before he closed the door on the thing and turned the lock with a satisfying click.

Back to the box.

The next layer was his pictures. They weren't of any of his kids; he wasn't that stupid. Nothing in this box would ever connect him with the guy they were calling the "Sunday-school killer" because he left them dressed in Sunday best, clean and shining, in places like parks and beaches, looking as if they'd just come from church.

But the pictures were the best the Internet had to offer, and a lot of these kids looked like the ones he'd had. Pretty kids, real pretty.

He took them out in the proper order, starting with the simple ones, letting the excitement build in his groin as he savored each one. First, the nudes—ten of them, he knew them all by heart. Then the nudes with the kids "playing" together, culled from the "My Little Fishie" newsletter of a nut-case religious cult that believed in kid-sex.

Then the good ones.

Halfway through, he slipped his hand into his pants without taking his eyes off the pictures.

This was going to be a good one. Molly looked just like the kid in the best of his pictures. She was going to be perfect; the last of the season, the best of the season.

He was pretty well occuppied as he got to the last set, though he noted absently that it sounded as if Molly was up and moving around again. This was the bondage-and-snuff set, very hard to get, and the only reason he had them at all was because he'd stolen them from a storage-locker. He wouldn't have taken the risk of getting them personally, but they'd given him some of his best ideas.

Molly must be awake by now. But this wasn't to be hurried—there wouldn't be any Mollys or Jeffreys until next year, next spring, summer, and fall. He had to make this one last.

He savored the emotions in the pictured eyes as he would savor Molly's fear; savored their pleading expressions, their helplessness. Such pretty little things, like her, like all his kids.

They wanted it, anybody knew that. Freud said so—that had been in that psychology course he took by correspondence when he was trying to figure himself out. Look at the way kids played "doctor" the minute you turned your back on them. That religious cult had it right; kids wanted it, needed it, and the only thing getting in the way was the way a bunch of repressed old men felt about it.

He'd show her what it was she wanted, show her good. He'd make it last, take it slow. Then, once she was all his and would do anything he said, he'd make sure nobody else would ever have her again. He'd keep her his, forever. Not even her parents would have her the way he did.

Under the last layer of pictures was the knife, the beautiful, shining filleting knife, the best made. Absolutely stainless, rustproof, with a pristine black handle. He laid it reverently beside the leather straps, then zipped up his pants and rose to his feet.

No doubt, she was shuffling around on the other side of the door, moving uncertainly back and forth. She should be just dazed enough that he'd get her gagged before she knew enough to scream.

He paused a moment to order his thoughts and his face before putting his hand on the doorknob. Next to the moment when the kid lay trussed-up under him, this was the best moment.

He flung the door wide open. "*Hel*-lo, Mo—"

That was as far as he got.

The screams brought the neighbors to break down the door. There were two sets of screams; his, and those of a terrified little girl pounding on the closet door.

A dozen of them gathered in the hall before they got

up the courage to break in, and by then Jim wasn't screaming anymore. What they found in the living-room made the first inside run back out the way they had come.

One managed to get as far as the bedroom to release the child, a pale young woman who lived at the other end of the floor, whose maternal instincts over-rode her stomach long enough to rescue the weeping child.

Molly fell out of the closet into her arms, sobbing with terror. The young woman recognized her from news; how could she not? Her picture had been everywhere.

Meanwhile one of the others who had fled the whimpering thing on the living-room floor got to a phone and called the cops.

The young woman closed the bedroom door on the horror in the next room, took the hysterical, shivering child into her arms, and waited for help to arrive, absently wondering at her own, hitherto unsuspected courage.

While they were waiting, the thing on the floor mewled, gasped, and died.

Although the young woman hadn't known what to make of the tangle of leather she'd briefly glimpsed on the carpet, the homicide detective knew exactly what it meant. He owed a candle to Saint Jude for the solving of his most hopeless case and another to the Virgin for saving *this* child before anything had happened to her.

And a third to whatever saint had seen to it that there would be no need for a trial.

"You say there was no sign of anything or anyone else?" he asked the young woman. She'd already told him that she was a librarian—that was shortly after she'd taken advantage of their arrival to close herself into the bathroom and throw up. He almost took her to task for possibly destroying evidence, but what was the point? This was one murder he didn't really want to solve.

She was sitting in the only chair in the living-room, carefully not looking at the outline on the carpet, or the blood-spattered mess of pictures and leather straps a little distance from her feet. He'd asked the same question at least a dozen times already.

"Nothing, no one." She shook her head. "There's no back door, just the hatches to the crawl-space, in each closet."

He looked where she pointed, at the open closet door with the kitchen stool still inside it. He walked over to the closet and craned his head around sideways, peering upward.

"Not too big, but a skinny guy could get up there," he said, half to himself. "Is that attic divided at all?"

"No, it runs all along the top floor; I never put anything up there because anybody could get into it from any other apartment." She shivered. "And I put locks on all my hatches. Now I'm glad I did. Once a year they fumigate, so they need the hatches to get exhaust fans up there."

"A skinny guy, one real good with a knife—maybe a 'Nam Vet. A SEAL, a Green Beret—" he was talking mostly to himself. "It might not have been a knife; maybe claws, like in the karate rags. Ninja claws. That could be what he used—"

He paced back to the center of the living room. The librarian rubbed her hands along her arms, watching him out of sick blue eyes.

"Okay, he knows what this sicko is up to—maybe he *just* now found out, doesn't want to call the cops for whatever reason. He comes down into the bedroom, locks the kid in the closet to keep her safe—"

"She told me that a bear locked her into the closet," the woman interrupted.

The detective laughed. "Lady, that kid has a knot the size of a baseball on her skull; she could have seen Luke

Skywalker lock her in that closet!" He went back to his deductions. "Okay, he locks the kid in, then makes enough noise so joy-boy thinks she finally woke up. Then when the door opens—yeah. It'll fly." He nodded. "Then he gets back out by this hatch." He sighed, regretful that he wouldn't ever get a chance to thank this guy. "Won't be any fingerprints; guy like this would be too smart to leave any."

He stared at the outline on the blood-soaked carpet pensively. The librarian shuddered.

"Look, officer," she said, asserting herself, "If you don't need me anymore—"

"Hey, Pete—" the detective's partner poked his head in through the door. "The kid's parents are here. The kid wants her teddy—she's raising a real howl about it, and the docs at the hospital don't want to sedate her if they don't have to."

"Shit, the kid misses being a statistic by a couple of minutes, and all she can think about is her toy!" He shook his head, and refocused on the librarian. "Go ahead, miss. I don't think you can tell us anything more. You might want to check into the hospital yourself, get checked over for shock. Either that, or pour yourself a stiff one. Call in sick tomorrow."

He smiled, suddenly realizing that she was pretty, in a wilted sort of way—and after what she'd just been through, no wonder she was wilted.

"That was what I had in mind already, Detective," she replied, and made good her escape before he changed his mind.

"Pete, her folks say she won't be able to sleep without it," his partner persisted.

"Yeah, yeah, go ahead and take it," he responded absently. If things had gone differently—they'd be shaking out that toy for hair and fiber samples, if they found it at all.

He handed the bear to his partner.

"Oh—before you give it back—"

"What?"

"There's blood on the paws," he replied, already looking for trace evidence that would support his theories. "Wouldn't want to shake her up any further, so make sure you wash it off first."

Okay, so I don't always take Diana Tregarde very seriously. When this story appeared in Marion Zimmer Bradley's Fantasy Magazine, *however, there was a reader (a self-proclaimed romance writer) who took it seriously, and was quite irate at the rather unflattering picture I painted of romance writers. She wrote a long and angry letter about it to the editor.*

The editor, who like me has seen *romance writers at a romance convention, declined to comment.*

A note: The character of Robert Harrison and the concept of "whoopie witches" was taken from the excellent supernatural role-playing game, Stalking the Night Fantastic *by Richard Tucholka and used with the creator's permission. There is also a computer game version,* Bureau Thirteen. *Both are highly recommended!*

Satanic, Versus . . .

"Mrs. Peel," intoned a suave, urbane tenor voice from the hotel doorway behind Di Tregarde, "We're needed."

The accent was faintly French rather than English, but the inflection was dead-on.

Di didn't bother to look in the mirror, although she knew there *would* be a reflection there. Andre LeBrel might be a 200-year-old vampire, but he cast a perfectly good reflection. She was too busy trying to get her false eyelashes to stick.

"In a minute, lover. The glue won't hold. I can't understand it—I bought the stuff last year for that unicorn costume and it was fine then—"

"Allow me." A thin, graceful hand appeared over her shoulder, holding a tiny tube of surgical adhesive. "I had the sinking feeling that you would forget. This glue, *cherie,* it does not age well."

"Piffle. Figure a back-stage haunt would know that." She took the white plastic tube from Andre, and proceeded to attach the pesky lashes properly. This time they obliged by staying put. She finished her preparations with a quick application of liner, and spun around to face her partner. "Here," she said, posing, feeling more than a little smug about how well the black leather jumpsuit fit, "How do I look?"

Andre cocked his bowler to the side and leaned on his umbrella. "Ravishing. And I?" His dark eyes twinkled merrily. Although he looked a great deal more like Timothy Dalton than Patrick Macnee, anyone seeing the two of them together would have no doubt who he was supposed to be costumed as. Di was very glad they had a "pair" costume, and blessed Andre's infatuation with old TV shows.

And they're damned well going to see us together all the time, Di told herself firmly. *Why I ever agreed to this fiasco . . .*

"You look altogether too good to make me feel comfortable," she told him, snapping off the light over the mirror. "I hope you realize what you're letting yourself in for. You're going to think you're a drumstick in a pool of piranha."

Andre made a face as he followed her into the hotel room from the dressing alcove. "*Cherie,* these are only romance writers. They—"

"Are for the most part over-imaginative middle-aged *hausfraus,* married to guys that are going thin on top and thick on the bottom, and you're likely going to be one of a handful of males in the room. And the rest are going to be middle-aged copies of their husbands, agents, or gay." She raised an eyebrow at him. "So where do you think that leaves you?"

"Like Old Man Kangaroo, very much run after." He had the audacity to laugh at her. "Have no fear, *cherie.* I shall evade the sharp little piranha teeth."

"I just hope *I* can," she muttered under her breath. Under most circumstances she avoided the Romance Writers of the World functions like the plague, chucked the newsletter in the garbage without reading it, and paid her dues only because Morrie pointed out that it would look really strange if she didn't belong. The RWW, she had found, was a hotbed of infighting and jealousy, and "my advances are bigger than your advances, so I am writing Deathless Prose and you are writing tripe." The general attitude seemed to be, "the publishers are out to get you, the agents are out to get you and your fellow writers are out to get you." Since Di got along perfectly well with agent and publishers, and really didn't *care* how well or poorly other writers were doing, she didn't see the point.

But somehow Morrie had talked her into attending the RWW Halloween party. And for the life of her, she couldn't remember why or how.

"Why am I doing this?" she asked Andre, as she snatched up her purse from the beige-draped bed, transferred everything really necessary into a black-leather belt-pouch, and slung the latter around her hips, making very sure the belt didn't interfere with the holster on her other hip. "You were the one who talked to Morrie on the phone."

"Because M'sieur Morrie wishes you to give his client Robert Harrison someone to talk to," the vampire reminded her. "M'sieur Harrison agreed to escort Valentine Vervain to the party in a moment of weakness equal to yours."

"Why in Hades did he agree to *that*?" she exclaimed, giving the sable-haired vampire a look of profound astonishment.

"Because Miss Vervain—*cherie,* that is not her *real* name, is it?—is one of Morrie's best clients, is newly divorced and alone and Morrie claims most insecure, and M'sieur Harrison was kind to her," Andre replied.

Di took a quick look around the hotel room, to make sure she hadn't forgotten anything. One thing about combining her annual "make nice with the publishers" trip with Halloween, she had a chance to get together with all her old New York buddies for a *real* Samhain celebration and avoid the Christmas and Thanksgiving crowds and bad weather. "I remember. That was when she did that crossover thing, and the sci-fi people took her apart for trying to claim it was the best thing since Tolkien." She chuckled heartlessly. "The less said about that, the better. Her magic system had holes I could drive a Mack truck through. But Harrison was a gentleman and kept the bloodshed to a minimum. But Morrie doesn't know Valentine—and no, sexy, her name used to be Edith Bowman until she changed it legally—if he thinks she's as insecure as she's acting. Three quarters of what La Valentine does is an act. And everything is in Technicolor and Dolby enhanced sound. So what's Harrison doing in town?"

She snatched up the key from the desk, and stuffed it into the pouch, as Andre held the door open for her.

"I do not know," he replied, twirling the umbrella once and waving her past. "You should ask him."

"I hope Valentine doesn't eat him alive," she said, striding down the beige hall, and frankly enjoying the appreciative look a hotel room-service clerk gave her as she sauntered by. "I wonder if she's going to wear the outfit from the cover of her last book—if she does, Harrison may decide he wants to spend the rest of the party in the men's room." She reached the end of the hall a fraction of a second before Andre, and punched the button for the elevator.

"I gather that is what we are to save him from, *cherie*," Andre pointed out wryly, as the elevator arrived.

"Oh well," she sighed, stepping into the mirror-walled cubicle. "It's only five hours, and it can't be that bad. How much trouble can a bunch of romance writers get into, anyway?"

There was enough lace, chiffon, and satin to outfit an entire Busby Berkeley musical. Di counted fifteen Harem Girls, nine Vampire Victims, three Southern Belles (the South was Out this year), a round dozen Ravished Maidens of various time periods (none of them peasants), and assorted Frills and Furbelows, and one "witch" in a black chiffon outfit clearly purchased from the Frederick's catalog. Aside from the "witch," she and Andre were the only ones dressed in black—and they *were* the only ones covered from neck to toes—though in Di's case, that was problematical; the tight black leather jumpsuit really didn't leave anything to the imagination.

The Avengers outfits had been Andre's idea, when she realized she really *had* agreed to go to this party. She *had* suggested Dracula for him and a witch for her—but he had pointed out, logically, that there was no point in coming as what they really were.

Besides, I've always wanted a black leather jumpsuit, and this made a good excuse to get it. And since I'm doing this as a favor to Morrie, I might *be able to deduct it. . . .*

And even if I can't, the looks *I'm getting are worth twice the price.*

Most of the women here—and as she'd warned Andre, the suite at the Henley Palace that RWW had rented for this bash contained about eighty percent women—were in their forties at best. Most of them demonstrated amply the problems with having a sedentary job. And most of them were wearing outfits that might have been worn by their favorite heroines, though few of them went to the extent that Valentine Vervain did, and copied the exact dress from the front of the latest book. The problem was, their heroines were all no older than twenty-two, and as described, weighed *maybe* ninety-five pounds. Since a great many of the ladies in question weighed *at least* half again that, the results were not what the wearers intended.

The sour looks Di was getting were just as flattering as the wolf-whistle the bellboy had sent her way.

A quick sail through the five rooms of the suite with Andre at her side ascertained that Valentine and her escort had not yet arrived. A quick glance at Andre's face proved that he was having a very difficult time restraining his mirth. She decided then that discretion was definitely the better part of valor, and retired to the balcony with Andre in tow and a couple of glasses of Perrier.

It was a beautiful night; one of those rare, late-October nights that made Di regret—briefly—moving to Connecticut. Clear, cool and crisp, with just enough wind to sweep the effluvium of city life from the streets. Below them, hundreds of lights created a jewelbox effect. If you looked hard, you could even see a few stars beyond the light-haze.

The sliding glass door to the balcony had been opened to vent some of the heat and overwhelming perfume (Di's nose said, nothing under a hundred dollars a bottle), and Di left it that way. She parked her elbows on the balcony railing and looked down, Andre at her side, and sighed.

He chuckled. "You warned me, and I did not believe. I apologize, *cherie.* It is—most remarkable."

"Hmm. Exercise that vampiric hearing of yours, and you'll get an ear-full," she said, watching the car-lights crawl by, twenty stories below. "When they aren't slaughtering each other and playing little power-trip games, they're picking apart their agents and their editors. If you've ever wondered why I've never bothered going after the big money, it's because to get it I'd have to play by *those* rules."

"Then I devoutly urge you to remain with modest ambitions, *cherie*," he said, fervently. "I—"

"Excuse me?" said a masculine voice from the balcony door. It had a distinct note of desperation in it. "Are you Diana Tregarde?"

Di turned. Behind her, peering around the edge of the doorway, was a harried-looking fellow in a baggy, tweedy sweater and slacks—not a costume—with a shock of prematurely graying, sandy-brown hair, glasses and a moustache. And a look of absolute misery.

"Robert Harrison, I presume?" she said, archly. "Come, join us in the sanctuary. It's too cold out here for chiffon."

"Thank God." Harrison ducked onto the balcony with the agility of a man evading Iraqi border-guards, and threw himself down in an aluminum patio chair out of sight of the windows. "I think the password is, 'Morrie sent me.'"

"Recognized; pass, friend. Give the man credit; he gave you an ally and an escape-route," Di chuckled. "Don't tell me; she showed up as the Sacred Priestess Askenazy."

"In a nine-foot chiffon train and see-through harem pants, yes," Harrison groaned. "And let me know I was Out of the Royal Favor for *not* dressing as What's-His-Name."

"Watirion," Di said helpfully. "Do you realize you can pronounce that as 'what-tire-iron'? I encourage the notion."

"But that wasn't the worst of it!" Harrison shook his head, distractedly, as if he was somewhat in a daze. "The worst was the monologue in the cab on the way over here. Every other word was Crystal this and Vibration that, Past Life Regression, and Mystic Rituals. The woman's a whoopie witch!"

Di blinked. That was a new one on *her.* "A what?"

Harrison looked up, and for the first time, seemed to see her. "Uh—" he hesitated. "Uh, some of what Morrie said—uh, he seemed to think you—well, you've seen things—uh, he said you know things—"

She fished the pentagram out from under the neck of her jumpsuit and flashed it briefly. "My religion is non-traditional, yes, and there are more things in heaven and earth, etcetera. Now what in Tophet is a whoopie witch?"

"It's—uh—a term some friends of mine use. It's kind of hard to explain." Harrison's brow furrowed. "Look, let me give you examples. Real witches have grimorie, sometimes handed down through their families for centuries. Whoopie witches have books they picked up at the supermarket. Usually right at the check-out counter."

"Real witches have carefully researched spells—" Di prompted.

"Whoopie witches draw a baseball diamond in chalk on the living room floor and recite random passages from the *Satanic Bible*."

"When real witches make substitutions, they do so knowing the exact difference the substitute will make—"

"Whoopie witches slop taco sauce in their pentagram because it looks like blood."

"Real witches gather their ingredients by hand—" Di was beginning to enjoy this game.

"Whoopie witches have a credit card, and *lots* of catalogues." Harrison was grinning, and so was Andre.

"Real witches spend hours in meditation—"

"Whoopie witches sit under a pyramid they ordered from a catalogue and watch *Knot's Landing*."

"Real witches cast spells knowing that any change they make in someone's life will come back at them three-fold, for good or ill—"

"Whoopie witches call up the Hideous Slime from

Yosotha to eat their neighbor's poodle because the bitch got the last carton of Haagen-Daaz double-chocolate at the Seven-Eleven."

"I think I've got the picture. So dear Val decided to take the so-called research she did for the Great Fantasy Novel seriously?" Di leaned back into the railing and laughed. "Oh, Robert, I pity you! Did she try to tell you that the two of you just *must* have been priestly lovers in a past life in Atlantis?"

"Lemuria," Harrison said, gloomily. "My God, she must be supporting half the crystal miners in Arkansas."

"Don't feel too sorry for her, Robert," Di warned him. "With her advances, she can afford it. And I know some perfectly nice people in Arkansas who should only soak her for every penny they can get. Change the subject; you're safe with us—and if she decides to hit the punch-bowl hard enough, you can send her back to her hotel in a cab and she'll never know the difference. What brings you to New York?"

"Morrie wants me to meet the new editors at Berkley; he thinks I've got a shot at selling them that near-space series I've been dying to do. And I had some people here in the City I really needed to see." He sighed. "And, I'll admit it, I'd been thinking about writing bodice-rippers under a pseudonym. When you know they're getting ten times what I am—"

Di shrugged. "I don't think you'd be happy doing it, unless you've written strictly to spec before. There's a lot of things you have to conform to that you might not feel comfortable doing. Listen, Harrison, you seem to know quite a bit about hot-and-cold-running esoterica—how did you—"

Someone in one of the other rooms screamed. Not the angry scream of a woman who has been insulted, but the soul-chilling shriek of pure terror that brands itself on the air and stops all conversation dead.

"What in—" Harrison was on his feet, staring in the direction of the scream. Di ignored him and launched herself at the patio door, pulling the Glock 19 from the holster on her hip, and thankful she'd loaded the silver-tipped bullets in the first clip.

Funny how everybody thought it couldn't be real because it was plastic. . . .

"Andre—the next balcony!" she called over her shoulder, knowing the vampire could easily scramble over the concrete divider and come in through the next patio door, giving them a two-pronged angle of attack.

The scream hadn't been what alerted her—simultaneous with the scream had been the wrenching feeling in her gut that was the signal that someone had breached the fabric of the Otherworld in her presence. She didn't know who, or what—but from the stream of panicked chiffon billowing towards the door at supersonic speed, it probably wasn't nice, and it probably had a great deal to do with one of the party-goers.

Three amply-endowed females (one Belle, one Ravished and one Harem) had reached the door to the next room at the same moment, and jammed it, and rather than one of them pulling free, they all three kept shoving harder, shrieking at the tops of their lungs in tones their agents surely recognized.

You'd think their advances failed to pay out! Di kept the Glock in her hand, but sprinted for the door. She grabbed the nearest flailing arm (Harem), planted her foot in the midsection of her neighbor (Belle) and shoved and pulled at the same time. The clot of feminine hysteria came loose with a sound of ripping cloth; a crinoline parted company with its wearer. The three women tumbled through the door, giving Di a clear launching path into the next room. She took it, diving for the shelter of a huge wooden coffee table, rolling, and aiming for the door of the last room with the Glock. And her elbow hit someone.

"What are *you* doing here?" asked Harrison, and Di, simultaneously. Harrison cowered—no, *had taken cover*, there was a distinct difference—behind the sofa beside the coffee table, his own huge magnum aimed at the same doorway.

"My *job*," they said—also simultaneously.

"*What?*" (Again in chorus).

"This is all a very amusing study in synchronicity," said Andre, crouching just behind Harrison, bowler tipped and sword from his umbrella out and ready, "but I suggest you both pay attention to that most boorish party-crasher over there—"

Something very large occluded the light for a moment in the next room, then the lights went out, and Di distinctly heard the sound of the chandelier being torn from the ceiling and thrown against the wall. She winced.

There go my dues up again.

"I got a glimpse," Andre continued. "It was very large, perhaps ten feet tall, and—*cherie*, looked like nothing so much as a rubber creature from a very bad movie. Except that I do not think it was rubber."

At just that moment, there was a thrashing from the other room, and Valentine Vervain, long red hair liberally beslimed, minus nine-foot train and one of her sleeves, scrambled through the door and plastered herself against the wall, where she promptly passed out.

"Valentine?" Di murmured—and snapped her head towards Harrison when he moaned—"Oh *no*," in a way that made her *sure* he knew something.

"Harrison!" she snapped. "Cough it up!"

There was a sound of things breaking in the other room, as if something was fumbling around in the dark, picking up whatever it encountered, and smashing it in frustration.

"Valentine—she said something about getting some of her 'friends' together tonight and 'calling up her soul-mate' so she could 'show that ex of hers.' I gather he appeared at the divorce hearing with a twenty-one-year-old blonde." Harrison gulped. "I figured she was just blowing it off—I never thought she had any power—"

"You'd be amazed what anger will do," Di replied grimly, keeping her eyes on the darkened doorway. "Sometimes it even transcends a total lack of talent. Put that together with the time of year—All Hallow's E'en—Samhain—is tomorrow. The Wall Between the Worlds is especially thin, and power flows are heavy right now. That's a recipe for disaster if I ever heard one."

"And here comes M'sieur Soul-Mate," said Andre, warningly.

What shambled in through the door was nothing that Di had ever heard of. It was, indeed, about ten feet tall. It was a very dark brown. It was covered with luxuriant brown hair—all over. Otherwise, it was nude. If there were any eyes, the hair hid them completely. It was built something along the lines of a powerful body-builder, taken to exaggerated lengths, and it drooled. It also stank, a combination of sulfur and musk so strong it would have brought tears to the eyes of a skunk.

"Wah-wen-ine!" it bawled, waving its arms around, as if it were blind. "Wah-wen-ine!"

"Oh goddess," Di groaned, putting two and two together and coming up with—*she called a soul-mate, and specified parameters. But she forgot to specify "human."* "Are you thinking what I'm thinking?"

The other writer nodded. "Tall, check. Dark, check. Long hair, check. Handsome—well, I suppose in some circles." Harrison stared at the thing in fascination.

"Some—thing—that will accept her completely as she is, and love her completely. Young, sure, he can't be more than five minutes old." Di watched the thing fumble for the doorframe and cling to it. "Look at that, he can't see. So love *is* blind. Strong and as masculine as you can get. And not too bright, which I bet she also specified. Oh, my ears and whiskers."

Valentine came to, saw the thing, and screamed.

"*Wah-wen-ine!*" it howled, and lunged for her. Reflexively, Di and Harrison both shot. He emptied his cylinder, and one speed-loader; Di gave up after four shots, when it was obvious they *were* hitting the thing, to no effect.

Valentine scrambled on hands and knees over the carpet, still screaming—but crawling in the wrong direction, towards the balcony, not the door.

"*Merde!*" Andre flung himself between the creature's clutching hands and its summoner, before Di could do anything.

And before Di could react to *that*, the thing backhanded Andre into a wall hard enough to put him through the plasterboard.

Valentine passed out again. Andre was already out for the count. There are some things even a vampire has a little trouble recovering from.

"Jesus!" Harrison was on his feet, fumbling for something in his pocket. Di joined him, holstering the Glock, and grabbed his arm.

"Harrison, distract it, make a noise, anything!" She pulled the atheme from her boot sheath and began cutting Sigils in the air with it, getting the Words of Dismissal out as fast as she could without slurring the syllables.

Harrison didn't even hesitate; he grabbed a couple of tin serving trays from the coffee table, shook off their contents, and banged them together.

The thing turned its head toward him, its hands just inches away from its goal. "Wah-wen-ine?" it said.

Harrison banged the trays again. It lunged toward the sound. It was a lot faster than Di had thought it was.

Evidently Harrison made the same error in judgment. It missed him by inches, and he scrambled out of the way by the width of a hair, just as Di concluded the Ritual of Dismissal.

To no effect.

"Hurry *up*, will you?" Harrison yelped, as the thing threw the couch into the wall and lunged again.

"I'm *trying!*" she replied through clenched teeth—

though not loud enough to distract the thing, which had concluded either (a) Harrison was Valentine or (b) Harrison was keeping it from Valentine. Whichever, it had gone from wailing Valentine's name to simply wailing, and lunging after Harrison, who was dodging with commendable agility in a man of middle age.

Of course, he has a lot of incentive.

She tried three more dismissals, still with no effect, the room was trashed, and Harrison was getting winded, and running out of heavy, expensive things to throw. . . .

And the only thing she could think of was the "incantation" she used—as a joke—to make the stop-lights change in her favor.

Oh hell—a cockamamie incantation pulled it up—

"By the Seven Rings of Zsa Zsa Gabor and the Rock of Elizabeth Taylor I command thee!" she shouted, stepping between the thing and Harrison (who was beginning to stumble). "By the Six Wives of Eddie Fisher and the Words of Karnak the Great I compel thee! *Freeze, buddy!*"

Power rose, through her, crested over her—and hit the thing. And the thing—stopped. It whimpered, and struggled a little against invisible bonds, but seemed unable to move.

Harrison dropped to the carpet, right on top of a spill of guacamole and ground-in tortilla chips, whimpering a little himself.

I have to get rid of this thing, quick, before it breaks the compulsion— She closed her eyes and trusted to instinct, and shouted the first thing that came into her mind. The Parking Ritual, with one change. . . .

"Great Squat, send him *to* a spot, and I'll send you three nuns—"

Mage-energies raged through the room, whirling about her, invisible, intangible to eyes and ears, but she felt them. She was the heart of the whirlwind, she and the other—

There was a *pop* of displaced air; she opened her eyes to see that the creature was gone—but the mage-energies continued to whirl—faster—

"Je-*sus*," said Harrison, "How did you—"

She waved him frantically to silence as the energies sensed his presence and began to circle in on him.

"Great Squat, thanks for the spot!" she yelled desperately, trying to complete the incantation before Harrison could be pulled in. *"Your nuns are in the mail!"*

The energies swirled up and away, satisfied. Andre groaned, stirred, and began extracting himself from the powdered sheetrock wall. Harrison stumbled over to give him a hand.

Just as someone pounded on the outer door of the suite.

"Police!" came a muffled voice. "Open the door!"

"It's open!" Di yelled back, unzipping her belt-pouch and pulling out her wallet.

Three people, two uniformed NYPD and one fellow in a suit with an impressive .357 Magnum in his hand, peered cautiously around the doorframe.

"Jee-zus Christ," one said in awe.

"Who?" the dazed Valentine murmured, hand hanging limply over her forehead. "Wha' hap . . ."

Andre appeared beside Di, bowler in hand, umbrella spotless and innocent-looking again.

Di fished her Hartford PD Special OPs ID out of her wallet and handed it to the man in the suit. "This lady," she said angrily, pointing to Valentine, "played a little Halloween joke that got out of hand. Her accomplices went out the back door, then down the fire escape. If you hurry you might be able to catch them."

The two NYCPD officers looked around at the destruction, and didn't seem any too inclined to chase after whoever was responsible. Di checked out of the corner of her eye; Harrison's own .44 had vanished as mysteriously as it had appeared.

"Are you certain this woman is responsible?" asked

the hard-faced, suited individual with a frown, as he holstered his .357. He wasn't paying much attention to the plastic handgrip in the holster at Di's hip, for which she was grateful.

House detective, I bet. With any luck, he's never seen a Glock.

Di nodded. "These two gentlemen will back me up as witnesses," she said. "I suspect some of the ladies from the party will be able to do so as well, once you explain that Ms. Vervain was playing a not-very-nice joke on them. Personally, I think she ought to be held accountable for the damages."

And keep my RWW dues from going through the roof.

"Well, I think so too, miss." The detective hauled Valentine ungently to her feet. The writer was still confused, and it wasn't an act this time. "Ma'am," he said sternly to the dazed redhead, "I think you'd better come with me. I think we have a few questions to ask you."

Di projected outraged innocence and harmlessness at them as hard as she could. The camouflage trick worked, which after this evening, was more than she expected. The two uniformed officers didn't even look at her weapon; they just followed the detective out without a single backwards glance.

Harrison cleared his throat, audibly. She turned and raised an eyebrow at him.

"You—I thought you were just a writer—"

"And I thought *you* were just a writer," she countered. "So we're even."

"But—" He took a good look at her face, and evidently thought better of prying. "What did you do with that—thing? That was the strangest incantation I've ever heard!"

She shrugged, and began picking her way through the mess of smashed furniture, spilled drinks, and crushed and ground-in refreshments. "I have *no* idea. Valentine brought it in with something screwy, I got rid of it the same way. And that critter has no idea how lucky he was."

"Why?" asked Harrison, as she and Andre reached the door.

"Why?" She turned and smiled sweetly. "Do you have any idea how hard it is to get a parking place in Manhattan at this time of night?"

This is the very first attempted professional appearance of Diana Tregarde, my occult detective. I've always enjoyed occult detectives, but there is a major problem with them—what are they supposed to do for a living*? Ghosts don't pay very well! So Di writes romances for a living and saves the world on the side. This story was originally rejected by the anthology I submitted it to; it became the basis for* Children of the Night *by* Another Company, *and was then published in this form by* Marion Zimmer Bradley's Fantasy Magazine.

Nightside

It was early spring, but the wind held no hint of verdancy, not even the promise of it—it was chill and odorless, and there were ghosts of dead leaves skittering before it. A few of them jittered into the pool of weak yellow light cast by the aging streetlamp—a converted gaslight that was a relic of the previous century. It was old and tired, its pea-green paint flaking away; as weary as this neighborhood, which was older still. Across the street loomed an ancient church, its congregation dwindled over the years to a handful of little old women and men who appeared like scrawny blackbirds every Sunday, and then scattered back to the shabby houses that stood to either side of it until Sunday should come again. On the side of the street that the lamp tried (and failed) to illuminate, was the cemetery.

Like the neighborhood, it was very old—in this case, fifty years shy of being classified as "Colonial." There were few empty gravesites now, and most of those belonged to the same little old ladies and men that had lived and would die here. It was protected from vandals by a thorny hedge as well as a ten-foot wrought-iron fence. Within its confines, as seen through the leafless branches of the hedge, granite cenotaphs and enormous Victorian monuments bulked shapelessly against the bare sliver of a waning moon.

The church across the street was dark and silent; the houses up and down the block showed few lights, if any. There was no reason for anyone of this neighborhood to be out in the night.

So the young woman waiting beneath the lamp-post seemed that much more out-of-place.

Nor could she be considered a typical resident of this neighborhood by any stretch of the imagination—for one thing, she was young; perhaps in her mid-twenties, but no more. Her clothing was neat but casual, too casual for someone visiting an elderly relative. She wore dark, knee-high boots, old, soft jeans tucked into their tops, and a thin windbreaker open at the front to show a leotard beneath. Her attire was far too light to be any real protection against the bite of the wind, yet she seemed unaware of the cold. Her hair was long, down to her waist, and straight—in the uncertain light of the lamp it was an indeterminate shadow, and it fell down her back like a waterfall. Her eyes were large and oddly slanted, but not Oriental; catlike, rather. Even the way she held herself was feline; poised, expectant—a graceful tension like a dancer's or a hunting predator's. She was not watching for something—no, her eyes were unfocused with concentration. She was *listening*.

A soft whistle, barely audible, carried down the street

on the chill wind. The tune was of a piece with the neighborhood—old and timeworn.

Many of the residents would have smiled in recollection to hear "Lili Marlene" again.

The tension left the girl as she swung around the lamp-post by one hand to face the direction of the whistle. She waved, and a welcoming smile warmed her eyes.

The whistler stepped into the edge of the circle of light. He, too, was dusky of eye and hair—and heart-breakingly handsome. He wore only dark jeans and a black turtleneck, no coat at all—but like the young woman, he didn't seem to notice the cold. There was an impish glint in his eyes as he finished the tune with a flourish.

"A flair for the dramatic, Diana, *mon cherie*?" he said mockingly. "Would that you were here for the same purpose as the lovely Lili! Alas, I fear my luck cannot be so good. . . ."

She laughed. His eyes warmed at the throaty chuckle. "Andre," she chided, "don't you ever think of anything else?"

"Am I not a son of the City of Light? I must uphold her reputation, *mais non*?" The young woman raised an ironic brow. He shrugged. "Ah well—since it is you who seek me, I fear I must be all business. A pity. Well, what lures you to my side this unseasonable night? What horror has *mademoiselle* Tregarde unearthed this time?"

Diana Tregarde sobered instantly, the laughter fleeing her eyes. "I'm afraid you picked the right word this time, Andre. It *is* a horror. The trouble is, I don't know what kind."

"Say on. I wait in breathless anticipation." His expression was mocking as he leaned against the lamp-post, and he feigned a yawn.

Diana scowled at him and her eyes darkened with anger. He raised an eyebrow of his own. "If this weren't so serious," she threatened, "I'd be tempted to pop you one—Andre, people are dying out there. There's a 'Ripper' loose in New York."

He shrugged, and shifted restlessly from one foot to the other. "So? This is new? Tell me when there is *not*! That sort of criminal is as common to the city as a rat. Let your police earn their salaries and capture him."

Her expression hardened. She folded her arms tightly across the thin nylon of her windbreaker; her lips tightened a little. "Use your head, Andre! If this was an ordinary slasher-killer, would *I* be involved?"

He examined his fingernails with care. "And what is it that makes it *extraordinaire,* eh?"

"The victims had no souls."

"I was not aware," he replied wryly, "that the dead possessed such things anymore."

She growled under her breath, and tossed her head impatiently, and the wind caught her hair and whipped it around her throat. "You are *deliberately* being difficult! I have half a mind—"

It finally seemed to penetrate the young man's mind that she was truly angry—and truly frightened, though she was doing her best to conceal the fact; his expression became contrite. "Forgive me, *cherie*. I *am* being recalcitrant."

"You're being a pain in the ass," she replied acidly. "Would I have come to you if I wasn't already out of my depth?"

"Well—" he admitted. "No. But—this business of souls, *cherie*, how can you determine such a thing? I find it most difficult to believe."

She shivered, and her eyes went brooding. "So did I. Trust me, my friend, I know what I'm talking about. There isn't a shred of doubt in my mind. There are at least six victims who no longer exist in *any* fashion anymore."

The young man finally evidenced alarm. "But—how?" he said, bewildered. "How is such a thing possible?"

She shook her head violently, clenching her hands

on the arms of her jacket as if by doing so she could protect herself from an unseen—but not unfelt—danger. "I don't know, I don't know! It seems incredible even now—I keep thinking it's a nightmare, but—Andre, it's real, it's not my imagination—" Her voice rose a little with each word, and Andre's sharp eyes rested for a moment on her trembling hands.

"*Eh bien,*" he sighed, "I believe you. So there is something about that devours souls—and mutilates bodies as well, since you mentioned a 'Ripper' persona?"

She nodded.

"Was the devouring before or after the mutilation?"

"Before, I think—it's not easy to judge." She shivered in a way that had nothing to do with the cold.

"And you came into this how?"

"Whatever it is, it took the friend of a friend; I—happened to be there to see the body afterwards, and I knew immediately there was something wrong. When I unshielded and used the Sight—"

"Bad." He made it a statement.

"Worse. I—I can't describe what it felt like. There were still residual emotions, things left behind when—" Her jaw clenched. "Then when I started checking further I found out about the other five victims—that what I had discovered was no fluke. Andre, whatever it is, it has to be stopped." She laughed again, but this time there was no humor in it. "After all, you could say stopping it is in my job description."

He nodded soberly. "And so you become involved. Well enough, if you must hunt this thing, so must I." He became all business. "Tell me of the history. When, and where, and who does it take?"

She bit her lip. " 'Where'—there's no pattern. 'Who' seems to be mostly a matter of opportunity; the only clue is that the victims were always out on the street and entirely alone, there were no witnesses whatsoever, so the thing needs total privacy and apparently can't strike where it will. And 'when'—is moon-dark."

"Bad." He shook his head. "I have no clue at the moment. The *loup-garou* I know, and others, but I know nothing that hunts beneath the dark moon."

She grimaced. "You think I do? That's why I need your help; you're sensitive enough to feel something out of the ordinary, and you can watch and hunt undetected. I can't. And I'm not sure I *want* to go trolling for this thing alone—without knowing what it is, I could end up as a late-night snack for it. But if that's what I have to do, I will."

Anger blazed up in his face like a cold fire. "You go hunting alone for this creature over my dead body!"

"That's a little redundant, isn't it?" Her smile was weak, but genuine again.

"Pah!" he dismissed her attempt at humor with a wave of his hand. "Tomorrow is the first night of moon-dark; *I* shall go a-hunting. Do *you* remain at home, else I shall be most wroth with you. I know where to find you, should I learn anything of note."

"You ought to—" Diana began, but she spoke to the empty air.

The next night was warmer, and Diana had gone to bed with her windows open to drive out some of the stale odors the long winter had left in her apartment. Not that the air of New York City was exactly fresh—but it was better than what the heating system kept recycling through the building. She didn't particularly like leaving her defenses open while she slept, but the lingering memory of Katy Rourk's fish wafting through the halls as she came in from shopping had decided her. Better exhaust fumes than burned haddock.

She hadn't had an easy time falling asleep, and when she finally managed to do so, tossed restlessly, her dreams uneasy and readily broken—

—as by the sound of someone in the room.

Before the intruder crossed even half the distance between the window and her bed, she was wide awake, and moving. She threw herself out of bed, somersaulted across her bedroom, and wound up crouched beside the door, one hand on the lightswitch, the other holding a polished dagger she'd taken from beneath her pillow.

As the lights came on, she saw Andre standing in the center of the bedroom, blinking in surprise, wearing a sheepish grin.

Relief made her knees go weak. "Andre, you *idiot*!" She tried to control her tone, but her voice was shrill and cracked a little. "You could have been *killed*!"

He spread his hands wide in a placating gesture. "Now, Diana—"

"'Now Diana' my eye!" she growled. "Even *you* would have a hard time getting around a severed spine!" She stood up slowly, shaking from head to toe with released tension.

"I didn't wish to wake you," he said, crestfallen.

She closed her eyes and took several long, deep, calming breaths; focusing on a mantra, moving herself back into stillness until she knew she would be able to reply without screaming at him.

"Don't," she said carefully, "Ever. Do. That. Again." She punctuated the last word by driving the dagger she held into the doorframe.

"*Certainement, mon petite*," he replied, his eyes widening a little as he began to calculate how fast she'd moved. "The next time I come in your window when you sleep, I shall blow a trumpet first."

"You'd be a *lot* safer. *I'd* be a lot happier," she said crossly, pulling the dagger loose with a snap of her wrist. She palmed the light-switch and dimmed the lamps down to where they would be comfortable to his light-sensitive eyes, then crossed the room, the plush brown carpet warm and soft under her bare feet. She bent slightly, and put the silver-plated dagger back under her pillow. Then with a sigh she folded her long legs beneath her to sit on her rumpled bed. This was the first time Andre had ever caught her asleep, and she was irritated far beyond what her disturbed dreams warranted. She was somewhat obsessed with her privacy and with keeping her night-boundaries unbreached—she and Andre were off-and-on lovers, but she'd never let him stay any length of time.

He approached the antique wooden bed slowly. "*Cherie*, this was no idle visit—"

"I should bloody well hope not!" she interrupted, trying to soothe her jangled nerves by combing the tangles out of her hair with her fingers.

"—I have seen your killer."

She froze.

"It is nothing I have ever seen or heard of before."

She clenched her hands on the strand of hair they held, ignoring the pull. "Go on—"

"It—no, *he*—I could not detect until he made his first kill tonight. I found him then, found him just before he took his hunting-shape, or I never would have discovered him at all; for when he is in that shape there is nothing about him that *I* could sense that marked him as different. So ordinary—a man, an Oriental; Japanese, I think, and like many others—not young, not old; not fat, not thin. So unremarkable as to be invisible. I followed him—he was so normal I found it difficult to believe what my own eyes had seen a moment before; then, not ten minutes later, he found yet another victim and—fed again."

He closed his eyes, his face thoughtful. "As I said, I have never seen or heard of his like, yet—yet there was something familiar about him. I cannot even tell you what it was, and yet it was familiar."

"You said you saw him attack—*how*, Andre?" she leaned forward, her face tight with urgency as the bed creaked a little beneath her.

"The second quarry was—the—is it 'bag lady' you say?" At her nod he continued. "He smiled at her—just smiled, that was all. She froze like the frightened rabbit. Then he—changed—into dark, dark smoke; only smoke, nothing more. The smoke enveloped the old woman until I could see her no longer. Then—he fed. I—I can understand your feelings now, *cherie.* It was—nothing to the eye, but—what I felt *within*—"

"Now you see," she said gravely.

"*Mais oui*, and you have no more argument from me. This thing is abomination, and must be ended."

"The question is—" She grimaced.

"How? I have given some thought to this. One cannot fight smoke. But in his hunting form—I think perhaps he is vulnerable to physical measures. As you say, even *I* would have difficulty in dealing with a severed spine or crushed brain. I think maybe it would be the same for him. Have you the courage to play the wounded bird, *mon petite*?" He sat beside her on the edge of the bed and regarded her with solemn and worried eyes.

She considered that for a moment. "Play bait while you wait for him to move in? It sounds like the best plan to me—it wouldn't be the first time I've done that, and I'm not exactly helpless, you know," she replied, twisting a strand of hair around her fingers.

"I think you have finally proved that to me tonight!" There was a hint of laughter in his eyes again, as well as chagrin. "I shall never again make the mistake of thinking you to be a fragile flower. *Bien.* Is tomorrow night too soon for you?"

"Tonight wouldn't be too soon," she stated flatly.

"Except that he has already gone to lair, having fed twice." He took one of her hands, freeing it from the lock of hair she had twisted about it. "No, we rest—I know where he is to be found, and tomorrow night we face him at full strength." Abruptly he grinned. "*Cherie*, I have read one of your books—"

She winced, and closed her eyes in a grimace. "Oh Lord—I was afraid you'd ferret out one of my pseudonyms. You're as bad as the Elephant's Child when it comes to 'satiable curiosity."

"It was hardly difficult to guess the author when she

used one of my favorite expressions for the title—and then described me so very intimately not three pages from the beginning."

Her expression was woeful. "Oh *no*! Not *that* one!"

He shook an admonishing finger at her. "I do not think it kind, to make me the villain, and all because I told you I spent a good deal of the Regency in London."

"But—but—Andre, these things follow *formulas*, I didn't really have a choice—anybody French in a Regency romance *has* to be either an expatriate aristocrat or a villain—" She bit her lip and looked pleadingly at him. "—I needed a villain and I didn't have a clue—I was in the middle of that phony medium thing *and* I had a deadline—and—" Her words thinned down to a whisper, "—to tell you the truth, I didn't think you'd ever find out. You—you aren't angry, are you?"

He lifted the hair away from her shoulder, cupped his hand beneath her chin and moved close beside her. "I *think* I may possibly be induced to forgive you—"

The near-chuckle in his voice told her she hadn't offended him. Reassured by that, she looked up at him, slyly. "Oh?"

"You could—" He slid her gown off her shoulder a little, and ran an inquisitive finger from the tip of her shoulderblade to just behind her ear "—write another, and let me play the hero—"

"Have you any—suggestions?" she replied, finding it difficult to reply when his mouth followed where his finger had been.

"In that 'Burning Passions' series, perhaps?"

She pushed him away, laughing. "The soft-core porn for housewives? Andre, you can't be serious!"

"Never more." He pulled her back. "Think of how much enjoyable the research would be—"

She grabbed his hand again before it could resume its explorations. "Aren't we supposed to be resting?"

He stopped for a moment and his face and eyes were

deadly serious. "*Cherie*, we must face this thing at strength. You need sleep—and to relax. Can you think of any better way to relax body and spirit than—"

"No," she admitted. "I always sleep like a rock when you get done with me."

"Well then. And I—I have needs; I have not tended to those needs for too long, if I am to have full strength, and I should not care to meet this creature at less than that."

"Excuses, excuses—" She briefly contemplated getting up long enough to take care of the lights—then decided a little waste of energy was worth it, and extinguished them with a thought. "C'mere, you—let's do some research."

He laughed deep in his throat as they reached for one another with the same eager hunger.

She woke late the next morning—so late that in a half hour it would have been "afternoon"—and lay quietly for a long, contented moment before wriggling out of the tumble of bedclothes and Andre. No fear of waking him—he wouldn't rouse until the sun went down. She arranged him a bit more comfortably and tucked him in, thinking that he looked absurdly young with his hair all rumpled and those long, dark lashes of his lying against his cheek—he looked much better this morning, now that she was in a position to pay attention. Last night he'd been pretty pale and hungry-thin. She shook her head over him. Someday his gallantry was going to get him into trouble. "Idiot—" she whispered, touching his forehead, "—all you ever have to do is *ask*—"

But there were other things to take care of—and to think of. A fight to get ready for; and she had a premonition it wasn't going to be an easy one.

So she showered and changed into a leotard, and took herself into her barren studio at the back of the apartment to run through her *katas* three times—once slow, twice at full speed—and then into some *Tai Chi* exercises to rebalance everything. She followed that with a half hour of meditation, then cast a circle and charged herself with all of the Power she thought she could safely carry.

Without knowing what it was she was to face, that was all she could do, really—that, and have a really good dinner—

She showered and changed again into a bright red sweatsuit and was just finishing that dinner when the sun set and Andre strolled into the white-painted kitchen, shirtless, and blinking sleepily.

She gulped the last bite of her liver and waggled her fingers at him. "If you want a shower, you'd better get a fast one—I want to get in place before he comes out for the night."

He sighed happily over the prospect of a hot shower. "The perfect way to start one's—day. *Petite,* you may have difficulty in dislodging me now that you have let me stay overnight—"

She showed her teeth. "Don't count your chickens, kiddo. I can be very nasty!"

"*Mon petite—I—*" He suddenly sobered, and looked at her with haunted eyes.

She saw his expression and abruptly stopped teasing. "Andre—please don't say it—I can't give you any better answer now than I could when you first asked—if I—cared for you as more than a friend."

He sighed again, less happily. "Then I will say no more, because you wish it—but—what of this notion—would you permit me to stay with you? No more than that. I could be of some use to you, I think, and I would take nothing from you that you did not offer first. I do not like it that you are so much alone. It did not matter when we first met, but you are collecting powerful enemies, *cherie*."

"I—" She wouldn't look at him, but only at her hands, clenched white-knuckled on the table.

"Unless there are others—" he prompted, hesitantly.

"No—no, there isn't anyone but you." She sat in silence for a moment, then glanced back up at him with one eyebrow lifted sardonically. "You *do* rather spoil a girl for anyone else's attentions."

He was genuinely startled. "*Mille pardons, cherie,*" he stuttered, "I—I did not know—"

She managed a feeble chuckle. "Oh Andre, you idiot—I *like* being spoiled! I don't get many things that are just for me—" she sighed, then gave in to his pleading eyes. "All right then, move in if you want—"

"It is what *you* want that concerns me."

"I want," she said, very softly. "Just—the commitment—don't ask for it. I've got responsibilities as well as Power, you know that; I—can't see how to balance them with what you offered before—"

"Enough," he silenced her with a wave of his hand. "The words are unsaid, we will speak of this no more unless you wish it. I seek the embrace of warm water—"

She turned her mind to the dangers ahead, resolutely pushing the dangers *he* represented into the back of her mind. "And I will go bail the car out of the garage."

He waited until he was belted in on the passenger's side of the car to comment on her outfit. "I did not know you planned to race him, Diana," he said with a quirk of one corner of his mouth.

"Urban camouflage," she replied, dodging two taxis and a kamikaze panel truck. "Joggers are everywhere, and they run at night a lot in deserted neighborhoods. Cops won't wonder about me or try to stop me, and our boy won't be surprised to see me alone. One of his other victims was out running. His boyfriend thought he'd had a heart attack. Poor thing. He wasn't one of us, so I didn't enlighten him. There are some things it's better the survivors don't know."

"*Oui.* Left here, *cherie.*"

The traffic thinned down to a trickle, then to nothing. There are odd little islands in New York at night; places as deserted as the loneliest country road. The area where Andre directed her was one such; by day it was small warehouses, one floor factories, an odd store or two. None of them had enough business to warrant running second or third shifts, and the neighborhood had not been gentrified yet, so no one actually lived here. There were a handful of night-watchmen, perhaps, but most of these places depended on locks, burglar-alarms, and dogs that were released at night to keep out intruders.

"There—" Andre pointed at a building that appeared to be home to several small manufactories. "He took the smoke-form and went to roost in the elevator control house at the top. That is why I did not advise going against him by day."

"Is he there now?" Diana peered up through the glare of sodium-vapor lights, but couldn't make out the top of the building.

Andre closed his eyes, a frown of concentration creasing his forehead. "No," he said after a moment. "I think he has gone hunting."

She repressed a shiver. "Then it's time to play bait."

Diana found a parking space marked dimly with the legend "President"—she thought it unlikely it would be wanted within the next few hours. It was deep in the shadow of the building Andre had pointed out, and her car was dead-black; with any luck, cops coming by wouldn't even notice it was there and start to wonder.

She hopped out, locking her door behind her, looking now exactly like the lone jogger she was pretending to be, and set off at an easy pace. She did not look back

If absolutely necessary, she knew she'd be able to keep this up for hours. She decided to take all the north-south streets first, then weave back along the east-west. Before the first hour was up she was wishing she'd dared bring a "walk-thing"—every street was like every other street; blank brick walls broken by dusty, barred windows and metal doors, alleys with only the occasional dumpster visible, refuse blowing along the gutters. She was bored; her nervousness had worn off, and she was lonely. She ran from light to darkness, from darkness to light, and saw and heard nothing but the occasional rat.

Then he struck, just when she was beginning to get a little careless. Careless enough not to see him arrive.

One moment there was nothing, the next, he was before her, waiting halfway down the block. She knew it was him—he was exactly as Andre had described him, a nondescript Oriental man in a dark windbreaker and slacks. He was tall for an Oriental—taller than she by several inches. His appearance nearly startled her into stopping—then she remembered that she was supposed to be an innocent jogger, and resumed her steady trot.

She knew he meant her to see him, he was standing directly beneath the streetlight and right in the middle of the sidewalk. She would have to swerve out of her path to avoid him.

She started to do just that, ignoring him as any real jogger would have—when he raised his head and smiled at her.

She was stopped dead in her tracks by the purest terror she had ever felt in her life. She froze, as all of his other victims must have—unable to think, unable to cry out, unable to run. Her legs had gone numb, and nothing existed for her but that terrible smile and those hard, black eyes that had no bottom—

Then the smile vanished, and the eyes flinched away. Diana could move again, and staggered back against the brick wall of the building behind her, her breath coming in harsh pants, the brick rough and comforting in its reality beneath her hands.

"Diana?" It was Andre's voice behind her.

"I'm—all right—" she said, not at all sure that she really was.

Andre strode silently past her, face grim and

purposeful. The man seemed to sense his purpose, and smiled again—

But Andre never faltered for even the barest moment.

The smile wavered and faded; the man fell back a step or two, surprised that his weapon had failed him—

Then he scowled, and pulled something out of the sleeve of his windbreaker; and to Diana's surprise, charged straight for Andre, his sneakered feet scuffing on the cement—

And something suddenly blurring about his right hand. As it connected with Andre's upraised left arm, Diana realized what it was—almost too late.

"Andre—he has nunchuks—they're *wood*," she cried out urgently as Andre grunted in unexpected pain. "He can *kill* you with them! Get the *hell* out of here!"

Andre needed no second warning. In the blink of an eye, he was gone.

Leaving Diana to face the creature alone.

She dropped into guard-stance as he regarded her thoughtfully, still making no sound, not even of heavy breathing. In a moment he seemed to make up his mind, and came for her.

At least he didn't smile again in that terrible way—perhaps the weapon was only effective once.

She hoped fervently he wouldn't try again—as an empath, she was doubly-vulnerable to a weapon forged of fear.

They circled each other warily, like two cats preparing to fight—then Diana thought she saw an opening—and took it.

And quickly came to the conclusion that she was overmatched, as he sent her tumbling with a badly bruised shin. The next few moments reinforced that conclusion—as he continued scatheless while she picked up injury after painful injury.

She was a brown-belt in karate—but he was a black-belt in kung-fu, and the contest was a pathetically uneven match. She knew before very long that he was toying with her—and while he still swung the wooden nunchuks, Andre did not dare move in close enough to help.

She realized, (as fear dried her mouth, she grew more and more winded, and she searched frantically for a means of escape) that she was as good as dead.

If only she could get those damn 'chucks away from him!

And as she ducked and stumbled against the curb, narrowly avoiding the strike he made at her, an idea came to her. He knew from her moves—as she knew from his—that she was no amateur. He would never expect an amateur's move from her—something truly stupid and suicidal—

So the next time he swung at her, she stood her ground. As the 'chuk came at her she took one step forward, smashing his nose with the heel of her right hand and lifting her left to intercept the flying baton.

As it connected with her left hand with a sickening crunch, she whirled and folded her entire body around hand and weapon, and went limp, carrying it away from him.

She collapsed in a heap at his feet, hand afire with pain, eyes blurring with it, and waited for either death or salvation.

And salvation in the form of Andre rose behind her attacker. With one *savate* kick he broke the man's back; Diana could hear it cracking like green wood—and before her assailant could collapse, a second double-handed blow sent him crashing into the brick wall, head crushed like an eggshell.

Diana struggled to her feet, and waited for some arcane transformation.

Nothing.

She staggered to the corpse, face flat and expressionless—a sign she was suppressing pain and shock with utterly implacable iron will. Andre began to move forward as if to stop her, then backed off again at the look in her eyes.

She bent slightly, just enough to touch the shoulder of the body with her good hand—and released the Power.

Andre pulled her back to safety as the corpse exploded into flame, burning as if it had been soaked in oil. She watched the flames for one moment, wooden-faced; then abruptly collapsed.

Andre caught her easily before she could hurt herself further, lifting her in his arms as if she weighed no more than a kitten. "*Mon pauvre petite*," he murmured, heading back towards the car at a swift but silent run, "It is the hospital for you, I think—"

"Saint—Francis—" she gasped, every step jarring her hand and bringing tears of pain to her eyes, "One of us—is on the night-staff—Dr. Crane—"

"*Bien*," he replied. "Now be silent—"

"But—how are you—"

"In your car, foolish one. I have the keys you left in it."

"But—"

"I can drive."

"But—"

"*And* I have a license. Will you be silent?"

"How?" she said, disobeying him.

"Night school," he replied succinctly, reaching the car, putting her briefly on her feet to unlock the passenger-side door, then lifting her into it. "You are not the only one who knows of urban camouflage."

This time she did not reply—mostly because she had fainted from pain.

The emergency room was empty—for which Andre was very grateful. His invocation of Dr. Crane brought a thin, bearded young man around to the tiny examining cubicle in record time.

"Good godalmighty! What did you tangle with, a

bus?" he exclaimed, when stripping the sweatsuit jacket and pants revealed that there was little of Diana that was not battered and black-and-blue.

Andre wrinkled his nose at the acrid antiseptic odors around them, and replied shortly. "No. Your 'Ripper.'"

The startled gaze the doctor fastened on him revealed that Andre had scored. "Who—won?" he asked at last.

"We did. I do not think he will prey upon anyone again."

The doctor's eyes closed briefly; Andre read prayerful thankfulness on his face as he sighed with relief. Then he returned to business. "You must be Andre, right? Anything I can supply?"

Andre laughed at the hesitation in his voice. "Fear not, your blood supply is quite safe, and I am unharmed. It is Diana who needs you."

The relief on the doctor's face made Andre laugh again.

Dr. Crane ignored him. "Right," he said, turning to the work *he* knew best.

She was lightheaded and groggy with the Demerol Dr. Crane had given her as Andre deftly stripped her and tucked her into her bed; she'd dozed all the way home in the car.

"I just wish I knew *what* that thing was—" she said inconsequentially, as he arranged her arm in its light Fiberglas cast a little more comfortably. "—I won't be happy until I *know*—"

"Then you are about to be happy, *cherie*, for I have had the brainstorm—" Andre ducked into the livingroom and emerged with a dusty leather-bound book. "Remember I said there was something familiar about it? Now I think I know what it was." He consulted the index, and turned pages rapidly—found the place he sought, and read for a few moments. "As I thought—listen. 'The *gaki*—also known as the Japanese vampire—also takes its nourishment only from the living. There are many kinds of *gaki*, extracting their sustenance from a wide variety of sources. The most harmless are the "perfume" and "music" *gaki*—and they are by far the most common. Far deadlier are those that require blood, flesh—or souls.' "

"Souls?"

"Just so. 'To feed, or when at rest, they take their normal form of a dense cloud of dark smoke. At other times, like the *kitsune*, they take on the form of a human being. Unlike the *kitsune*, however, there is no way to distinguish them in this form from any other human. In the smoke form, they are invulnerable—in the human form, however, they can be killed; but to permanently destroy them, the body must be burned—preferably in conjunction with or solely by Power.' I said there was something familiar about it—it seems to have been a kind of distant cousin." Andre's mouth smiled, but his eyes reflected only a long-abiding bitterness.

"There is *no way* you have any relationship with that—thing!" she said forcefully. "It had no more honor, heart or soul than a rabid beast!"

"I—I thank you, *cherie*," he said, slowly, the warmth returning to his eyes. "There are not many who would think as you do."

"Their own closed-minded stupidity."

"To change the subject—what was it made you burn it as you did? I would have abandoned it. It seemed dead enough."

"I don't know—it just seemed the thing to do," she yawned. "Sometimes my instincts just work . . right. . . ."

Suddenly her eyes seemed too leaden to keep open. "Like they did with you. . . ." She fought against exhaustion and the drug, trying to keep both at bay.

But without success. Sleep claimed her for its own.

He watched her for the rest of the night, until the leaden lethargy of his own limbs told him dawn was near. He had already decided not to share her bed, lest any movement on his part cause her pain—instead, he made up a pallet on the floor beside her.

He stood over her broodingly while he in his turn fought slumber, and touched her face gently. "Well—" he whispered, holding off torpor far deeper and heavier than hers could ever be—while she was mortal. "You are not aware to hear, so I may say what I will and you cannot forbid. Dream; sleep and dream—I shall see you safe—my only love."

And he took his place beside her, to lie motionless until night should come again.

This was originally for a Susan Shwartz anthology, Sisters of Fantasy 2.

Wet Wings

Katherine watched avidly, chin cradled in her old, arthritic hands, as the chrysalis heaved, and writhed, and finally split up the back. The crinkled, sodden wings of the butterfly emerged first, followed by the bloated body. She breathed a sigh of wonder, as she always did, and the butterfly tried to flap its useless wings in alarm as it caught her movement.

"Silly thing," she chided it affectionately. "You know you can't fly with wet wings!" Then she exerted a little of her magic; just a little, brushing the butterfly with a spark of calm that jumped from her trembling index finger to its quivering antenna.

The butterfly, soothed, went back to its real job, pumping the fluid from its body into the veins of its wings, unfurling them into their full glory. It was not a particularly rare butterfly, certainly not an endangered one; nothing but a common Buckeye, a butterfly so ordinary that no one even commented on seeing them when she was a child. But Katherine had always found the markings exquisite, and she had used this species and the Sulfurs more often than any other to carry her magic.

Magic. That was a word hard to find written anymore. No one approved of magic these days. Strange that in a country that gave the Church of Gaia equal rights with the Catholic Church, that no one believed in magic.

But magic was not "correct." It was not given equally to all, nor could it be given equally to all. And that which could not be made equal, must be destroyed. . . .

"We always knew that there would be repression and a burning time again," she told the butterfly, as its wings unfolded a little more. "But we never thought that the ones behind the repression would come from our own ranks."

Perhaps she should have realized it would happen. So many people had come to her over the years, drawn by the magic in her books, demanding to be taught. Some had the talent and the will; most had only delusions. How they had cursed her when she told them the truth! They had wanted to be like the heroes and heroines of her stories; *special, powerful.*

She remembered them all; the boy she had told, regretfully, that his "telepathy" was only observation and the ability to read body-language. The girl whose "psychic attacks" had been caused by potassium imbalances. The would-be "bardic mage" who had nothing other than a facility to delude himself. And the many who could not tell a tale, because they would not let themselves see the tales all around them. They were neither powerful nor special, at least not in terms either of the power of magic, nor the magic of storytelling. More often than not, they would go to someone else, demanding to be taught, unwilling to hear the truth.

Eventually, they found someone; in one of the many movements that sprouted on the fringes like parasitic mushrooms. She, like the other mages of her time, had simply shaken her head and sighed for them. But what she had not reckoned on, nor had anyone else, was that these movements had gained strength and a life of their own—and had gone political.

Somehow, although the process had been so gradual she had never noticed when it had become unstoppable, those who cherished their delusions began to legislate some of those delusions. "Politically correct" they called it—and *some* of the things they had done she had welcomed, seeing them as the harbingers of more freedom, not less.

But they had gone from the reasonable to the unreasoning; from demanding and getting a removal of sexism to a denial of sexuality and the differences that should have been celebrated. From legislating the humane treatment of animals to making the possession of any animal or animal product without licenses and yearly inspections a crime. Fewer people bothered with owning a pet these days—no, not a pet, an "Animal Companion," and one did not "own" it, one "nurtured" it. Not when inspectors had the right to come into your home day or night, make certain that you were giving your Animal Companion all the rights to which it was entitled. And the rarer the animal, the more onerous the conditions. . . .

"That wouldn't suit you, would it, Horace?" she asked the young crow perched over the window. Horace was completely illegal; there was no way she could have gotten a license for him. She lived in an apartment, not on a farm; she could never give him the four-acre "hunting preserve" he required. Never mind that he had come to her, lured by her magic, and that he was free to come and go through her window, hunting and exercising at will. He also came and went with her little spell-packets, providing her with eyes on the world where she could not go, and bringing back the cocoons and chrysalises that she used for her butterfly-magics.

She shook her head, and sighed. They had sucked all the juice of life out of the world, that was what they had done. Outside, the gray overcast day mirrored the gray sameness of the world they had created. There were no bright colors anymore to draw the eye, only pastels. No passion, no fire, nothing to arouse any kind of emotions. They had decreed that everyone *must* be equal, and no one must be offended, ever. And they had begun the burning and the banning. . . .

She had become alarmed when the burning and banning started; she knew that her own world was doomed when it reached things like "Hansel and Gretel"—banned, not because there was a witch in it, but because the witch was evil, and that might offend witches. She had known that her own work was doomed when a book that had been lauded for its portrayal of a young gay hero was banned because the young gay hero was unhappy and suicidal. She had not even bothered to argue. She simply announced her retirement, and went into seclusion, pouring all her energies into the magic of her butterflies.

From the first moment of spring to the last of autumn, Horace brought her caterpillars and cocoons. When the young butterflies emerged, she gave them each a special burden and sent them out into the world again.

Wonder. Imagination. Joy. Diversity. Some she sent out to wake the gifts of magic in others. Some she sent to wake simple stubborn will.

Discontent. Rebellion. She sowed her seeds, here in this tiny apartment, of what she hoped would be the next revolution. She would not be here to see it—but the day would come, she hoped, when those who *were* different and special would no longer be willing or content with sameness and equality at the expense of diversity.

Her door-buzzer sounded, jarring her out of her reverie.

She got up, stiffly, and went to the intercom. But the face there was that of her old friend Piet, the "Environmental Engineer" of the apartment building, and he wore an expression of despair.

"Kathy, the Psi-cops are coming for you," he said, quickly, casting a look over his shoulder to see if there was anyone listening. "They made me let them in—"

The screen darkened abruptly.

Oh Gods— She had been so careful! But—in a way, she had expected it. She had been a world-renowned fantasy writer; she had made no secret of her knowledge of real-world magics. The Psi-cops had not made any spectacular arrests lately. Possibly they were running out of victims; she should have known they would start looking at peoples' pasts.

She glanced around at the apartment reflexively—

No. There was no hope. There were too many thing she had that were contraband. The shelves full of books, the feathers and bones she used in her magics, the freezer full of meat that she shared with Horace and his predecessors, the wool blankets—

For that matter, they could arrest her on the basis of her jewelry alone, the fetish-necklaces she carved and made, the medicine-wheels and shields, and the prayer-feathers. She was not Native American; she had no right to make these things even for private use.

And she knew what would happen to her. The Psi-cops would take her away, confiscate all her property, and "re-educate" her.

Drugged, brainwashed, wired and probed. There would be nothing left of her when they finished. They had "re-educated" Jim three years ago, and when he came out, everything, even his magic and his ability to tell a story, was gone. He had not even had the opportunity to gift it to someone else; they had simply crushed it. He had committed suicide less than a week after his release.

She had a few more minutes at most, before they zapped the lock on her door and broke in. She had to save something, anything!

Then her eyes lighted on the butterfly, his wings fully unfurled and waving gently, and she knew what she would do.

First, she freed Horace. He flew off, squawking indignantly at being sent out into the overcast. But there was no other choice; if they found him, they would probably cage him up and send him to a forest preserve somewhere. He did not know how to find food in a wilderness—let him at least stay here in the city, where he knew how to steal food from birdfeeders, and where the best dumpsters were.

Then she cupped her hands around the butterfly, and gathered all of her magic. *All* of it this time; a great burden for one tiny insect, but there was no choice.

Songs and tales, magic and wonder; power, vision, will, strength— She breathed them into the butterfly's wings, and he trembled as the magic swirled around him, in a vortex of sparkling mist.

Pride. Poetry. Determination. Love. Hope—

She heard them at the door, banging on it, ordering her to open in the name of the Equal State. She ignored them. There was at least a minute or so left.

The gift of words. The gift of difference—

Finally she took her hands away, spent and exhausted, and feeling as empty as an old paper sack. The butterfly waved his wings, and though she could no longer see it, she knew that a drift of sparkling power followed the movements.

There was a whine behind her as the Psi-cops zapped the lock.

She opened the window, coaxed the butterfly onto her hand, and put him outside. An errant ray of sunshine broke through the overcast, gilding him with a glory that mirrored the magic he carried.

"Go," she breathed. "Find someone worthy."

He spread his wings, tested the breeze, and lifted off her hand, to be carried away.

And she turned, full of dignity and empty of all else, to face her enemies.

Here is the only *Valdemar short story I have ever done, largely because I hate to waste a good story idea on something as small as a short story! This first appeared in the anthology,* Horse Fantastic.

Stolen Silver

Silver stamped restively as another horse on the picket-line shifted and blundered into his hindquarters. Alberich clucked to quiet him and patted the stallion's neck; the beast swung his head about to blow softly into the young Captain's hair. Alberich smiled a little, thinking wistfully that the stallion was perhaps the only creature in the entire camp that felt anything like friendship for him.

And possibly the only creature that isn't waiting for me to fail.

Amazingly gentle, for a stallion, Silver had caused no problems either in combat or here, on the picket-line. Which was just as well, for if he had, Alberich would have had him gelded or traded off for a more tractable mount, gift of the Voice of Vkandis Sunlord or no. Alberich had enough troubles without worrying about the behavior of his beast.

He wasn't sure where the graceful creature had come

from; *Shin'a'in-bred,* they'd told him. Chosen for him out of a string of animals "liberated from the enemy." Which meant war-booty, from one of the constant conflicts along the borders. Silver hadn't come from one of the bandit-nests, that was sure—the only beasts the bandits owned were as disreputable as their owners. Horses "liberated" from the bandits usually weren't worth keeping. Silver probably came from Menmellith via Rethwellan; the King was rumored to have some kind of connection with the horse-breeding, blood-thirsty Shin'a'in nomads.

Whatever; when Alberich lost his faithful old Smoke a few weeks ago he hadn't expected to get anything better than the obstinate, intractable gelding he'd taken from its bandit-owner.

But fate ruled otherwise; the Voice chose to "honor" him with a superior replacement along with his commission, the letter that accompanied the paper pointing out that Silver was the perfect mount for a Captain of light cavalry. It was also another evidence of favoritism from above, with the implication that he had earned that favoritism outside of performance in the field. Not a gift that was likely to increase his popularity with some of the men under his command, and a beast that was going to make him pretty damned conspicuous in any encounter with the enemy.

Plus one that's an unlucky color. Those witchy-Heralds of Valdemar ride white horses, and the blue-eyed beasts may be witches too, for all I know.

The horse nuzzled him again, showing as sweet a temper as any lady's mare. He scratched its nose, and it sighed with content; he wished *he* could be as contented. Things had been bad enough before getting this commission. Now—

There was an uneasy, prickly sensation between his shoulder-blades as he went back to brushing his new mount down. He glanced over his shoulder, to intercept the glare of Leftenant Herdahl; the man dropped his gaze and brushed his horse's flank vigorously, but not quickly enough to prevent Alberich from seeing the hate and anger in the hot blue eyes.

The Voice had done Alberich no favors in rewarding him with the Captaincy and this prize mount, passing over Herdahl and Klaus, both his seniors in years of service, if not in experience. Neither of them had expected that *he* would be promoted over their heads; during the week's wait for word to come from Headquarters, they had saved their rivalry for each other.

Too bad they didn't murder each other, he thought resentfully, then suppressed the rest of the thought. It was said that some of the priests of Vkandis could pluck the thoughts from a man's head. It could have been thoughts like that one that had led to Herdahl's being passed over for promotion. But it could also be that this was a test, a way of flinging the ambitious young Leftenant Alberich into deep water, to see if he would survive the experience. If he did, well and good; he was of suitable material to continue to advance, perhaps even to the rank of Commander. If he did not—well, that was too bad. If his ambition undid him, then he wasn't fit enough for the post.

That was the way of things, in the armies of Karse. You rose by watching your back, and (if the occasion arose) sticking careful knives into the backs of your less-cautious fellows, and insuring other enemies took the punishment. All the while, the priests of the Sunlord, who were the ones who were truly in charge, watched and smiled and dispensed favors and punishments with the same dispassionate aloofness displayed by the One God.

But Alberich had given a good account of himself along the border, at the corner where Karse met Menmellith and the witch-nation Valdemar, in the campaign against the bandits there. He'd *earned* his rank, he told himself once again, as Silver stamped and shifted his weight beneath the strokes of Alberich's brush. The spring sun burned down on his head, hotter than he expected without the breeze to cool him.

There was no reason to feel as if he'd cheated to get where he was. He'd led more successful sorties against the bandits in his first year in the field than the other two had achieved in their entire careers together. He'd cleared more territory than anyone of Leftenant rank ever had in that space of time—and when Captain Anberg had met with one too many arrows, the men had seemed willing that the Voice chose him over the other two candidates.

It had been the policy of late to permit the brigands to flourish, provided they confined their attentions to Valdemar and the Menmellith peasantry and left the inhabitants of Karse unmolested. A stupid policy, in Alberich's opinion; you couldn't trust bandits, that was the whole reason why they became bandits in the first place. If they could be trusted, they'd be in the army themselves, or in the Temple Guard, or even have turned mercenary. He'd seen the danger back when he was a youngster in the Academy, in his first tactics classes. He'd even said as much to one of his teachers—phrased as a question, of course—and had been ignored.

But as Alberich had predicted, there had been trouble from the brigands, once they began to multiply; problems that escalated past the point where they were useful. With complete disregard for the unwritten agreements between them and Karse, they struck everyone, and when they finally began attacking villages, the authorities deemed it time they were disposed of.

Alberich had just finished cavalry training as an officer when the troubles broke out; he'd spent most of his young life in the Karsite military schools. The ultimate authority was in the hands of the Voices, of course; the highest anyone not of the priesthood could expect to rise was to Commander. But officers were never taken from the ranks; many of the rank-and-file were conscripts, and although it was never openly stated, the

Voices did not trust their continued loyalty if they were given power.

Alberich, and many others like him, had been selected at the age of thirteen by a Voice sent every year to search out young male-children, strong of body and quick of mind, to school into officers.

Alberich had both those qualities, developing expertise in many weapons with an ease that was the envy of his classmates, picking up his lessons in academic subjects with what seemed to be equal ease.

It wasn't ease; it was the fact that Alberich studied long and hard, knowing that there was no way for the bastard son of a tavern whore to advance in Karse except in the army. There was no place for him to go, no way to get into a trade, no hope for any but the most menial of jobs. The Voices didn't care about a man's parentage once he was chosen as an officer, they cared only about his abilities and whether or not he would use them in service to his God and country. It was a lonely life, though—his mother had loved and cared for him to the best of her abilities, and he'd had friends among the other children of similar circumstances. When he came to the Academy, he had no friends, and his mother was not permitted to contact him, lest she "distract him," or "contaminate his purity of purpose." Alberich had never seen her again, but both of them had known this was the only way for him to live a better life than she had.

Alberich had no illusions about the purity of the One God's priesthood. There were as many corrupt and venal priests as there were upright, and more fanatic than there were forgiving. He had seen plenty of the venal kind in the tavern; had hidden from one or two that had come seeking pleasures strictly forbidden by the One God's edicts. He had known they were coming, looking for him, and had managed to make himself scarce long before they arrived. Just as, somehow, he had known when the Voice was coming to look for young male children for the Academy, and had made certain he was noticed and questioned—

And that he had known which customers it was safe to cadge for a penny in return for running errands—

Or that he had known that drunk was going to try to set the stable afire.

Somehow. That was Alberich's secret. He knew things were going to happen. That was a witch-power, and forbidden by the Voices of the One God. If anyone knew he had it—

But he had also known, as surely as he had known all the rest, that he had to conceal the fact that he had this power, even before he knew the law against it.

He'd succeeded fairly well over the years, though it was getting harder and harder all the time. The power struggled inside him, wanting to break free, once or twice overwhelming him with visions so intense that for a moment he was blind and deaf to everything else. It was getting harder to concoct reasons for knowing things he had no business knowing, like the hiding places of the bandits they were chasing, the bolt-holes and escape routes. But it was harder still to ignore them, especially when subsequent visions showed him innocent people suffering because he didn't act on what he knew.

He brushed Silver's neck vigorously, the dust tickling his nose and making him want to sneeze—

—and between one brush-stroke and the next, he lost his sense of balance, went light-headed, and the dazzle that heralded a vision-to-come sparkled between his eyes and Silver's neck.

Not here! he thought desperately, clinging to Silver's mane and trying to pretend there was nothing wrong. *Not now, not with Herdahl watching—*

But the witch-power would not obey him, not this time.

A flash of blue light, blinding him. *The bandits he'd thought were south had slipped behind him, into the north, joining with two more packs of the curs, becoming a group large enough to take on his troops and give them an even fight. But first, they wanted a secure base. They were going to make Alberich meet them on ground of their choosing. Fortified ground.*

That this ground was already occupied was only a minor inconvenience . . . one that would soon be dealt with.

He fought free of the vision for a moment, clinging to Silver's shoulder like a drowning man, both hands full of the beast's silky mane, while the horse curved his head back and looked at him curiously. The big brown eyes flickered blue, briefly, like a half-hidden flash of lightning, reflecting—

—another burst of sapphire. *The bandits' target was a fortified village, a small one, built on the top of a hill, above the farm-fields. Ordinarily, these people would have no difficulty in holding off a score of bandits. But there were three times that number ranged against them, and a recent edict from the High Temple decreed that no one but the Temple Guard and the Army could possess anything but the simplest of weapons. Not three weeks ago, a detachment of priests and a Voice had come through here, divesting them of everything but knives, farm-implements, and such simple bows and arrows as were suitable for waterfowl and small game. And while they were at it, a third of the able-bodied men had been conscripted for the regular Army.*

These people didn't have a chance.

The bandits drew closer, under the cover of a brush-filled ravine.

Alberich found himself on Silver's back, without knowing how he'd gotten there, without remembering that he'd flung saddle and bridle back on the beast—

No, not bridle; Silver still wore the hackamore he'd had on the picket-line. Alberich's bugle was in his hand; presumably he'd blown the muster, for his men were running towards him, buckling on swords and slinging quivers over their shoulders.

Blinding flash of cerulean—

The bandits attacked the village walls, overpowering the poor man who was trying to bar the gate against them, and swarming inside.

It hadn't happened yet, he knew that with the surety with which he knew his own name. It wasn't even going to happen in the next few moments. But it was going to happen *soon*—

They poured inside, cutting down anyone who resisted them, then throwing off what little restraint they had shown and launching into an orgy of looting and rapine. Alberich gagged as one of them grabbed a pregnant woman and with a single slash of his sword, murdered the child that ran to try and protect her, followed through to her—

The vision released him, and he found himself surrounded by dust and thunder, still on Silver's back—

—but leaning over the stallion's neck as now he led his troops up the road to the village of Sunsdale at full gallop. Hooves pounded the packed-earth of the road, making it impossible to hear or speak; the vibration thrummed into his bones as he shifted his weight with the stallion's turns. Silver ran easily, with no sign of distress, though all around him and behind him the other horses streamed saliva from the corners of their mouths, and their flanks ran with sweat and foam, as they strained to keep up.

The lack of a bit didn't seem to make any difference to the stallion; he answered to neck-rein and knee so readily he might have been anticipating Alberich's thoughts.

Alberich dismissed the uneasy feelings *that* prompted. Better not to think that he might have a second witch-power along with the first. He'd never shown any ability to control beasts by thought before. There was no reason to think he could now. The stallion was just superbly trained, that was all. And he had more important things to worry about.

They topped the crest of a hill; Sunsdale lay atop the next one, just as he had seen in his vision, and the brush-filled ravine beyond it.

There was no sign of trouble.

This time it's been a wild hare, he thought, disgusted at himself for allowing blind panic to overcome him. And for what? A daytime-nightmare? *Next time I'll probably see trolls under my bed,* he thought, just about to pull Silver up and bring the rest of his men to a halt—

When a flash of sunlight on metal betrayed the bandits' location.

He grabbed for the bugle dangling from his left wrist instead, and pulled his blade with the right; sounded the charge, and led the entire troop down the hill, an unstoppable torrent of hooves and steel, hitting the brigands' hidden line like an avalanche.

Sword in hand, Alberich limped wearily to another body sprawled amid the rocks and trampled weeds of the ravine, and thrust it through to make death certain. His sword felt heavy and unwieldy, his stomach churned, and there was a sour taste in his mouth. He didn't think he was going to lose control of himself, but he was glad he was almost at the end of the battle-line. He hated this part of the fighting—which wasn't fighting at all; it was nothing more than butchery.

But it was necessary. This scum was just as likely to be feigning death as to actually be dead. Other officers hadn't been that thorough—and hadn't lived long enough to regret it.

Silver was being fed and watered along with the rest of the mounts by the youngsters of Sunsdale; the finest fodder and clearest spring water, and a round dozen young boys to brush and curry them clean. And the men were being fed and made much of by the older villagers. Gratitude had made them forgetful of the loss of their weapons and many of their men. Suddenly the army that had conscripted their relatives was no longer their adversary. Or else, since the troops had arrived out of nowhere like Vengeance of the Sunlord Himself, they assumed the One God had a hand in it, and it would be prudent to resign themselves to the sacrifice. And meanwhile, the instrument of their rescue probably ought to be well treated. . . .

Except for the Captain, who was doing a dirty job he refused to assign to anyone else.

Alberich made certain of two more corpses and looked dully around for more.

There weren't any, and he saw to his surprise that the sun was hardly more than a finger-breadth from the horizon. Shadows already filled the ravine, the evening breeze had picked up, and it was getting chilly. Last year's weeds tossed in the freshening wind as he gazed around at the long shadows cast by the scrubby trees. More time had passed than he thought—and if he didn't hurry, he was going to be late for SunDescending.

He scrambled over the slippery rocks of the ravine, cursing under his breath as his boots (meant for riding) skidded on the smooth, rounded boulders. The last thing he needed now was to be late for a Holy Service, especially this one. The priest here was bound to ask him for a Thanks-Prayer for the victory. If he was late, it would look as if he was arrogantly attributing the victory to his own abilities, and not the Hand of the Sunlord. And with an accusation like that hanging over his head, he'd be in danger not only of being deprived of his current rank, but of being demoted into the ranks, with no chance of promotion, a step up from stable-hand, but not a big one.

He fought his way over the edge, and half-ran, half-limped to the village gates, reaching them just as the sun touched the horizon. He put a little more speed into his weary, aching legs, and got to the edge of the crowd in the village square a scant breath before the priest began the First Chant.

He bowed his head with the others, and not until he raised his head at the end of it did he realize that the robes the priest wore were not black, but red. This was no mere village priest—this was a Voice!

He suppressed his start of surprise, and the shiver of fear that followed it. He didn't know what this village meant, or what had happened to require posting a Voice here, but there was little wonder now why they had submitted so tamely to the taking of their men and the confiscation of their weapons. No one sane would contradict a Voice.

The Voice held up his hand, and got instant silence; a silence so profound that the sounds of the horses on the picket-line came clearly over the walls. Horses stamped and whickered a little, and in the distance, a few lonely birds called, and the breeze rustled through the new leaves of the trees in the ravine. Alberich longed suddenly to be able to mount Silver and ride away from here, far away from the machinations of Voices and the omnipresent smell of death and blood. He yearned for somewhere clean, somewhere that he wouldn't have to guard his back from those he should be able to trust. . . .

"Today this village was saved from certain destruction," the Voice said, his words ringing out, but without passion, without any inflection whatsoever. "And for that, we offer Thanks-giving to Vkandis Sunlord, Most High, One God, to whom all things are known. The instrument of that salvation was Captain Alberich, who mustered his men in time to catch our attackers in the very act. It seems a miracle—"

During the speech, some of the men had been moving closer to Alberich, grouping themselves around him to bask in the admiration of the villagers.

Or so he thought. Until the Voice's tone hardened, and his next words proved their real intent.

"It *seems* a miracle—but it was not!" he thundered. "You were saved by the power of the One God, whose wrath destroyed the bandits, but Alberich betrayed the Sunlord by using the unholy powers of witchcraft! *Seize him*!"

The men grabbed him as he turned to run, throwing him to the ground and pinning him with superior numbers. He fought them anyway, struggling furiously, until someone brought the hilt of a knife down on the back of his head.

He didn't black out altogether, but he couldn't move or see; his eyes wouldn't focus, and a gray film obscured everything. He felt himself being dragged off by the arms—heaved into darkness—felt himself hitting a hard surface—heard the slamming of a door.

Then heard only confused murmurs as he lay in shadows, trying to regain his senses and his strength. Gradually his sight cleared, and he made out walls on all sides of him, close enough to touch. He raised his aching head cautiously, and made out the dim outline of an ill-fitting door. The floor, clearly, was dirt. And smelled unmistakably of birds.

They must have thrown him into some kind of shed, something that had once held chickens or pigeons. He was under no illusions that this meant his prison would be easy to escape; out here, the chicken-sheds were frequently built better than the houses, for chickens were more valuable than children.

Still, once darkness descended, it might be possible to get away. If he could overpower whatever guards that the Voice had placed around him. If he could find a way out of the shed. . . .

If he could get past the Voice himself. There were stories that the Voices had other powers than plucking the thoughts from a man's head—stories that they commanded the services of demons tamed by the Sunlord—

While he lay there gathering his wits, another smell invaded the shed, overpowering even the stench of old bird-droppings. A sharp, thick smell . . . it took a moment for him to recognize it.

But when he did, he clawed his way up the wall he'd been thrown against, to stand wide-eyed in the darkness, nails digging into the wood behind him, heart pounding with stark terror.

Oil. They had poured oil around the foundations, splashed it up against the sides of the shed. And now he heard them out there, bringing piles of dry brush and wood to stack against the walls. The punishment for witchery was burning, and they were taking no chances; they were going to burn him now.

The noises outside stopped; the murmur of voices faded as his captors moved away—

Then the Voice called out, once—a set of three sharp, angry words—

And every crack and crevice in the building was outlined in yellow and red, as the entire shed was engulfed in flames from outside.

Alberich cried out, and staggered away from the wall he'd been leaning against. The shed was bigger than he'd thought—but not big enough to protect him. The oil they'd spread so profligately made the flames burn hotter, and the wood of the shed was old, weathered, probably dry. Within moments, the very air scorched him; he hid his mouth in a fold of his shirt, but his lungs burned with every breath. His eyes streamed tears of pain as he turned, staggering, searching for an escape that didn't exist.

One of the walls burned through, showing the flames leaping from the wood and brush piled beyond it. He couldn't hear anything but the roar of the flames. At any moment now, the roof would cave in, burying him in burning debris—

:Look out!:

How he heard the warning—or how he knew to stagger back as far as he could without being incinerated on the spot—he did not know. But a heartbeat after that warning shout in his mind, a huge, silver-white shadow lofted through the hole in the burning wall, and landed beside him. It was still wearing his saddle and hackamore—

And it turned huge, impossibly *blue* eyes on him as he stood there gaping at it. It? No. *Him.*

:On!: the stallion snapped at him. *:The roof's about to go!:*

Whatever fear he had of the beast, he was more afraid of a death by burning. With hands that screamed with pain, he grabbed the saddle-bow and threw himself onto it. He hadn't even found the stirrups when the stallion turned on his hind feet.

There was a crack of collapsing wood, as fire engulfed them. Burning thatch fell before and behind them, sparks showering as the air was sucked into the blaze, hotter. . . .

But, amazingly, no fire licked at his flesh once he had mounted. . . .

Alberich sobbed with relief as the cool air surged into his lungs—the stallion's hooves hit the ground beyond the flames, and he gasped with pain as he was flung forward against the saddle-bow.

Then the real pain began, the torture of half-scorched skin, and the broken bones of his capture, jarred into agony by the stallion's headlong gallop into the night. The beast thundered towards the villagers, and they screamed and parted before it; soldiers and Voice alike were caught unawares, and not one of them raised a weapon in time to stop the flight.

:Stay on,: the stallion said grimly, into his mind, as the darkness was shattered by the red lightning of his own pain. *:Stay on, stay with me; we have a long way to go before we're safe. Stay with me. . . .:*

Safe where? he wanted to ask—but there was no way to ask around the pain. All he could do was to hang on, and hope he could do what the horse wanted.

An eternity later—as dawn rose as red as the flames that had nearly killed him—the stallion had slowed to a walk. Dawn was on their right, which meant that the stallion was heading north, across the border, into the witch-kingdom of Valdemar. Which only made sense, since what he'd thought was a horse had turned out to be one of the blue-eyed witch-beasts. . . .

None of it mattered. Now that the stallion had slowed to a walk, his pain had dulled, but he was exhausted and out of any energy to think or even feel with. What could the witches do to him, after all? Kill him? At the moment, that would be a kindness. . . .

The stallion stopped, and he looked up, trying to see through the film that had come over his vision. At first he thought he was seeing double; two white witch-beasts and two white-clad riders blocked the road. But then he realized that there *were* two of them, hastily dismounting, reaching for him.

He let himself slide down into their hands, hearing nothing he could understand, only a babble of strange syllables.

Then, in his mind—

:Can you hear me?:

:I—what?: he replied, without thinking.

:Taver says his name's Alberich,: came a second voice in his head. *:Alberich? Can you stay with us a little longer? We need to get you to a Healer. You're going into shock; fight it for us. Your Companion will help you, if you let him.:*

His what? He shook his head; not in negation, in puzzlement. Where was he? All his life he'd heard that the witches of Valdemar were evil—but—

:And all our lives we've heard that nothing comes out of Karse but brigands and bad weather,: said the first voice, full of concern, but with an edge of humor to it. He shook his head again and peered up at the person supporting him on his right. A woman, with many laugh-lines etched around her generous mouth. She seemed to fit that first voice in his head, somehow. . . .

:So, which are you, Alberich?: she asked, as he fought to stay awake, feeling the presence of the stallion *(his*

Companion?) like a steady shoulder to lean against, deep inside his soul. *:Brigand, or bad weather?:*

:Neither . . . I hope . . .: he replied, absently, as he clung to consciousness as she'd asked.

:Good. I'd hate to think of a Companion Choosing a brigand to be a Herald,: she said, with her mouth twitching a little, as if she was holding back a grin, *:And a thunderstorm in human guise would make uncomfortable company.:*

:Choosing?: he asked. *:What—what do you mean?:*

:I mean that you're a Herald, my friend,: she told him. *:Somehow your Companion managed to insinuate himself across the Border to get you, too. That's how Heralds of Valdemar are made; Companions Choose them—:* She looked up and away from him, and relief and satisfaction spread over her face at whatever it was she saw. *:—and the rest of it can wait. Aren's brought the Healer. Go ahead and let go, we'll take over from here.:*

He took her at her word, and let the darkness take him. But her last words followed him down into the shadows, and instead of bringing the fear they *should* have given him, they brought him comfort, and a peace he never expected.

:It's a hell of a greeting, Herald Alberich, and a hell of a way to get here—but welcome to Valdemar, brother. Welcome . . .:

This odd little story was first published in Marion Zimmer Bradley's Fantasy Magazine. *It's the one I always use as an example when people ask me where I get my ideas. This one literally came as I was driving to work, saw a piece of cardboard skitter across the road in front of me as if it was alive, and thought, "Now what if it* was *alive?"*

Roadkill

A gust of wind hit the side of George Randal's van and nearly tore the steering wheel out of his hands. He cursed as the vehicle lurched sideways, and wrestled it back into his own lane.

It was a good thing there weren't too many people on the road. It was just a damned good thing that Mingo Road *was* a four-lane at this point, or he'd have been in the ditch. A mile away, it wasn't, but all the shift traffic from the airline maintenance base, the Rockwell plant and the McDonald-Douglas plant where he worked would have put an intolerable strain on a two-lane road.

The stoplight at Mingo and 163rd turned yellow, and rather than push his luck, he obeyed it, instead of doing an "Okie caution" ("Step on the gas, Fred, she's fixin' to turn red"). This was going to be another typical late spring Oklahoma day. Wind gusting up to 60 per, and rain off and on. Used to be, when he was a kid, it'd be dry as old bones by this late in the season, but not anymore. All the flood-control projects and water-management dams had changed the micro-climate, and it was unlikely this part of Oklahoma would ever see another Dust-Bowl.

Although with winds like this, he could certainly extrapolate what it had been like, back then during the thirties.

The habit of working a mental simulation was so ingrained it was close to a reflex; once the thought occurred, his mind took over, calculating wind-speed, type of dust, carrying capacity of the air. He was so intent on the internal calculations that he hardly noticed when the light turned green, and only the impatient honk of the car behind him jolted him out of his reverie. He pulled the van out into the intersection, and the red sports-car behind him roared around him, driver giving him the finger as he passed.

"You son of a—" he noted with satisfaction the MacDac parking permit in the corner of the rear window: the vanity plate was an easy one to remember, "HOTONE." He'd tell a little fib to the guard at the guard shack, and have the jerk cited for reckless driving in the parking-lot. That would go on his work-record, and serve him right, too.

If it hadn't been for the combination of the wind gust and the fool in the red IROC, he would never have noticed the strange behavior of that piece of cardboard in the median strip.

But because of the gust, he *knew* which direction the wind was coming from. When the IROC screamed right over the center-line, heading straight toward a piece of flattened box, and the box skittered just barely out of the way as if the wind had picked it up and moved it in time, something went off in his brain.

As he came up even to where the box had been, he

saw what the thing had been covering; roadkill, a dead 'possum. At that exact moment he knew what had been wrong with the scene a second before, when the box had moved. Because it had moved *against* the wind.

He cast a startled glance in his rear-view mirror just in time to see the box skitter back, with the wind this time, and stop just covering the dead animal.

That brought all the little calculations going on in his head to a screeching halt. George was an orderly man, a career engineer, whose one fervent belief was that everything could be explained in terms of physics if you had enough data.

Except that this little incident was completely outside his ordered universe.

He was so preoccupied with trying to think of an explanation for the box's anomalous behavior that he didn't remember to report the kid in the sports-car at the guard-shack. He couldn't even get his mind on the new canard specs he'd been so excited about yesterday. Instead he sat at his desk, playing with the CAD/CAM computer, trying to find *some* way for that box to have done what it did.

And coming up dry. It should not, *could* not, have moved that way, and the odds against it moving back to exactly the same place where it had left were unbelievable.

He finally grabbed his gym-bag, left his cubicle, and headed for the tiny locker-room MacDac kept for those employees who had taken up running or jogging on their lunch-breaks. Obviously he was not going to get anything done until he checked the site out, and he might just as well combine that with his lunch-time exercise. Today he'd run out on Mingo instead of around the base.

A couple of Air National Guard A-4s cruised by overhead, momentarily distracting him. He'd forgotten exactly where the roadkill had been, and before he was quite ready for it, he was practically on top of it. Suddenly he was no longer quite sure that he wanted to do this. It seemed silly, a fantasy born of too many late-night movies. But as long as he was out here . . .

The box was nowhere in sight. Feeling slightly foolish, he crossed to the median and took a good look at the body.

It was half-eaten, which wasn't particularly amazing. Any roadkill that was relatively fresh was bound to get chewed on.

Except that the last time he'd seen roadkill on the median, it had stayed there until it bloated, untouched. Animals didn't like the traffic; they wouldn't go after carrion in the middle of the road if they could help it.

And there was something wrong with the way the bite-marks looked too. Old Boy Scout memories came back, tracking and identifying animals by signs. . . .

The flesh hadn't been bitten off so much as carved off—as if the carcass had been chewed by something with enormous buck teeth, like some kind of carnivorous horse, or beaver. Nothing in his limited experience made marks like that.

As a cold trickle ran down his spine, a rustle in the weeds at the side of the road made him jump. He looked up.

The box was there, in the weeds. He hadn't seen it, half-hidden there, until it had moved. It almost seemed as if the thing was watching him; the way it had a corner poked out of the weeds like a head. . . .

His reaction was stupid and irrational, and he didn't care. He bolted, ran all the way back to the guard-shack with a chill in his stomach that all his running couldn't warm.

He didn't stop until he reached the guard-shack and the safety of the fenced-in MacDac compound, the sanity and rational universe of steel and measurement where nothing existed that could not be simulated on a computer screen.

He slowed to a gentle jog as he passed the shack; he'd have liked to stop, because his heart was pounding so hard he couldn't hear anything, but if he did, the guards would ask him what was wrong. . . .

He waited until he was just out of sight, and then dropped to a walk. He remembered from somewhere, maybe one of his jogging tapes, that it was a bad idea just to stop, that his muscles would stiffen. Actually he had the feeling if he went to his knees on the verge like he wanted to, he'd never get up again.

He reached the sanctuary of his air-conditioned office and slumped down into his chair, still panting. He waited with his eyes closed for his heart to stop pounding, while the sweat cooled and dried in the gust of metallic-flavored air from the vent over his chair. He tried to summon up laughter at himself, a grown man, for finding a flattened piece of cardboard so frightening, but the laughter wouldn't come.

Instead other memories of those days as a Boy Scout returned, of the year he'd spent at camp where he'd learned those meager tracking skills. One of the counselors had a grandfather who was—or so the boy claimed—a full Cherokee medicine man. He'd persuaded the old man to make a visit to the camp. George had found himself impressed against his will, as had the rest of the Scouts; the old man still wore his hair in two long, iron-gray braids and a bone necklace under his plain work-shirt. He had a dignity and self-possession that kept all of the rowdy adolescents in awe of him and silent when he spoke.

He'd condescended to tell stories at their campfire several times. Most of them were tales of what his life had been like as a boy on the reservation at the turn of the century—but once or twice he'd told them bits of odd Indian lore, not all of it Cherokee.

Like the shape-changers. George didn't remember what he'd called them, but he did recall what had started the story. One of the boys had seen *I Was A Teen-age Werewolf* before he'd come to camp, and he was regaling all of them with a vivid description of

Michael Landon's transformation into the monster. The old man had listened, and scoffed. That was no kind of shape-changer, he'd told them scornfully. Then he had launched into a new story.

George no longer recalled the words, but he remembered the gist of it. How the shape-changers would prey upon the Indians in a peculiar fashion; stealing what they wanted by deception. If one wanted meat, for instance, he would transform himself into a hunter's game-bag and wait for the Indian to stuff the "bag" full, then shift back and carry the game off while the hunter's back was turned. If one wanted a new buffalo-robe, he would transform himself into a stretching-frame—or if very ambitious, into a tipi, and make off with all of the inhabitant's worldly goods.

"Why didn't they just turn into horses and carry everything off?" he'd wanted to know. The old man had shaken his head. "Because they cannot take a living form," he'd said, "only a dead one. And you do not want to catch them, either. Better for you to pretend it never happened."

But he wouldn't say what would happen if someone *did* catch the thief at work. He only looked, for a brief instant, very frightened, as if he had not intended to say that much.

George felt suddenly sick. What if these things, these shape-changers, *weren't* just legend. What could they be living on now? They wouldn't be able to sneak into someone's house and counterfeit a refrigerator.

But there was all that roadkill, enough dead animals along Mingo alone each year to keep someone going, if that someone wasn't too fastidious.

And what would be easier to mimic than an old, flattened box?

He wanted to laugh at himself, but the laughter wouldn't come. This was such a stupid fantasy, built out of nothing but a boy's imagination and a box that didn't behave the way it ought to.

Instead, he only felt sicker, and more frightened. Now he could recall the one thing the old man had said about the creatures and their fear of discovery.

"*They do not permit it*," he'd said, as his eyes widened in that strange flicker of fear. "*They do not permit it.*"

Finally he just couldn't sit there anymore. He picked up the phone and mumbled something to his manager about feeling sick, grabbed his car keys and headed for the parking lot. Several of the others on the engineering staff looked at him oddly as he passed their desks; the secretary even stopped him and asked him if he felt all right. He mumbled something at her that didn't change her look of concern, and assured her that he was going straight home.

He told himself that he was going to do just that. He even had his turn-signal on for a right-hand turn, fully intending to take the on-ramp at Pine and take the freeway home.

But instead he found himself turning left, where the roadkill was still lying.

He saw it as he came up over the rise; and the box was lying on top of it once again.

Suddenly desperate to prove to himself that this entire fantasy he'd created around a dead 'possum and a piece of cardboard was nothing more than that, he jerked the wheel over and straddled the median, gunning the engine and heading straight for the dingy brown splotch of the flattened box.

There was no wind now; if the thing moved, it would have to do so under its own power.

He floored the accelerator, determined that the thing wasn't going to escape his tires.

It didn't move; he felt a sudden surge of joy—

Then the thing struck.

It leapt up at the last possible second, landing with a *splat,* splayed across his windshield. He had a brief, horrifying impression of some kind of face, flattened and distorted, red eyes and huge, beaver-like teeth as long as his hand—

Then it was gone, and the car was out of control, tires screaming, wheel wrenching under his hands.

He pumped his brakes—once, twice—then the pedal went flat to the floor.

And as the car heeled over on two wheels, beginning a high-speed roll that could have only one ending, that analytical part of his mind that was not screaming in terror was calculating just how easy it would be for a pair of huge, chisel-like teeth to shear through a brake-line.

Larry and I wrote this for the Keith Laumer "Bolo" anthology, but it stands pretty well alone. All you have to know is that Bolos are fairly unstoppable, self-aware, intelligent tanks.

Operation Desert Fox

Mercedes Lackey & Larry Dixon

Siegfried O'Harrigan's name had sometimes caused confusion, although the Service tended to be color-blind. He was black, slight of build and descended from a woman whose African tribal name had been long since lost to her descendants.

He wore both Caucasian names—Siegfried and O'Harrigan—as badges of high honor, however, as had all of that lady's descendants. Many times, although it might have been politically correct to do so, Siegfried's ancestors had resisted changing their name to something more ethnic. Their name was a gift—and not a badge of servitude to anyone. One did not return a gift, especially not one steeped in the love of ancestors. . . .

Siegfried had heard the story many times as a child,

and had never tired of it. The tale was the modern equivalent of a fairy-tale, it had been so very unlikely. *O'Harrigan* had been the name of an Irish-born engineer, fresh off the boat himself, who had seen Siegfried's many-times-great grandmother and her infant son being herded down the gangplank and straight to the Richmond Virginia slave market. She had been, perhaps, thirteen years old when the Arab slave-traders had stolen her. That she had survived the journey at all was a miracle. And she was the very first thing that O'Harrigan set eyes on as he stepped onto the dock in this new land of freedom.

The irony had not been lost on him. Sick and frightened, the woman had locked eyes with Sean O'Harrigan for a single instant, but that instant had been enough.

They had shared neither language nor race, but perhaps Sean had seen in her eyes the antithesis of everything he had come to America to find. *His* people had suffered virtual slavery at the hands of the English landlords; he knew what slavery felt like. He was outraged, and felt that he had to do *something.* He could not save all the slaves offloaded this day—but he could help these two.

He had followed the traders to the market and bought the woman and her child "off the coffle," paying for them before they could be put up on the auction-block, before they could even be warehoused. He fed them, cared for them until they were strong, and then put them on *another* boat, this time as passengers, before the woman could learn much more than his name. The rest the O'Harrigans learned later, from Sean's letters, long after.

The boat was headed back to Africa, to the newly-founded nation of Liberia, a place of hope for freed slaves, whose very name meant "land of liberty." Life there would not be easy for them, but it would not be a life spent in chains, suffering at the whims of men who called themselves "Master."

Thereafter, the woman and her children wore the name of O'Harrigan proudly, in memory of the stranger's kindness—as many other citizens of the newly-formed nation would wear the names of those who had freed them.

No, the O'Harrigans would not change their name for any turn of politics. Respect earned was infinitely more powerful than any messages beaten into someone by whips or media.

And as for the name "Siegfried"—that was also in memory of a stranger's kindness; this time a member of Rommel's Afrika Korps. Another random act of kindness, this time from a first lieutenant who had seen to it that a captured black man with the name O'Harrigan was correctly identified as Liberian and not as American. He had then seen to it that John O'Harrigan was treated well and released.

John had named his first-born son for that German, because the young lieutenant had no children of his own. The tradition and the story that went with it had continued down the generations, joining that of Sean O'Harrigan. Siegfried's people remembered their debts of honor.

Siegfried O'Harrigan's name was at violent odds with his appearance. He was neither blond and tall, nor short and red-haired—and in fact, he was not Caucasian at all.

In this much, he matched the colonists of Bachman's World, most of whom were of East Indian and Pakistani descent. In every other way, he was totally unlike them.

He had been in the military for most of his life, and had planned to stay in. He was happy in uniform, and for many of the colonists here, that was a totally foreign concept.

Both of those stories of his ancestors were in his mind as he stood, travel-weary and yet excited, before a massive piece of the machinery of war, a glorious hulk of purpose-built design. It was larger than a good many of the buildings of this far-off colony at the edges of human space.

Bachman's World. A poor colony known only for its single export of a medicinal desert plant, it was not a place likely to attract a tourist trade. Those who came here left because life was even harder in the slums of Calcutta, or the perpetually typhoon-swept mud-flats of Bangladesh. They were farmers, who grew vast acreages of the "saje" for export, and irrigated just enough land to feed themselves. A hot, dry wind blew sand into the tight curls of his hair and stirred the short sleeves of his desert-khaki uniform. It occurred to him that he could not have chosen a more appropriate setting for what was likely to prove a life-long exile, considering his hobby—his obsession. And yet, it was an exile he had chosen willingly, even eagerly.

This behemoth, this juggernaut, this mountain of gleaming metal, was a Bolo. Now, it was *his* Bolo, his partner. A partner whose workings he knew intimately . . . and whose thought processes suited his so uniquely that there might not be a similar match in all the Galaxy.

RML-1138. Outmoded now, and facing retirement—which, for a Bolo, meant *deactivation.*

Extinction, in other words. Bolos were more than "super-tanks," more than war machines, for they were inhabited by some of the finest AIs in human space. When a Bolo was "retired," so was the AI. Permanently.

There were those, even now, who were lobbying for AI rights, who equated deactivation with murder. They were opposed by any number of special-interest groups, beginning with religionists, who objected to the notion than anything housed in a "body" of electronic circuitry could be considered "human" enough to "murder." No matter which side won, nothing would occur soon enough to save this particular Bolo.

Siegfried had also faced retirement, for the same reason. *Outmoded.* He had specialized in weapons'-systems repair, the specific, delicate tracking and targeting systems.

Which were now outmoded, out-of-date; *he* had been

deemed too old to retrain. He had been facing an uncertain future, relegated to some dead-end job with no chance for promotion, or more likely, given an "early-out" option. He had applied for a transfer, listing, in desperation, everything that might give him an edge somewhere. On the advice of his superiors, he had included his background and his hobby of military strategy of the pre-Atomic period.

And to his utter amazement, it had been that background and hobby that had attracted the attention of someone in the Reserves, someone who had been looking to make a most particular match. . . .

The wind died; no one with any sense moved outside during the heat of midday. The port might have been deserted, but for a lone motor running somewhere in the distance.

The Bolo was utterly silent, but Siegfried knew that he—*he,* not *it*—was watching him, examining him with a myriad of sophisticated instruments. By now, he probably even knew how many fillings were in his mouth, how many grommets in his desert-boots. He had already passed judgment on Siegfried's service record, but there was this final confrontation to face, before the partnership could be declared a reality.

He cleared his throat, delicately. Now came the moment of truth. It was time to find out if what one administrator in the Reserves—and one human facing early-out and a future of desperate scrabbling for employment—thought was the perfect match really *would* prove to be the salvation of that human and this huge marvel of machinery and circuits.

Siegfried's hobby was the key—desert warfare, tactics, and most of all, the history and thought of one particular desert commander.

Erwin Rommel. The "Desert Fox," the man his greatest rival had termed "the last chivalrous knight." Siegfried knew everything there was to know about the great tank-commander. He had fought and refought every campaign Rommel had ever commanded, and his admiration for the man whose life had briefly touched on that of his own ancestor's had never faded, nor had his fascination with the man and his genius.

And there was at least one other being in the universe whose fascination with the Desert Fox matched Siegfried's. This being; the intelligence resident in this particular Bolo, the Bolo that called *himself* "Rommel." Most, if not all, Bolos acquired a name or nickname based on their designations—LNE became "Lenny," or "KKR" became "Kicker." Whether this Bolo had been fascinated by the Desert Fox because of his designation, or had noticed the resemblance of "RML" to "Rommel" because of his fascination, it didn't much matter. Rommel was as much an expert on his namesake as Siegfried was.

Like Siegfried, RML-1138 was scheduled for "early-out," but like Siegfried, the Reserves offered him a reprieve. The Reserves didn't usually take or need Bolos; for one thing, they were dreadfully expensive. A Reserve unit could requisition a great deal of equipment for the "cost" of one Bolo. For another, the close partnership required between Bolo and operator precluded use of Bolos in situations where the "partnerships" would not last past the exercise of the moment. Nor were Bolo partners often "retired" to the Reserves.

And not too many Bolos were available to the Reserves. Retirement for both Bolo and operator was usually permanent, and as often as not, was in the front lines.

But luck (good or ill, it remained to be seen) was with Rommel; he had lost his partner to a deadly virus, he had not seen much in the way of combat, and he was in near-new condition.

And Bachman's World wanted a Reserve battalion. They could not field their own—every able-bodied human here was a farmer or engaged in the export trade. A substantial percentage of the population was of some form of pacifistic religion that precluded bearing arms—Janist, Buddhist, some forms of Hindu.

Bachman's World was *entitled* to a Reserve force; it was their right under the law to have an on-planet defense force supplied by the regular military. Just because Bachman's World was back-of-beyond of nowhere, and even the most conservative of military planners thought their insistence on having such a force in place to be paranoid in the extreme, that did not negate their right to have it. Their charter was clear. The law was on their side.

Sending them a Reserve battalion would be expensive in the extreme, in terms of maintaining that battalion. The soldiers would be full-timers, on full pay. There was no base—it would have to be built. There was no equipment—that would all have to be imported.

That was when one solitary bean-counting accountant at High Command came up with the answer that would satisfy the letter of the law, yet save the military considerable expense.

The law had been written stipulating, not numbers of personnel and equipment, but a monetary amount. That unknown accountant had determined that the amount so stipulated, meant to be the equivalent value of an infantry battalion, exactly equaled the worth of one Bolo and its operator.

The records-search was on.

Enter one Reserve officer, searching for a Bolo in good condition, about to be "retired," with no current operator-partner—

—and someone to match him, familiar with at least the rudiments of mech-warfare, the insides of a Bolo, and willing to be exiled for the rest of his life.

Finding RML-1138, called "Rommel," and Siegfried O'Harrigan, hobbyist military historian.

The government of Bachman's World was less than pleased with the response to their demand, but there was little they could do besides protest. Rommel was shipped to Bachman's World first; Siegfried was given a crash-course in Bolo operation. He followed on the first regularly-scheduled freighter as soon as his training was over. If, for whatever reason, the pairing did not work, he would leave on the same freighter that brought him.

Now, came the moment of truth.

"Guten tag, Herr Rommel," he said, in careful German, the antique German he had learned in order to be able to read first-hand chronicles in the original language. *"Ich bin Siegfried O'Harrigan."*

A moment of silence—and then, surprisingly, a sound much like a dry chuckle.

"*Wie geht's, Herr O'Harrigan.* I've been expecting you. Aren't you a little dark to be a Storm Trooper?"

The voice was deep, pleasant, and came from a point somewhere above Siegfried's head. And Siegfried knew the question was a trap, of sorts. Or a test, to see just how much he really *did* know, as opposed to what he claimed to know. A good many pre-Atomic historians could be caught by that question themselves.

"Hardly a Storm Trooper," he countered. "Field-Marshall Erwin Rommel would not have had one of *those* under his command. And no Nazis, either. Don't think to trap *me* that easily."

The Bolo uttered that same dry chuckle. "Good for you, Siegfried O'Harrigan. *Willkommen.*"

The hatch opened, silently; a ladder descended just as silently, inviting Siegfried to come out of the hot, desert sun and into Rommel's controlled interior. Rommel had replied to Siegfried's response, but had done so with nothing unnecessary in the way of words, in the tradition of his namesake.

Siegfried had passed the test.

Once again, Siegfried stood in the blindingly hot sun, this time at strict attention, watching the departing back of the mayor of Port City. The interview had not been pleasant, although both parties had been strictly polite; the mayor's back was stiff with anger. He had not cared for what Siegfried had told him.

"They do not much care for us, do they, Siegfried?" Rommel sounded resigned, and Siegfried sighed. It was impossible to hide anything from the Bolo; Rommel had already proven himself to be an adept reader of human body-language, and of course, anything that was broadcast over the airwaves, scrambled or not, Rommel could access and read. Rommel was right; he and his partner were not the most popular of residents at the moment.

What amazed Siegfried, and continued to amaze him, was how *human* the Bolo was. He was used to AIs of course, but Rommel was something special. Rommel cared about what people did and thought; most AIs really didn't take a great interest in the doings and opinions of mere humans.

"No, Rommel, they don't," he replied. "You really can't blame them; they thought they were going to get a battalion of conventional troops, not one very expensive piece of equipment and one single human."

"But we are easily the equivalent of a battalion of conventional troops," Rommel objected, logically. He lowered his ladder, and now that the mayor was well out of sight, Siegfried felt free to climb back into the cool interior of the Bolo.

He waited until he was settled in his customary seat, now worn to the contours of his own figure after a year, before he answered the AI he now consciously considered to be his best friend as well as his assigned partner. Inside the cabin of the Bolo, everything was clean, if a little worn—cool—the light dimmed the way Siegfried liked it. This was, in fact, the most comfortable quarters Siegfried had ever enjoyed. Granted, things were a bit cramped, but he had everything he needed in here, from shower and cooking facilities to multiple kinds of entertainment. And the Bolo did not need to worry about "wasting" energy; his power-plant was geared to supply full-combat needs in any and all climates; what Siegfried needed to keep cool and comfortable was miniscule. Outside, the ever-present desert sand blew everywhere, the heat was enough to drive even the most patient person mad, and the sun bleached everything to a bone-white. Inside was a compact world of Siegfried's own.

Bachman's World had little to recommend it. That was the problem.

"It's a complicated issue, Rommel," he said. "If a battalion of conventional troops had been sent here, there would have been more than the initial expenditure—there would have been an ongoing expenditure to support them."

"Yes—that support money would come into the community. I understand their distress." Rommel would understand, of course; Field Marshal Erwin Rommel had understood the problems of supply only too well, and his namesake could hardly do less. "Could it be they demanded the troops in the first place in order to gain that money?"

Siegfried grimaced, and toyed with the controls on the panel in front of him. "That's what High Command thinks, actually. There never was any real reason to think Bachman's World was under any sort of threat, and after a year, there's even less reason than there was when they made the request. They expected something to bring in money from outside; you and I are hardly bringing in big revenue for them."

Indeed, they weren't bringing in any income at all. Rommel, of course, required no support, since he was not expending anything. His power-plant would supply all his needs for the next hundred years before it needed refueling. If there had been a battalion of men here, it would have been less expensive for High Command to set up a standard mess hall, buying their supplies from the local farmers, rather than shipping in food and other supplies. Further, the men would have been spending their pay locally. In fact, local suppliers would have been found for nearly everything except weaponry.

But with only one man here, it was far less expensive for High Command to arrange for his supplies to come in at regular intervals on scheduled freight-runs. The Bolo ate nothing. They didn't even use "local" water; the Bolo recycled nearly every drop, and distilled the rest from occasional rainfall and dew. Siegfried was not the usual soldier-on-leave; when he spent his pay, it was generally off-planet, ordering things to be shipped in, and not patronizing local merchants. He bought books, not beer; he didn't gamble, his interest in food was minimal and satisfied by the R.E.M.s (Ready-to-Eat-Meals) that were standard field issue and shipped to him by the crateful. And he was far more interested in that four-letter word for "intercourse" that began with a "t" than in intercourse of any other kind. He was an ascetic scholar; such men were not the sort who brought any amount of money into a community. He and his partner, parked as they were at the edge of the spaceport, were a continual reminder of how Bachman's World had been "cheated."

And for that reason, the mayor of Port City had suggested—stiffly, but politely—that his and Rommel's continuing presence so near the main settlement was somewhat disconcerting. He had hinted that the peace-loving citizens found the Bolo frightening (and never mind that they had requested some sort of defense from the military). And if they could not find a way to make themselves useful, perhaps they ought to at least *earn* their pay by pretending to go on maneuvers. It didn't matter that Siegfried and Rommel were perfectly capable of conducting such exercises without moving. That was hardly the point.

"You heard him, my friend," Siegfried sighed. "They'd like us to go away. Not that they have any authority to order us to do so—as I reminded the mayor. But I suspect seeing us constantly is something of an embarrassment to whoever it was that promised a battalion of troops to bring in cash and got us instead."

"In that case, Siegfried," Rommel said gently, "we probably should take the mayor's suggestion. How long do you think we should stay away?"

"When's the next ship due in?" Siegfried replied. "There's no real reason for us to be here until it arrives, and then we only need to stay long enough to pick up my supplies."

"True." With a barely-audible rumble, Rommel started his banks of motive engines. "Have you any destination in mind?"

Without prompting, Rommel projected the map of the immediate area on one of Siegfried's control-room screens. Siegfried studied it for a moment, trying to work out the possible repercussions of vanishing into the hills altogether. "I'll tell you what, old man," he said slowly, "we've just been playing at doing our job. Really, that's hardly honorable, when it comes down to it. Even if they don't need us and never did, the fact is that they asked for on-planet protection, and we haven't even planned how to give it to them. How about if we actually go out there in the bush and *do* that planning?"

There was interest in the AI's voice; he did not imagine it. "What do you mean by that?" Rommel asked.

"I mean, let's go out there and scout the territory ourselves; plan defenses and offenses, as if this dustball *was* likely to be invaded. The topographical surveys stink for military purposes; let's get a real war plan in place. What the hell—it can't hurt, right? And if the locals see us actually doing some work, they might not think so badly of us."

Rommel was silent for a moment. "They will still blame High Command, Siegfried. They did not receive what they wanted, even though they received what they were entitled to."

"But they won't blame *us*." He put a little coaxing

into his voice. "Look, Rommel, we're going to be here for the rest of our lives, and we really can't afford to have the entire population angry with us forever. I know our standing orders are to stay at Port City, but the mayor just countermanded those orders. So let's have some fun, and show'em we know our duty at the same time! Let's use Erwin's strategies around here, and see how they work! We can run all kinds of scenarios—let's assume in the event of a real invasion we could get some of these farmers to pick up a weapon; that'll give us additional scenarios to run. Figure troops against you, mechs against you, troops and mechs against you, plus untrained men against troops, men against mechs, you against another Bolo-type AI—"

"It would be entertaining." Rommel sounded very interested. "And as long as we keep our defensive surveillance up, and an eye on Port City, we would not technically be violating orders. . . ."

"Then let's do it," Siegfried said decisively. "Like I said, the maps they gave us stink; let's go make our own, then plot strategy. Let's find every wadi and overhang big enough to hide you. Let's act as if there really *was* going to be an invasion. Let's give them some options, log the plans with the mayor's office. We can plan for evacuations, we can check resources, there's a lot of things we can do. And let's start right now!"

They mapped every dry stream-bed, every dusty hill, every animal-trail. For months, the two of them rumbled across the arid landscape, with Siegfried emerging now and again to carry surveying instruments to the tops of hills too fragile to bear Rommel's weight. And when every inch of territory within a week of Port City had been surveyed and accurately mapped, they began playing a game of "hide and seek" with the locals.

It was surprisingly gratifying. At first, after they had vanished for a while, the local news-channel seemed to reflect an attitude of "and good riddance." But then, when *no one* spotted them, there was a certain amount of concern—followed by a certain amount of annoyance. After all, Rommel was "their" Bolo—what was Siegfried doing, taking him out for some kind of vacation? As if Bachman's World offered any kind of amusement. . . .

That was when Rommel and Siegfried began stalking farmers.

They would find a good hiding place and get into it well in advance of a farmer's arrival. When he would show up, Rommel would rise up, seemingly from out of the ground, draped in camouflage-net, his weaponry trained on the farmer's vehicle. Then Siegfried would pop up out of the hatch, wave cheerfully, retract the camouflage, and he and Rommel would rumble away.

Talk of "vacations" ceased entirely after that.

They extended their range, once they were certain that the locals were no longer assuming the two of them were "gold-bricking." Rommel tested all of his abilities to the limit, making certain everything was still up to spec. And on the few occasions that it wasn't, Siegfried put in a requisition for parts and spent many long hours making certain that the repairs and replacements *were* bringing Rommel up to like-new condition.

Together they plotted defensive and offensive strategies; Siegfried studied Rommel's manuals as if a time would come when he would have to rebuild Rommel from spare parts. They ran every kind of simulation in the book—and not just on Rommel's computers, but with Rommel himself actually running and dry-firing against plotted enemies. Occasionally one of the news-people would become curious about their whereabouts, and lie in wait for them when the scheduled supplies arrived. Siegfried would give a formal interview, reporting in general what they had been doing—and then, he would carefully file another set of emergency plans with the mayor's office. Sometimes it even made the evening news. Once, it was even accompanied by a clip someone had shot of Rommel roaring at top speed across a ridge.

Nor was that all they did. As Rommel pointed out, the presumptive "battalion" would have been available in emergencies—there was no reason why *they* shouldn't respond when local emergencies came up.

So—when a flash-flood trapped a young woman and three children on the roof of her vehicle, it was Rommel and Siegfried who not only rescued them, but towed the vehicle to safety as well. When a snowfall in the mountains stranded a dozen truckers, Siegfried and Rommel got them out. When a small child was lost while playing in the hills, Rommel found her by having all searchers clear out as soon as the sun went down, and using his heat-sensors to locate every source of approximately her size. They put out runaway brushfires by rolling over them; they responded to Maydays from remote locations when they were nearer than any other agency. They even joined in a manhunt for an escaped rapist—who turned himself in, practically soiling himself with fear, when he learned that Rommel was part of the search-party.

It didn't hurt. They were of no help for men trapped in a mine collapse; or rather, of no *more* help than Siegfried's two hands could make them. They couldn't rebuild bridges that were washed away, nor construct roads. But what they could do, they did, often before anyone thought to ask them for help.

By the end of their second year on Bachman's World, they were at least no longer the target of resentment. Those few citizens they had aided actually looked on them with gratitude. The local politicians whose careers had suffered because of their presence had found other causes to espouse, other schemes to pursue. Siegfried and Rommel were a dead issue.

But by then, the two of them had established a routine of monitoring emergency channels, running their private war-games, updating their maps, and adding changes in the colony to their defense and offense plans. There was no reason to go back to simply sitting beside the spaceport. Neither of them cared for sitting idle, and what they were doing was the nearest either of them would ever get to actually refighting the battles their idol had lost and won.

When High Command got their reports and sent recommendations for further "readiness" preparations, and *commendations* for their "community service"—Siegfried, now wiser in the ways of manipulating public opinion, issued a statement to the press about both.

After that, there were no more rumblings of discontent, and things might have gone on as they were until Siegfried was too old to climb Rommel's ladder.

But the fates had another plan in store for them.

Alarms woke Siegfried out of a sound and dreamless sleep. Not the synthesized pseudo-alarms Rommel used when surprising him for a drill, either, but the real thing—

He launched himself out of his bunk before his eyes were focused, grabbing the back of the com-chair to steady himself before he flung himself into it and strapped himself down. As soon as he moved, Rommel turned off all the alarms but one; the proximity alert from the single defense-satellite in orbit above them.

Interior lighting had gone to full-emergency red. He scrubbed at his eyes with the back of his hand, impatiently; finally they focused on the screens of his console, and he could read what was there. And he swore, fervently and creatively.

One unknown ship sat in geosynch orbit above Port City; a big one, answering no hails from the port, and seeding the skies with what appeared to his sleep-fogged eyes as hundreds of smaller drop-ships.

"The mother-ship has already neutralized the port air-to-ground defenses, Siegfried," Rommel reported grimly. "I don't know what kind of stealthing devices they have, or if they've got some new kind of drive, but they don't match anything in my records. They just appeared out of nowhere and started dumping drop-ships. I think we can assume they're hostiles."

They had a match for just this in their hundreds of plans; unknown ship, unknown attackers, dropping a pattern of offensive troops of some kind—

"What are they landing?" he asked, playing the console board. "You're stealthed, right?"

"To the max," Rommel told him. "I don't detect anything like life-forms on those incoming vessels, but my sensors aren't as sophisticated as they could be. The vessels themselves aren't all that big. My guess is that they're dropping either live troops or clusters of very small mechs, mobile armor, maybe the size of a Panzer."

"Landing pattern?" he asked. He brought up all of Rommel's weaponry; AIs weren't allowed to activate their own weapons. And they weren't allowed to fire on living troops without permission from a human, either. That was the only real reason for a Bolo needing an operator.

"Surrounding Port City, but starting from about where the first farms are." Rommel ran swift readiness-tests on the systems as Siegfried brought them up; the screens scrolled too fast for Siegfried to read them.

They had a name for that particular scenario. It was one of the first possibilities they had run when they began plotting invasion and counter-invasion plans.

"Operation Cattle Drive. Right." If the invaders followed the same scheme he and Rommel had anticipated, they planned to drive the populace into Port City, and either capture the civilians, or destroy them at leisure. He checked their current location; it was out beyond the drop-zone. "Is there anything landing close to us?"

"Not yet—but the odds are that something will soon." Rommel sounded confident, as well he should be—his ability to project landing-patterns was far better than any human's. "I'd say within the next fifteen minutes."

Siegfried suddenly shivered in a breath of cool air

from the ventilators, and was painfully aware suddenly that he was dressed in nothing more than a pair of fatigue-shorts. Oh well; some of the Desert Fox's battles had taken place with the men wearing little else. What they could put up with, he could. There certainly wasn't anyone here to complain.

"As soon as you think we can move without detection, close on the nearest craft," he ordered. "I want to see what we're up against. And start scanning the local freqs; if there's anything in the way of organized defense from the civvies, I want to know about it."

A pause, while the ventilators hummed softly, and glowing dots descended on several screens. "They don't seem to have anything, Siegfried," Rommel reported quietly. "Once the ground-to-space defenses were fried, they just collapsed. Right now, they seem to be in a complete state of panic. They don't even seem to remember that *we're* out here—no one's tried to hail us on any of our regular channels."

"Either that—or they think we're out of commission," he muttered absently. "Or just maybe they are giving us credit for knowing what we're doing and are trying *not* to give us away. I hope so. The longer we can go without detection, the better chance we have to pull something out of a hat."

An increase in vibration warned him that Rommel was about to move. A new screen lit up, this one tracking a single vessel. "Got one," the Bolo said shortly. "I'm coming in behind his sensor sweep."

Four more screens lit up; enhanced front, back, top, and side views of the terrain. Only the changing views on the screens showed that Rommel was moving; other than that, there was no way to tell from inside the cabin what was happening. It would be different if Rommel had to execute evasive maneuvers of course, but right now, he might have still been parked. The control cabin and living quarters were heavily shielded and cushioned against the shocks of ordinary movement. Only if

Rommel took a direct hit by something impressive would Siegfried feel it. . . .

And if he takes a direct hit by something more than impressive—we're slag. Bolos are the best, but they can't take everything.

"The craft is down."

He pushed the thought away from his mind. This was what Rommel had been built to do—this moment justified Rommel's very existence. And *he* had known from the very beginning that the possibility, however remote, had existed that he too would be in combat one day. That was what being in the military was all about. There was no use in pretending otherwise.

Get on with the job. That's what they've sent me here to do. Wasn't there an ancient royal family whose motto was "God, and my Duty?" Then let that be his.

"Have you detected any sensor scans from the mothership?" he asked, his voice a harsh whisper. "Or anything other than a forward scan from the landing craft?" He didn't know why he was whispering—

"Not as yet, Siegfried," Rommel replied, sounding a little surprised. "Apparently, these invaders are confident that there is no one out here at all. Even that forward scan seemed mainly to be a landing-aid."

"Nobody here but us chickens," Siegfried muttered. "Are they offloading yet?"

"Wait—yes. The ramp is down. We will be within visual range ourselves in a moment—there—"

More screens came alive; Siegfried read them rapidly—

Then read them again, incredulously.

"Mechs?" he said, astonished. *"Remotely controlled* mechs?"

"So it appears." Rommel sounded just as mystified. "This does not match any known configuration. There is one limited AI in that ship. Data indicates it is hardened against any attack conventional forces at the port could mount. The ship seems to be digging in—

look at the seismic reading on 4-B. The limited AI is in control of the mechs it is deploying. I believe that we can assume this will be the case for the other invading ships, at least the ones coming down at the moment, since they all appear to be of the same model."

Siegfried studied the screens; as they had assumed, the mechs were about the size of pre-Atomic Panzers, and seemed to be built along similar lines. "Armored mechs. Good against anything a civilian has. Is that ship hardened against anything *you* can throw?" he asked finally.

There was a certain amount of glee in Rommel's voice. "I think not. Shall we try?"

Siegfried's mouth dried. There was no telling what weaponry that ship packed—or the mother-ship held. The mother-ship might be monitoring the drop-ships, watching for attack. *God and my Duty,* he thought.

"You may fire when ready, Herr Rommel."

They had taken the drop-ship by complete surprise; destroying it before it had a chance to transmit distress or tactical data to the mother-ship. The mechs had stopped in their tracks the moment the AI's direction ceased.

But rather than roll on to the next target, Siegfried had ordered Rommel to stealth again, while he examined the remains of the mechs and the controlling craft. He'd had an idea—the question was, would it work?

He knew weapons systems; knew computer-driven control. There were only a limited number of ways such controls could work. And if he recognized any of those here—

He told himself, as he scrambled into clothing and climbed the ladder out of the cabin, that he would give himself an hour. The situation would not change much in an hour; there was very little that he and Rommel could accomplish in that time in the way of mounting a campaign. As it happened, it took him fifteen minutes more than that to learn all he needed to know. At the end of that time, though, he scrambled back into Rommel's guts with mingled feelings of elation and anger.

The ship and mechs were clearly of human origin, and some of the vanes and protrusions that made them look so unfamiliar had been tacked on purely to make both the drop-ships and armored mechs look alien in nature. Someone, somewhere, had discovered something about Bachman's World that suddenly made it valuable. From the hardware interlocks and the programming modes he had found in what was left of the controlling ship, he suspected that the "someone" was not a government, but a corporation.

And a multiplanet corporation could afford to mount an invasion force fairly easily. The best force for the job would, of course, be something precisely like this—completely mechanized. There would be no troops to "hush up" afterwards; no leaks to the interstellar press. Only a nice clean invasion—and, in all probability, a nice, clean extermination at the end of it, with no humans to protest the slaughter of helpless civilians.

And afterwards, there would be no evidence anywhere to contradict the claim that the civilians had slaughtered each other in some kind of local conflict.

The mechs and the AI itself were from systems he had studied when he first started in this specialty—outmoded even by his standards, but reliable, and when set against farmers with hand-weapons, perfectly adequate.

There was one problem with this kind of setup . . . from the enemy's standpoint. It was a problem they didn't know they had.

Yet.

He filled Rommel in on what he had discovered as he raced up the ladder, then slid down the handrails into the command cabin. "Now, here's the thing—I got the access code to command those mechs with a little fiddling in the AI's memory. Nice of them to leave in so many manual overrides for me. I reset the command interface freq to one you have, and hardwired it so they shouldn't be able to change it—"

He jumped into the command chair and strapped in; his hands danced across the keypad, keying in the frequency and the code. Then he saluted the console jauntily. "Congratulations, Herr Rommel," he said, unable to keep the glee out of his voice. "You are now a Field Marshal."

"*Siegfried!*" Yes, there was astonishment in Rommel's synthesized voice. "You just gave me command of an armored mobile strike force!"

"I certainly did. And I freed your command circuits so that you can run them without waiting for my orders to do something." Siegfried couldn't help grinning. "After all, you're not going against living troops, you're going to be attacking AIs and mechs. The next AI might not be so easy to take over, but if you're running in the middle of a swarm of 'friendlies,' you might not be suspected. And when we knock out *that* one, we'll take over again. I'll even put the next bunch on a different command freq so you can command them separately. Sooner or later they'll figure out what we're doing, but by then I hope we'll have at least an equal force under our command."

"This is good, Siegfried!"

"You bet it's good, *mein Freund*," he retorted. "What's more, we've studied the best—they can't possibly have that advantage. All right—let's show these amateurs how one of the old masters handles armor!"

The second and third takeovers were as easy as the first. By the fourth, however, matters had changed. It might have dawned on either the AIs on the ground or whoever was in command of the overall operation in the mother-ship above that the triple loss of AIs and mechs was not due to simple malfunction, but to an unknown and unsuspected enemy.

In that, the hostiles were following in the mental footsteps of another pre-Atomic commander, who had once stated, "Once is happenstance, twice is circumstance, but three times is enemy action."

So the fourth time their forces advanced on a ship, they met with fierce resistance.

They lost about a dozen mechs, and Siegfried had suffered a bit of a shakeup and a fair amount of bruising, but they managed to destroy the fourth AI without much damage to Rommel's exterior. Despite the danger from unexploded shells and some residual radiation, Siegfried doggedly went out into the wreckage to get that precious access code.

He returned to bad news. "They know we're here, Siegfried," Rommel announced. "That last barrage gave them a silhouette upstairs; they know I'm a Bolo, so now they know what they're up against."

Siegfried swore quietly, as he gave Rommel his fourth contingent of mechs. "Well, have they figured out exactly what we're doing yet? Or can you tell?" Siegfried asked while typing in the fourth unit's access codes.

"I can't—I—can't—Siegfried—" the Bolo replied, suddenly without any inflection at all. "Siegfried. There is a problem. Another. I am stretching my—resources—"

This time Siegfried swore with a lot less creativity. That was something he had not even considered! The AIs they were eliminating were much less sophisticated than Rommel—

"Drop the last batch!" he snapped. To his relief, Rommel sounded like himself again as he released control of the last contingent of mechs.

"That was not a pleasurable experience," Rommel said mildly.

"What happened?" he demanded.

"As I needed to devote more resources to controlling the mechs, I began losing higher functions," the Bolo replied simply. "We should have expected that; so far

I am doing the work of three lesser AIs and all the functions you require, *and* maneuvering of the various groups we have captured. As I pick up more groups, I will inevitably lose processing functions."

Siegfried thought, frantically. There were about twenty of these invading ships; their plan absolutely required that Rommel control at least eight of the groups to successfully hold the invasion off Port City. There was no way they'd be anything worse than an annoyance with only three; the other groups could outflank them. "What if you shut down things in here?" he asked. "Run basic life-support, but nothing fancy. And I could drive—run your weapons' systems."

"You could. That would help." Rommel pondered for a moment. "My calculations are that we can take the required eight of the groups if you also issue battle orders and I simply carry them out. But there is a further problem."

"Which is?" he asked—although he had the sinking feeling that he knew what the problem was going to be.

"Higher functions. One of the functions I will lose at about the seventh takeover is what you refer to as my personality. A great deal of my ability to maintain a personality is dependent on devoting a substantial percentage of my central processor to that personality. And if it disappears—"

The Bolo paused. Siegfried's hands clenched on the arms of his chair.

"—it may not return. There is a possibility that the records and algorithms which make up my personality will be written over by comparison files during strategic control calculations." Again Rommel paused. "Siegfried, this is our duty. I am willing to take that chance."

Siegfried swallowed, only to find a lump in his throat and his guts in knots. "Are you sure?" he asked gently. "Are you very sure? What you're talking about is—is a kind of deactivation."

"I am sure," Rommel replied firmly. "The Field Marshal would have made the same choice."

Rommel's manuals were all on a handheld reader. He had studied them from front to back—wasn't there something in there? "Hold on a minute—"

He ran through the index, frantically keyword searching. This was a memory function, right? Or at least it was software. The designers didn't encourage operators to go mucking around in the AI functions . . . what would a computer jock call what he was looking for?

Finally he found it; a tiny section in programmerese, not even listed in the index. He scanned it, quickly, and found the warning that had been the thing that had caught his eye in the first place.

This system has been simulation proven in expected scenarios, but has never been fully field-tested.

What the hell did that mean? He had a guess; this was essentially a full-copy backup of the AI's processor. He suspected that they had never tested the backup function on an AI with a full personality. There was no way of knowing if the restoration function would actually "restore" a lost personality.

But the backup memory-module in question had its own power-supply, and was protected in the most hardened areas of Rommel's interior. Nothing was going to destroy it that didn't slag him and Rommel together, and if "personality" was largely a matter of memory—

It might work. It might not. It was worth trying, even if the backup procedure was fiendishly hard to initiate. They really *didn't* want operators mucking around with the AIs.

Twenty command-strings later, a single memory-mod began its simple task; Rommel was back in charge of the fourth group of mechs, and Siegfried had taken over the driving.

He was not as good as Rommel was, but he was better than he had thought.

They took groups five, and six, and it was horrible—

listening to Rommel fade away, lose the vitality behind the synthesized voice. If Siegfried hadn't had his hands full already, literally, it would have been worse.

But with group seven—

That was when he just about lost it, because in reply to one of his voice-commands, instead of a "Got it, Siegfried," what came over the speakers was the metallic "Affirmative" of a simple voice-activated computer.

All of Rommel's resources were now devoted to self-defense and control of the armored mechs.

God and my Duty. Siegfried took a deep breath, and began keying in the commands for mass armor deployment.

The ancient commanders were right; from the ground, there was no way of knowing when the moment of truth came. Siegfried only realized they had won when the mother-ship suddenly vanished from orbit, and the remaining AIs went dead. Cutting their losses; there was nothing in any of the equipment that would betray *where* it came from. Whoever was in charge of the invasion force must have decided that there was no way they would finish the mission before *someone*, a regularly scheduled freighter or a surprise patrol, discovered what was going on and reported it.

By that time, he had been awake for fifty hours straight; he had put squeeze-bulbs of electrolytic drink near at hand, but he was starving and still thirsty. With the air-conditioning cut out, he must have sweated out every ounce of fluid he drank. His hands were shaking and every muscle in his neck and shoulders were cramped from hunching over the boards.

Rommel was battered and had lost several external sensors and one of his guns. But the moment that the mother-ship vanished, he had only one thought.

He manually dropped control of every mech from Rommel's systems, and waited, praying, for his old friend to "come back."

But nothing happened—other than the obvious things that any AI would do, restoring all the comfort-support and life-support functions, and beginning damage checks and some self-repair.

Rommel was gone.

His throat closed; his stomach knotted. But—

It wasn't tested. That doesn't mean it won't work.

Once more, his hands moved over the keyboard, with another twenty command-strings, telling that little memory-module in the heart of his Bolo to initiate full restoration. He hadn't thought he had water to spare for tears—yet there they were, burning their way down his cheeks. Two of them.

He ignored them, fiercely, shaking his head to clear his eyes, and continuing the command-sequence.

Damage checks and self-repair aborted. Life-support went on automatic.

And Siegfried put his head down on the console to rest his burning eyes for a moment. Just for a moment—

Just—

"*Ahem.*"

Siegfried jolted out of sleep, cracking his elbow on the console, staring around the cabin with his heart racing wildly.

"I believe we have visitors, Siegfried," said that wonderful, familiar voice. "They seem most impatient."

Screens lit up, showing a small army of civilians approaching, riding in everything from outmoded sandrails to tractors, all of them cheering, all of them heading straight for the Bolo.

"We seem to have their approval at least," Rommel continued.

His heart had stopped racing, but he still trembled. And once again, he seemed to have come up with the moisture for tears. He nodded, knowing Rommel would see it, unable for the moment to get any words out.

"Siegfried—before we become immersed in grateful

civilians—how *did* you bring me back?" Rommel asked. "I'm rather curious—I actually seem to remember fading out. An unpleasant experience."

"How did I get you back?" he managed to choke out—and then began laughing.

He held up the manual, laughing, and cried out the famous quote of George Patton—

"'Rommel, you magnificent bastard, *I read your book!*'"

Sometimes we write for odd markets; I wrote this piece for a magazine called Pet Bird Report, *which is bird behaviorist Sally Blanchard's outlet for continuing information on parrot behavior and psychology. It's a terrific magazine, and if you have a bird but haven't subscribed, I suggest you would find it worth your while. With twelve birds, I need all the help I can get! At any rate, Sally asked me for some fiction, and I came up with this.*

Grey

For nine years, Sarah Jane Lyon-White lived happily with her parents in the heart of Africa. Her father was a physician, her mother, a nurse, and they worked at a Protestant mission in the Congo. She was happy there, not the least because her mother and father were far more enlightened than many another mission worker in the days when Victoria was Queen; taking the cause of healing as more sacred than that of conversion, they undertook to work *with* the natives, and made friends instead of enemies among the shamans and medicine-people. Because of this, Sarah was a cherished and protected child, although she was no stranger to the many dangers of life in the Congo.

When she was six, and far older in responsibility than most of her peers, one of the shaman brought her a parrot-chick still in quills; he taught her how to feed and care for it, and told her that while *it* was a child, she was to protect it, but when it was grown, it would protect and guide *her*. She called the parrot "Grey," and it became her best friend—and indeed, although she never told her parents, it became her protector as well.

But when she was nine, her parents sent her to live in England for the sake of her health. And because her mother feared that the climate of England would not be good for Grey's health, she had to leave her beloved friend behind.

Now, this was quite the usual thing in the days when Victoria was Queen and the great British Empire was so vast that there was never an hour when some part of it was not in sunlight. It was thought that English children were more delicate than their parents, and that the inhospitable humors of hot climes would make them sicken and die. Not that their *parents* didn't sicken and die quite as readily as the children, who were, in fact, far sturdier than they were given credit for—but it was thought, by anxious mothers, that the climate of England would be far kinder to them. So off they were shipped, some as young as two and three, torn away from their anxious mamas and native nurses and sent to live with relatives or even total strangers.

Now, as Mr. Kipling and Mrs. Hope-Hodgson have shown us, many of these total strangers—and no few of the relatives—were bad, wicked people, interested only in the round gold sovereigns that the childrens' parents sent to them for their care. There were many schools where the poor lonely things were neglected or even abused; where their health suffered far more than if they had stayed safely at the sides of their mamas.

But there were good schools too, and kindly people, and Sarah Jane's mama had been both wise and careful in her selection. In fact, Sarah Jane's mama had made a choice that was far wiser than even she had guessed. . . .

Nan—that was her only name, for no one had told her of any other—lurked anxiously about the back gate of the Big House. She was new to this neighborhood, for her slatternly mother had lost yet another job in a gin-mill and they had been forced to move all the way across Whitechapel, and this part of London was as foreign to Nan as the wilds of Australia. She had been told by more than one of the children hereabouts that if she hung about the back gate after tea, a strange man with a towel wrapped about his head would come out with a basket of food and give it out to any child who happened to be there. Now, there were not as many children willing to accept this offering as might have been expected, even in this poor neighborhood. They were afraid of the man, afraid of his piercing, black eyes, his swarthy skin, and his way of walking like a great hunting-cat. Some suspected poison in the food, others murmured that he and the woman of the house were foreigners, and intended to kill English children with terrible curses on the food they offered. But Nan was faint with hunger; she hadn't eaten in two days, and was willing to dare poison, curses, and anything else for a bit of bread.

Furthermore, Nan had a secret defense; under duress, she could often sense the intent and even dimly hear the thoughts of others. That was how she avoided her mother when it was most dangerous to approach her, as well as avoiding other dangers in the streets themselves. Nan was certain that if this man had any ill intentions, she would know it.

Still, as tea-time and twilight both approached, she hung back a little from the wrought-iron gate, beginning to wonder if it wouldn't be better to see what, if anything, her mother brought home. If she'd found a job—or a "gen'lmun"—there might be a farthing or two to spare for food before Aggie spent the rest on gin. Behind the high, grimy wall, the Big House loomed dark and ominous against the smoky, lowering sky, and the strange, carved creatures sitting atop every pillar in the wall and every corner of the House fair gave Nan the shivers whenever she looked at them. There were no two alike, and most of them were beasts out of a rummy's worst deliriums. The only one that Nan could see that looked at all normal was a big, grey bird with a fat body and a hooked beak that sat on top of the right-hand gatepost of the back gate.

Nan had no way to tell time, but as she waited, growing colder and hungrier—and more nervous—with each passing moment, she began to think for certain that the other children had been having her on. Teatime was surely long over; the tale they'd told her was nothing more than that, something to gull the newcomer with. It was getting dark, there were no other children waiting, and after dark it was dangerous even for a child like Nan, wise in the ways of the evil streets, to be abroad. Disappointed, and with her stomach a knot of pain, Nan began to turn away from the gate.

"I think that there is no one here, Missy S'ab," said a low, deep voice, heavily accented, sounding disappointed. Nan hastily turned back, and peering through the gloom, she barely made out a tall, dark form with a smaller one beside it.

"No, Karamjit—look there!" replied the voice of a young girl, and the smaller form pointed at Nan. A little girl ran up to the gate, and waved through the bars. "Hello! I'm Sarah—what's your name? Would you like some tea-bread? We've plenty!"

The girl's voice, also strangely accented, had none of the imperiousness that Nan would have expected coming from the child of a "toff." She sounded only friendly and helpful, and that, more than anything, was what drew Nan back to the wrought-iron gate.

"Indeed, Missy Sarah speaks the truth," the man said; and as Nan drew nearer, she saw that the other children had not exaggerated when they described him. His head was wrapped around in a cloth; he wore a long, high-collared coat of some bright stuff, and white trousers that were tucked into glossy boots. He was as fiercely erect as the iron gate itself; lean and angular as a hunting tiger, with skin so dark she could scarcely make out his features, and eyes that glittered at her like beads of black glass.

But strangest, and perhaps most ominous of all, Nan could sense nothing from the dark man. He might not even have been there; there was a blank wall where his thoughts should have been.

The little girl beside him was perfectly ordinary by comparison; a bright little wren of a thing, not pretty, but sweet, with a trusting smile that went straight to Nan's heart. Nan had a motherly side to her; the younger children of whatever neighborhood she lived in tended to flock to her, look up to her, and follow her lead. She in her turn tried to keep them out of trouble, and whenever there was extra to go around, she fed them out of her own scant stocks.

But the tall fellow frightened her, and made her nervous, especially when further moments revealed no more of his intentions than Nan had sensed before; the girl's bright eyes noted that, and she whispered something to the dark man as Nan withdrew a little. He nodded, and handed her a basket that looked promisingly heavy.

Then he withdrew out of sight, leaving the little girl alone at the gate. The child pushed the gate open enough to hand the basket through. "Please, won't you come and take this? It's awfully heavy."

In spite of the clear and open brightness of the little girl's thoughts, ten years of hard living had made Nan suspicious. The child might know nothing of what the dark man wanted. "Woi're yer givin' food away?" she asked, edging forward a little, but not yet quite willing to take the basket.

The little girl put the basket down on the ground and clasped her hands behind her back. "Well, Mem'sab says that she won't tell Maya and Selim to make less food for tea, because she won't have us going hungry while we're growing. And she says that old, stale toast is fit only for starlings, so people ought to have the good of it before it goes stale. And she says that there's no reason why children outside our gate have to go to bed hungry when we have enough to share, and my Mum and Da say that sharing is charity and Charity is one of the cardinal virtues, so Mem'sab is being virtuous, which is a good thing, because she'll go to heaven and she would make a good angel."

Most of that came out in a rush that quite bewildered Nan, especially the last, about cardinal virtues and heaven and angels. But she did understand that "Mem'sab," whoever that was, must be one of those daft religious creatures that gave away food free for the taking, and Nan's own Mum had told her that there was no point in letting other people take what you could get from people like that. So Nan edged forward and made a snatch at the basket-handle.

She tried, that is; it proved a great deal heavier than she'd thought, and she gave an involuntary grunt at the weight of it.

"Be careful," the little girl admonished mischievously. "It's heavy."

"Yer moight'o warned me!" Nan said, a bit indignant, and more than a bit excited. If this wasn't a trick—if there wasn't a brick in the basket—oh, she'd eat well tonight, and tomorrow, too!

"Come back tomorrow!" the little thing called, as she shut the gate and turned and skipped towards the house. "Remember me! I'm Sarah Jane, and I'll bring the basket tomorrow!"

"Thenkee, Sarah Jane," Nan called back, belatedly;

then, just in case these strange creatures would think better of their generosity, she made the basket and herself vanish into the night.

She came earlier the next day, bringing back the now-empty basket, and found Sarah Jane waiting at the gate. To her disappointment, there was no basket waiting beside the child, and Nan almost turned back, but Sarah saw her and called to her before she could fade back into the shadows of the streets.

"Karamjit is bringing the basket in a bit," the child said, "There's things Mem'sab wants you to have. And—what am I to call you? It's rude to call you 'girl,' but I don't know your name."

"Nan," Nan replied, feeling as if a cart had run over her. This child, though younger than Nan herself, had a way of taking over a situation that was all out of keeping with Nan's notion of how things were. "Wot kind'o place is this, anyway?"

"It's a school, a boarding-school," Sarah said promptly. "Mem'sab and her husband have it for the children of people who live in India, mostly. Mem'sab can't have children herself, which is very sad, but she says that means she can be a mother to us. Mem'sab came from India, and that's where Karamjit and Selim and Maya and the others are from, too; they came with her."

"Yer mean the black feller?" Nan asked, bewildered. "Yer from In'ju too?"

"No," Sarah said, shaking her head. "Africa. I wish I was back there." Her face paled and her eyes misted, and Nan, moved by an impulse she did not understand, tried to distract her with questions.

"Wot's it loik, then? Izit loik Lunnun?"

"Like London! Oh, no, it couldn't be less like London!" Nan's ploy worked; the child giggled at the idea of comparing the Congo with a metropolis, and she painted a vivid word-picture of the green jungles, teeming with birds and animals of all sorts; of the natives who came to her father and mother for medicines. "Mum and Da don't do what some of the others do—they went and talked to the magic men and showed them they weren't going to interfere in the magic work, and now whenever Mum and Da have a patient who thinks he's cursed, they call the magic man in to help, and when a magic man has someone that his magic can't help right away, he takes the patient to Mum and Da and they all put on feathers and Mum and Da give him White Medicine while the magic man burns his herbs and feathers and makes his chants, and everyone is happy. There haven't been any uprisings at our station for *ever* so long, and our magic men won't let anyone put black chickens at our door. One of them gave me Grey, and I wanted to bring her with me, but Mum said I shouldn't." Now the child sighed, and looked woeful again.

"Wot's a Grey?" Nan asked.

"She's a Polly, a grey parrot with the beautifullest red tail; the medicine man gave her to me when she was all prickles, he showed me how to feed her with mashed-up yams and things. She's *so* smart, she follows me about, and she can say, oh, hundreds of things. The medicine man said that she was to be my guardian and keep me from harm. But Mum was afraid the smoke in London would hurt her, and I couldn't bring her with me." Sarah looked up at the fat, stone bird on the gatepost above her. "That's why Mem'sab gave me *that* gargoyle, to be my guardian instead. We all have them, each child has her own, and that one's mine." She looked down again at Nan, and lowered her voice to a whisper. "Sometimes when I get lonesome, I come here and talk to her, and it's like talking to Grey."

Nan nodded her head, understanding. "Oi useta go an' talk t' a stachew in one'a the yards, 'til we 'adta move. It looked loik me grammum. Felt loik I was talkin' to 'er, I fair did."

A footstep on the gravel path made Nan look up, and

she jumped to see the tall man with the head-wrap standing there, as if he had come out of the thin air. She had not sensed his presence, and once again, even though he stood materially before her she *could not.* He took no notice of Nan, which she was grateful for; instead, he handed the basket he was carrying to Sarah Jane, and walked off without a word.

Sarah passed the basket to Nan; it was heavier this time, and Nan *thought* she smelled something like roasted meat. Oh, if *only* they'd given her the drippings from their beef! Her mouth watered at the thought.

"I hope you like these," Sarah said shyly, as Nan passed her the much-lighter empty. "Mem'sab says that if you'll keep coming back, I'm to talk to you and ask you about London; she says that's the best way to learn about things. She says otherwise, when I go out, I might get into trouble I don't understand."

Nan's eyes widened at the thought that the head of a school had said anything of the sort—but Sarah Jane hardly seemed like the type of child to lie. "All roit, I s'pose," she said dubiously. "If you'll be 'ere, so'll Oi."

The next day, faithful as the rising sun, Sarah was waiting with her basket, and Nan was invited to come inside the gate. She wouldn't venture any farther in than a bench in the garden, but as Sarah asked questions, she answered them as bluntly and plainly as she would any similar question asked by a child in her own neighborhood. Sarah learned about the dangers of the dark side of London first-hand—and oddly, although she nodded wisely and with clear understanding, they didn't seem to *frighten* her.

"Garn!" Nan said once, when Sarah absorbed the interesting fact that the opium den a few doors from where Nan and her mother had a room had pitched three dead men out into the street the night before. "Yer ain't never seen nothin' loik that!"

"You forget, Mum and Da have a hospital, and it's very dangerous where they are," Sarah replied matter-of-factly. "I've seen dead men, and dead women and even babies. When Nkumba came in clawed up by a lion, I helped bring water and bandages, while Mum and Da sewed him up. When there was a black-water fever, I saw lots of people die. It was horrid and sad, but I didn't fuss, because Nkumba and Da and Mum were worked nearly to bones and needed me to be good."

Nan's eyes widened again. "Wot else y'see?" she whispered, impressed in spite of herself.

After that, the two children traded stories of two very different sorts of jungles. Despite its dangers, Nan thought that Sarah's was the better of the two.

She learned other things as well; that "Mem'sab" was a completely remarkable woman, for she had a Sikh, a Gurkha, two Moslems, two Buddhists, and assorted Hindus working in peace and harmony together—"and Mum said in her letter that it's easier to get leopards to herd sheep than that!" Mem'sab was by no means a fool; the Sikh and the Gurkha shared guard duty, patrolling the walls by day and night. One of the Hindu women was the "ayah," who took care of the smallest children; the rest of the motley assortment were servants and even teachers.

She heard many stories about the remarkable Grey, who really *did* act as Sarah's guardian, if Sarah was to be believed. Sarah described times when she had inadvertently gotten lost; she had called frantically for Grey, who was allowed to fly free, and the bird had come to her, leading her back to familiar paths. Grey had kept her from eating some pretty but poisonous berries by flying at her and nipping her fingers until she dropped them. Grey alerted the servants to the presence of snakes in the nursery, always making a patrol before she allowed Sarah to enter. And once, according to Sarah, when she had encountered a lion on the path, Grey had flown off and made sounds like a young gazelle in distress, attracting the lion's attention before it could scent Sarah. "She led it away, and didn't come back to me until it was too far away to bother coming back," the little girl claimed solemnly, "Grey is *very* clever." Nan didn't know whether to gape at her or laugh; she couldn't imagine how a mere bird could be intelligent enough to talk, much less act with purpose.

Nan had breath to laugh with, nowadays, thanks to baskets that held more than bread. The food she found in there, though distinctly odd, was always good, and she no longer felt out of breath and tired all the time. She had stopped wondering and worrying about why "Mem'sab" took such an interest in her, and simply accepted the gifts without question. They might stop at any moment; she accepted that without question, too.

The only thing she couldn't accept so easily was the manservant's eerie mental silence.

"How is your mother?" Sarah asked, since yesterday Nan had confessed that Aggie been "on a tear" and had consumed, or so Nan feared, something stronger and more dangerous than gin.

Nan shook her head. "I dunno," she replied reluctantly. "Aggie didn' wake up when I went out. Tha's not roight, she us'lly at least waked up t'foind out wha' I got. She don' half loik them baskets, 'cause it means I don' go beggin' as much."

"And if you don't beg money, she can't drink," Sarah observed shrewdly. "You hate begging, don't you?"

"Mostly I don' like gettin' kicked an' cursed at," Nan temporized. "It ain't loik I'm gettin' underfoot . . ."

But Sarah's questions were coming too near the bone, tonight, and Nan didn't want to have to deal with them. She got to her feet and picked up her basket. "I gotter go," she said abruptly.

Sarah rose from her seat on the bench and gave Nan a penetrating look. Nan had the peculiar feeling that the child was looking at *her* thoughts, and deciding whether or not to press her further. "All right," Sarah said. "It *is* getting dark."

It wasn't, but Nan wasn't about to pass up the offer of a graceful exit. "'Tis, that," she said promptly, and squeezed through the narrow opening Karamjit had left in the gate.

But she had not gone four paces when two rough-looking men in shabby tweed jackets blocked her path. "You Nan Killian?" said one hoarsely. Then when Nan stared at him blankly, added, "Aggie Killian's girl?"

The answer was surprised out of her; she hadn't been expecting such a confrontation, and she hadn't yet managed to sort herself out. "Ye—es," she said slowly.

"Good," the first man grunted. "Yer Ma sent us; she's gone t' a new place, an' she wants us t'show y' the way."

Now, several thoughts flew through Nan's mind at that moment. The first was, that as they were paid up on the rent through the end of the week, she could not imagine Aggie ever vacating before the time was up. The second was, that even if Aggie *had* set up somewhere else, she would never have sent a pair of strangers to find Nan.

And third was that Aggie had turned to a more potent intoxicant than gin—which meant she would need a deal more money. And Aggie had only one thing left to sell.

Nan.

Their minds were such a roil that she couldn't "hear" any distinct thoughts, but it was obvious that they meant her no good.

"Wait a minnit—" Nan said, her voice trembling a little as she backed away from the two men, edging around them to get to the street. "Did'jer say Aggie *Killian's* gel? Me Ma ain't called Killian, yer got th' wrong gel—"

It was at that moment that one of the men lunged for her with a curse. He had his hands nearly on her, and would have gotten her, too, except for one bit of interference.

Sarah came shooting out of the gate like a little bullet. She body-slammed the fellow, going into the back of his knees and knocking him right off his feet. She danced out of the way as he fell in the nick of time, ran to Nan, and caught her hand, tugging her towards the street. "Run!" she commanded imperiously, and Nan ran.

The two of them scrabbled through the dark alleys and twisted streets without any idea where they were, only that they had to shake off their pursuers. Unfortunately, the time that Nan would have put into learning her new neighborhood like the back of her grimy little hand had been put into talking with Sarah, and before too long, even Nan was lost in the maze of dark, fetid streets. Then their luck ran out altogether, and they found themselves staring at the blank wall of a building, in a dead-end cul-de-sac.

They whirled around, hoping to escape before they were trapped, but it was already too late. The bulky silhouettes of the two men loomed against the fading light at the end of the street.

"Oo's yer friend, ducky?" the first man purred. "Think she'd loik t'come with?"

To Nan's astonishment, Sarah stood straight and tall, and even stepped forward a pace. "I think you ought to go away and leave us alone," she said clearly. "You're going to find yourselves in a lot of trouble."

The talkative man laughed. "Them's big words from such a little gel," he mocked. "We ain't leavin' wi'out we collect what's ours, an' a bit more fer th' trouble yer caused."

Nan was petrified with fear, shaking in every limb, as Sarah stepped back, putting her back to the damp wall. As the first man touched Sarah's arm, she shrieked out a single word.

"*Grey!*"

As Sarah cried out the name of her pet, Nan let loose a wordless prayer for something, *anything*, to come to their rescue.

Something screamed behind the man; startled and distracted for a moment, he turned. For a moment, a fluttering shape obscured his face, and *he* screamed in pain. He shook his head, violently.

"Get it off!" he screamed at his partner. "*Get it off!*"

"Get what off?" the man said, bewildered. "There ain't nothin' there!"

The man clawed frantically at the front of his face, but whatever had attacked him had vanished without a trace. But not before leading more substantial help to the rescue.

Out of the dusk and the first wisps of fog, Karamjit and another swarthy man ran on noiseless feet. In their hands were cudgels which they used to good purpose on the two who opposed them. Nor did they waste any effort, clubbing the two senseless with a remarkable economy of motion.

Then, without a single word, each of the men scooped up a girl in his arms, and bore them back to the school. At that point, finding herself safe in the arms of an unlooked-for rescuer, Nan felt secure enough to break down into hysterical tears.

Nor was that the end of it; she found herself bundled up into the sacred precincts of the school itself, plunged into the first hot bath of her life, wrapped in a clean flannel gown, and put into a real bed. Sarah was in a similar bed beside her. As she sat there, numb, a plain-looking woman with beautiful eyes came and sat down on the foot of Sarah's bed, and looked from one to the other of them.

"Well," the lady said at last, "what have you two to say for yourselves?"

Nan couldn't manage anything, but that was all right, since Sarah wasn't about to let her get in a word anyway. The child jabbered like a monkey, a confused speech about Nan's mother, the men she'd sold Nan to, the virtue of Charity, the timely appearance of Grey, and a great deal more besides. The lady listened and nodded, and when Sarah ran down at last, she turned to Nan.

"I believe Sarah is right in one thing," she said

gravely. "I believe we will have to keep you. Now, both of you—sleep."

And to Nan's surprise, she fell asleep immediately.

But that was not the end to the story. A month later, Sarah's mother arrived, with Grey in a cage. Nan had, by then, found a place where she could listen to what went on in the best parlor without being found, and she glued her ear to the crack in the pantry to listen when Sarah was taken into that hallowed room.

"—found Grey senseless beside her perch," Sarah's mother was saying. "I thought it was a fit, but the Shaman swore that Sarah was in trouble and the bird had gone to help. Grey awoke none the worse, and I would have thought nothing more of the incident, until your message arrived."

"And so you came, very wisely, bringing this remarkable bird." Mem'sab made chirping noises at the bird, and an odd little voice said, "Hello, bright eyes!"

Mem'sab chuckled. "How much of strangeness are you prepared to believe in, my dear?" she asked gently. "Would you believe me if I told you that I have seen this bird once before——fluttering and pecking at my window, then leading my men to rescue your child?"

"I can only answer with Hamlet," Sarah's mother said after a pause. "That there are more things in heaven and earth than I suspected."

"Good," Mem'sab replied decidedly. "Then I take it you are not here to remove Sarah from our midst."

"No," came the soft reply. "I came only to see that Sarah was well, and to ask if you would permit her pet to be with her."

"Gladly," Mem'sab said. "Though I might question which of the two was the pet!"

"Clever bird!" said Grey.

I enjoyed the characters in "Grey" so much that I decided to write another novella for this anthology using the same characters. You might think of Mem'sab Harton as the Victorian version of Diana Tregarde, sans *vampire boyfriend. I'm toying with the idea of doing an entire book about the Harton School, Nan, Sarah, and Grey, and I'd be interested to hear if anyone besides parrot-lovers would want to read it.*

Grey's Ghost

When Victoria was the Queen of England, there was a small, unprepossessing school for the children of expatriate Englishmen that had quite an interesting reputation in the shoddy Whitechapel neighborhood on which it bordered, a reputation that kept the students safer than all the bobbies in London.

Once, a young, impoverished beggar-girl named Nan Killian had obtained leftovers at the back gate, and most of the other waifs and gutter-rats of the neighborhood shunned the place, though they gladly shared in Nan's bounty when she dared the gate and its guardian.

But now another child picked up food at the back gate of the Harton School For Boys and Girls on the edge of Whitechapel in London, not Nan Killian. Children no longer shunned the back gate of the school, although they treated its inhabitants with extreme caution. Adults—particularly the criminal, disreputable criminals who preyed on children—treated the place and its inhabitants with a great deal more than mere caution. Word had gotten around that two child-pimps had tried to take one of the pupils, and had been found with arms and legs broken, beaten senseless. Word had followed that anyone who threatened another child protected by the school would be found dead—*if* he was found at all.

The two tall, swarthy "blackfellas" who served as the school's guards were rumored to have strange powers, or be members of the *thugee* cult, or worse. It was safer just to pretend the school didn't exist and go about one's unsavory business elsewhere.

Nan Killian was no longer a child of the streets; she was now a pupil at the school herself, a transmutation that astonished her every morning when she awoke. To find herself in a neat little dormitory room, papered with roses, curtained in gingham, made her often feel as if she was dreaming. To then rise with the other girls, dress in clean, fresh clothing, and go off to lessons in the hitherto unreachable realms of reading and writing was more than she had ever dared dream of.

Her best friend was still Sarah, the little girl from Africa who had brought her that first basket of leftovers. But now she slept in the next bed over from Sarah's, and they shared many late-night giggles and confidences, instead of leftover tea-bread.

Nan also had a job; she had discovered, somewhat to her own bemusement, that the littlest children instinctively trusted her and would obey her when they obeyed no-one else. So Nan "paid" for her tutoring and keep by helping Nadra, the babies' nurse, or "ayah," as they all called her. Nadra was from India, as were most of the servants, from the formidable guards, the Sikh Karamjit and the Gurkha Selim, to the cook, Maya. Mrs. Helen Harton—or Mem'sab, as everyone called her—

and her husband had once been expatriates in India themselves. Master Harton—called, with ultimate respect, Sahib Harton—now worked as an advisor to an import firm; his service in India had left him with a small pension, and a permanent limp. When he and his wife had returned and had learned quite by accident of the terrible conditions children returned to England often lived in, they had resolved that the children of their friends back in the Punjab, at least, would not have that terrible knowledge thrust upon them.

Here the children sent away in bewilderment by anxious parents fearing that they would sicken in the hot foreign lands found, not a cold and alien place with nothing they recognized, but the familiar sounds of Hindustani, the comfort and coddling of a native nanny, and the familiar curries and rice to eat. Their new home, if a little shabby, held furniture made familiar from their years in the bungalows. But most of all, they were not told coldly to "be a man" or "stop being a crybaby"—for here they found friendly shoulders to weep out their homesickness on. If there were no French Masters here, there *was* a great deal of love and care; if the furniture was unfashionable and shabby, the children were well-fed and rosy.

It never ceased to amaze Nan that more parents didn't send their children to the Harton School, but some folks mistakenly trusted relatives to take better care of their precious ones than strangers, and some thought that a school owned and operated by someone with a lofty reputation or a title was a wiser choice for a boy-child who would likely join the Civil Service when he came of age. And as for the girls, there would always be those who felt that lessons by French dancing-masters and language teachers, lessons on the harp and in water-color painting, were more valuable than a sound education in the same basics given to a boy.

Sometimes these parents learned their lessons the hard way.

✧ ✧ ✧

"Ready for m'lesson, Mem'sab," Nan called into the second-best parlor, which was Mem'sab's private domain. It was commonly understood that sometimes Mem'sab had to do odd things—"Important things that we don't need to know about," Sarah said wisely—and she might have to do them at a moment's notice. So it was better to announce oneself at the door before venturing over the threshold.

But today Mem'sab was only reading a book, and looked up at Nan with a smile that transformed her plain face and made her eyes bright and beautiful.

By now Nan had seen plenty of ladies who dressed in finer stuffs than Mem'sab's simple Artistic gown of common stuffs, made bright with embroidery courtesy of Maya. Nan had seen ladies who were acknowledged Beauties like Mrs. Lillie Langtry, ladies who obviously spent many hours in the hands of their dressers and hairdressers rather than pulling their hair up into a simple chignon from which little curling strands of brown-gold were always escaping. Mem'sab's jewelry was not of diamonds and gold, but odd, heavy pieces in silver and semi-precious gems. But in Nan's eyes, not one of those ladies was worth wasting a single glance upon.

Then again, Nan *was* a little prejudiced.

"Come in, Nan," the Headmistress said, patting the flowered sofa beside her invitingly. "You're doing much better already, you know. You have a quick ear."

"Thenkee, Mem'sab," Nan replied, flushing with pleasure. She, like any of the servants, would gladly have laid down her life for Mem'sab Harton; they all worshipped her blatantly, and a word of praise from their idol was worth more than a pocketful of sovereigns. Nan sat gingerly down on the chintz-covered sofa and smoothed her clean pinafore with an unconscious gesture of pride.

Mem'sab took a book of etiquette from the table beside her, and opened it, looking at Nan expectantly. "Go ahead, dear."

"Good morning, ma'am. How do you do? I am quite well. I trust your family is fine," Nan began, and waited for Mem'sab's response, which would be her cue for the next polite phrase. The point here was not that Nan needed to learn manners and mannerly speech, but that she needed to *lose* the dreadful cadence of the streets which would doom her to poverty forever, quite literally. Nan spoke the commonplace phrases slowly and with great care, as much care as Sarah took over her French. An accurate analogy, since the King's English, as spoken by the middle and upper classes, was nearly as much a foreign language to Nan as French and Latin were to Sarah.

She had gotten the knack of it by thinking of it exactly as a foreign language, once Mem'sab had proven to her how much better others would treat her if she didn't speak like a guttersnipe. She was still fluent in the language of the streets, and often went out with Karamjit as a translator when he went on errands that took him into the slums or Chinatown. But gradually her tongue became accustomed to the new cadences, and her habitual speech marked her less as "untouchable."

"Beautifully done," Mem'sab said warmly, when Nan finished her recitation. "Your new assignment will be to pick a poem and recite it to me, properly spoken, and memorized."

"I think I'd loike—*like*—to do one uv Mr. Kipling's, Mem'sab," Nan said shyly.

Mem'sab laughed. "I hope you aren't thinking of 'Gunga Din,' you naughty girl!" the woman mock-chided. "It had better be one from the *Jungle Book*, or *Puck of Pook's Hill*, not something written in Cockney dialect!"

"Yes, Mem'sab, I mean, no, Mem'sab," Nan replied quickly. "I'll pick a right'un. Mebbe the lullaby for the White Seal?" Ever since discovering Rudyard Kipling's stories, Nan had been completely enthralled; Mem'sab often read them to the children as a go-to-bed treat, for the stories often evoked memories of India for the children sent away.

"That will do very well. Are you ready for the other lesson?" Mem'sab asked, so casually that no one but Nan would have known that the "other lesson" was one not taught in any other school in this part of the world.

"I—think so." Nan got up and closed the parlor door, signaling to all the world that she and Mem'sab were not to be disturbed unless someone was dying or the house was burning down.

For the next half hour, Mem'sab turned over cards, and Nan called out the next card before she turned it over. When the last of the fifty-two lay in the face-up pile before her, Nan waited expectantly for the results.

"Not at all bad; you had almost half of them, and all the colors right," Mem'sab said with content. Nan was disappointed; she knew that Mem'sab could call out all fifty-two without an error, though Sarah could only get the colors correctly.

"Sahib brought me some things from the warehouse for you to try your 'feeling' on," Mem'sab continued. "I truly think that is where you true Gifts lie, dear."

Nan sighed mournfully. "But knowin' the cards would be a lot more *useful*," she complained.

"What, so you can grow up to cheat foolish young men out of their inheritances?" Now Mem'sab actually laughed out loud. "Try it, dear, and the Gift will desert you at the time you need it most! No, be content with what you have and learn to use it wisely, to help yourself and others."

"But card-sharpin' *would* help me, an' I could use takin's to help others," Nan couldn't resist protesting, but she held out her hand for the first object anyway.

It was a carved beetle; very interesting, Nan thought, as she waited to "feel" what it would tell her. It felt like pottery or stone, and it was of a turquoise-blue, shaded with pale brown. "It's old," she said finally. Then, "*Really* old. Old as—Methusalum! It was made for an important man, but not a king or anything."

She tried for more, but couldn't sense anything else. "That's all," she said, and handed it back to Mem'sab.

"Now this." The carved beetle that Mem'sab gave her was, for all intents and purposes, identical to the one she'd just held, but immediately Nan sensed the difference.

"Piff! That 'un's new!" She also felt something else, something of *intent,* a sensation she readily identified since it was one of the driving forces behind commerce in Whitechapel. "Feller as made it figgers he's put one over on somebody."

"Excellent, dear!" Mem'sab nodded. "They are both *scarabs,* a kind of good-luck carving found with mummies—which are, indeed, often as old as Methuselah. The first one I knew was real, as I helped unwrap the mummy myself. The second, however, was from a shipment that Sahib suspected were fakes."

Nan nodded, interested to learn that this Gift of hers had some practical application after all. "So could be I could tell people when they been gammoned?"

"Very likely, and quite likely that they would pay you for the knowledge, as long as they don't think that *you* are trying to fool them as well. Here, try this." The next object placed in Nan's hand was a bit of jewelry, a simple silver brooch with "gems" of cut iron. Nan dropped it as soon as it touched her hand, overwhelmed by fear and horror.

"Lummy!" she cried, without thinking. "He *killed* her!"

Who "they" were, she had no sense of; that would require more contact, which she did *not* want to have. But Mem'sab didn't seem at all surprised; she just shook her head very sadly and put the brooch back in a little box which she closed without a word.

She held out a child's locket on a worn ribbon. "Don't be afraid, Nan," she coaxed, when Nan was reluctant to accept it, "This one isn't bad, I promise you."

Nan took the locket gingerly, but broke out into a smile when she got a feeling of warmth, contentment, and happiness. She waited for other images to come, and sensed a tired, but exceedingly happy woman, a proud man, and one—no, *two* strong and lively mites with the woman.

Slyly, Nan glanced up at her mentor. "She's 'ad twins, 'asn't she?" Nan asked. "When was it?"

"I just got the letter and the locket today, but it was about two months ago," Mem'sab replied. "The lady is my best friend's daughter, who was given that locket by her mother for luck just before the birth of her children. She sent it to me to have it duplicated, as she would like to present one to each little girl."

"I'd 'ave it taken apart, an' put half of th' old 'un with half of the new 'un," Nan suggested, and Mem'sab brightened at the idea.

"An excellent idea, and I will do just that. Now, dear, are you feeling tired? Have you a headache? We've gone on longer than we did at your last lesson."

Nan nodded, quite ready to admit to both.

Mem'sab gave her still-thin shoulders a little hug, and sent her off to her afternoon lessons.

Figuring came harder to Nan than reading; she'd already had some letters before she had arrived, enough to spell out the signs on shops and stalls and the like and make out a word here and there on a discarded broadsheet. When the full mystery of letters had been disclosed to her, mastery had come as naturally as breathing, and she was already able to read her beloved Kipling stories with minimal prompting. But numbers were a mystery arcane, and she struggled with the youngest of the children to comprehend what they meant. Anything past one hundred baffled her for the moment, and Sarah did her best to help her friend.

After arithmetic came geography, but for a child to whom Kensington Palace was the end of the universe, it was harder to believe in the existence of Arabia than of Fairyland, and Heaven was quite as real and solid as South America, for she reckoned that she had an equal chance of seeing either. As for how all those odd names and shapes fit together . . . well!

History came easier, although she didn't yet grasp that it was as real as yesterday, for to Nan it was just a chain of linking stories. Perhaps that was why she loved the Kipling stories so much, for she often felt as out-of-place as Mowgli when the human-tribe tried to reclaim him.

At the end of lessons Nan usually went to help Nadra in the nursery; the children there, ranging in age from two to five, were a handful when it came to getting them bathed and put to bed. They tried to put off bedtime as long as possible; there were a half-dozen of them, which was just enough that when Nadra had finally gotten two of them into a bathtub, the other four had escaped, and were running about the nursery like dripping, naked apes, screaming joyfully at their escape.

But tonight, Karamjit came for Nan and Sarah as soon as the history lesson was over, summoning them with a look and a gesture. As always, the African parrot Grey sat on Sarah's shoulder; she was so well-behaved, even to the point of being housebroken, that he was allowed to be with her from morning to night. The handsome grey parrot with the bright red tail had adapted very well to this new sort of jungle when Sarah's mother brought her to her daughter; Sarah was very careful to keep her warm and out of drafts, and she ate virtually the same food that she did. Mem'sab seemed to understand the kind of diet that let her thrive; she allowed her only a little of the chicken and beef, and made certain that she filled up on carrots and other vegetables before she got any of the curried rice she loved so much. In fact, she often pointed to Grey as an example to the other children who would rather have had sweets than green stuffs, telling them that Grey was smarter than they were, for *she* knew what would make her grow big and strong. Being unfavorably compared to a bird often made the difference with the little boys in particular, who were behaving better at table since the parrot came to live at the school.

So Grey came along when Karamjit brought them to the door of Mem'sab's parlor, cautioning them to wait quietly until Mem'sab called them.

"What do you suppose can be going on?" Sarah asked curiously, while Grey turned her head to look at Nan with her penetrating pale-yellow eyes.

Nan shushed her, pressing her ear to the keyhole to see what she could hear. "There's another lady in there with Mem'sab, and she sounds sad," Nan said at last.

Grey cocked her head to one side, then turned his head upside down as she sometimes did when something puzzled her. "Hurt," she said quietly, and made a little sound like someone crying.

Nan had long since gotten used to the fact that Grey noticed everything that went on around her and occasionally commented on it like a human person. If the wolves in the *Jungle Book* could think and talk, she reasoned, why not a parrot? She accepted Grey's abilities as casually as Sarah, who had raised her herself and had no doubt of the intelligence of her feathered friend.

Had either of them acquired the "wisdom" of their elders, they might have been surprised that Mem'sab accepted those abilities too.

Nan jumped back as footsteps warned her that the visitor had risen and was coming towards the door; she and Sarah pressed themselves back against the wall as the strange woman passed them, her face hidden behind a veil. She took no notice of the children, but turned back to Mem'sab.

"Katherine, I believe going to this woman is a grave mistake on your part," Mem'sab told her quietly. "You and I have been friends since we were in school together; you know that I would never advise you against anything you felt so strongly about unless I thought you might be harmed by it. This woman does you no good."

The woman shook her head. "How could I be harmed by it?" she replied, her voice trembling. "What *possible* ill could come of this?"

"A very great deal, I fear," Mem'sab, her expression some combination of concern and other emotions that Nan couldn't read.

Impulsively, the woman reached out for Mem'sab's hand. "Then come *with* me!" she cried. "If this woman cannot convince *you* that she is genuine, and that she provides me with what I need more than breath, then I will not see her again."

Mem'sab's eyes looked keenly into her friend's, easily defeating the concealment of the veil about her features. "You are willing to risk her unmasking as a fraud, and the pain for you that will follow?"

"I am certain enough of her that I know that you will be convinced, even against your will," the woman replied with certainty.

Mem'sab nodded. "Very well, then. You and I—and these two girls—will see her together."

Only now did the woman notice Sarah and Nan, and her brief glance dismissed them as unimportant. "I see no reason why you wish to have children along, but if you can guarantee they will behave, and that is what it takes you to be convinced to see Madame Varonsky, then so be it. I will have an invitation sent to you for the next seance."

Mem'sab smiled, and patted her friend's hand. "Sometimes children see things more clearly than we adults do," was all she replied. "I will be waiting for that invitation."

The woman squeezed Mem'sab's hand, then turned and left, ushered out by one of the native servants. Mem'sab gestured to the two girls to precede her into the parlor, and shut the door behind them.

"What did you think of the lady, Nan?" asked their

teacher, as the two children took their places side-by-side, on the loveseat they generally shared when they were in the parlor together.

Nan assessed the woman as would any street-child; economics came first. "She's in mournin' an' she's gentry," Nan replied automatically. "Silk gowns fer mournin' is somethin' only gentry kin afford. I 'spect she's easy t' gammon, too; paid no attention t'us, an' I was near enough t' get me hand into 'er purse an' her never knowin' till she was home. An' she didn' ask fer a cab t' be brung, so's I reckon she keeps 'er carriage. That's not jest gentry, tha's *quality*."

"Right on all counts, my dear," Mem'sab said, a bit grimly. "Katherine has no more sense than one of the babies, and never had. Her parents didn't spoil her, but they never saw any reason to educate her in practical matters. They counted on her finding a husband who would do all her thinking for her, and as a consequence, she is pliant to any hand that offers mastery. She married into money; her husband has a very high position in the Colonial Government. Nothing but the best school would do for her boy, and a spoiled little lad he was, too."

Grey suddenly began coughing, most realistically, a series of terrible, racking coughs, and Sarah turned her head to look into her eyes. Then she turned back to Mem'sab. "He's dead, isn't he?" the child said, quite matter-of-factly. "He got sick, and died. That's who she's in mourning for."

"Quite right, and as Grey showed us, he caught pneumonia." Mem'sab looked grim. "Poor food, icy rooms, and barbaric treatment—" She threw up her hands, and shook her head. "There's no reason to go on; at least Katherine has decided to trust her twins to us instead of the school her husband wanted. She'll bring them to Nadra tomorrow, Nan, and they'll probably be terrified, so I'm counting on you to help Nadra soothe them."

Nan could well imagine that they would be terrified; not only were they being left with strangers, but they would know, at least dimly, that their brother had come away to school and died. They would be certain that the same was about to happen to them.

"That, however, is not why I sent for you," Mem'sab continued. "Katherine is seeing a medium; do either of you know what that is?"

Sarah and Nan shook their heads, but Grey made a rude noise. Sarah looked shocked, but Nan giggled and Mem'sab laughed.

"I am afraid that Grey is correct in her opinions, for the most part," the woman told them. "A *medium* is a person who claims to speak with the dead, and help the souls of the dead speak to the living." Her mouth compressed, and Nan sensed her carefully controlled anger. "All this is accomplished for a very fine fee, I might add."

"Ho! Like them gypsy palm-readers, an' the conjure-men!" Nan exclaimed in recognition. "Aye, there's a mort'a gammon there, and that's sure. You reckon this lady's been gammoned, then?"

"Yes I do, and I would like you two—*three*—" she amended, with a penetrating look at Grey, "—to help me prove it. Nan, if there is trickery afoot, do you think you could catch it?"

Nan had no doubt. "I bet I could," she said. "Can't be harder'n keepin' a hand out uv yer pocket—or grabbin' the wrist once it's in."

"Good girl—you *must* remember to speak properly, and only when you're spoken to, though," Mem'sab warned her. "If this so-called medium thinks you are anything but a gently-reared child, she might find an excuse to dismiss the seance." She turned to Sarah. "Now, if by some incredible chance this woman *is* genuine, could you and Grey tell?"

Sarah's head bobbed so hard her curls tumbled into her eyes. "Yes, Mem'sab," she said, with as much confidence as Nan. "M'luko, the Medicine Man that gave me Grey, said that Grey could tell when the spirits were there, and someday I might, too."

"Did he, now?" Mem'sab gave her a curious look. "How interesting! Well, if Grey can tell us if there are spirits or not, that will be quite useful enough for our purposes. Are either of you afraid to go with me? I expect the invitation will come quite soon." Again, Mem'sab had that grim look. "Katherine is too choice a fish to be allowed to swim free for long; the Madame will want to keep her under her control by 'consulting' with her as often as possible."

Sarah looked to Nan for guidance, and Nan thought that her friend might be a little fearful, despite her brave words. But Nan herself only laughed. "I ain't afraid of nobody's sham ghost," she said, curling her lip scornfully. "An' I ain't sure I'd be afraid uv a *real* one."

"Wisely said, Nan; spirits can only harm us as much as we permit them to." Nan thought that Mem'sab looked relieved, like maybe she hadn't wanted to count on their help until she actually got it. "Thank you, both of you." She reached out and took their hands, giving them a squeeze that said a great deal without words. "Now, both of you get back to whatever it was that I took you from. I will let you know in plenty of time when our excursion will be."

It was past the babies' bed-time, so Sarah and Nan went together to beg Maya for their delayed tea, and carried the tray themselves up to the now-deserted nursery. They set out the tea-things on one of the little tables, feeling a mutual need to discuss Mem'sab's strange proposition.

Grey had her tea, too; a little bowl of curried rice, carrots, and beans. They set it down on the table and Grey climbed carefully down from Sarah's shoulder to the table-top, where she selected a bean and ate it neatly, holding in on one claw while she took small bites, watching them both.

"Do you think there might be real ghosts?" Sarah asked immediately, shivering a little. "I mean, what if this lady can bring real ghosts up?"

Grey and Nan made the same rude noise at the same time; it was easy to tell where Grey had learned it. "Garn!" Nan said scornfully. "Reckon that Mem'sab only ast if you could tell as an outside bet. *But* the livin' people might be the ones as is dangerous." She ate a bite of bread-and-butter thoughtfully. "I dunno as Mem'sab's thought that far, but that Missus Katherine's a right easy mark, an' a fat 'un, too. People as is willin' t' gammon the gentry *might* not be real happy about bein' found out."

Sarah nodded. "Should we tell Karamjit?" she asked, showing a great deal more common sense than she would have before Nan came into her life. "Mem'sab's thinking hard about her friend, but she might not think a bit about herself."

"Aye, an' Selim an' mebbe Sahib, too." Nan was a little dubious about that, having only seen the lordly Sahib from a distance.

"I'll ask Selim to tell Sahib, if you'll talk to Karamjit," Sarah said, knowing the surest route to the Master from her knowledge of the School and its inhabitants. "But tell me what to look for! Three sets of eyes are better than two."

"Fust thing, whatever they *want* you t' look at is gonna be what makes a fuss—noises or voices or whatever," Nan said after a moment of thought. "I dunno how this *medium* stuff is gonna work, but that's what happens when a purse gets nicked. You gotta get the mark's attention, so he won't be thinkin' of his pocket. So whatever they *want* us to look at, we look away from. That's the main thing. Mebbe Mem'sab can tell us what these things is s'pposed to be like—if I know what's t' happen, I kin guess what tricks they're like t' pull." She finished her bread and butter, and began her own curry; she'd quickly acquired a taste for the spicy Indian dishes that the other children loved. "If there ain't ghosts, I bet they got somebody dressed up t' *look* like one." She grinned slyly at Grey. "An' I betcha a good pinch or a bite would make 'im yell proper!"

"And you couldn't hurt a real ghost with a pinch." Sarah nodded. "I suppose we're just going to have to watch and wait, and see what we can do."

Nan, as always, ate as a street-child would, although her manners had improved considerably since coming to the School; she inhaled her food rapidly, so that no one would have a chance to take it from her. She was already finished, although Sarah hadn't eaten more than half of her tea. She put her plates aside on the tray, and propped her head up on her hands with her elbows on the table. "We got to talk to Karamjit an' Selim, that's the main thing," she said, thinking out loud. "They might know what we should do."

"Selim will come home with Sahib," Sarah answered, "But Karamjit is probably leaving the basket at the back gate right now, and if you run, you can catch him alone."

Taking that as her hint, for Sarah had a way of knowing where most people were at any given time, Nan jumped to her feet and ran out of the nursery and down the back stairs, flying through the kitchen, much to the amusement of the cook, Maya. She burst through the kitchen door, and ran down the path to the back gate, so quickly she hardly felt the cold at all, though she had run outside without a coat. Mustafa swept the garden paths free of snow every day, but so soon after Boxing Day there were mounds of the stuff on either side of the path, snow with a faint tinge of gray from the soot that plagued London in almost every weather.

Nan saw the Sikh, Karamjit, soon enough to avoid bouncing off his legs. The tall, dark, immensely dignified man was bundled up to the eyes in a heavy quilted coat and two mufflers, his head wrapped in a dark brown turban. Nan no longer feared him, though she respected him as only a street child who has seen a superior fighter in action could. "Karamjit!" she called, as she slowed her headlong pace. "I need t' talk wi' ye!"

There was an amused glint in the Sikh's dark eyes, though only much association with him allowed Nan to see it. "And what does Missy Nan wish to speak of that she comes racing out into the cold like the wind from the mountains?"

"Mem'sab ast us t' help her with somethin'—there's this lady as is a *meedeeyum* that she thinks is gammonin' her friend. We—tha's Sarah an' Grey an' me—we says a'course, but—" Here Nan stopped, because she wasn't entirely certain how to tell an adult that she thought another adult didn't know what she was getting herself into. "I just got a bad feelin'," she ended, lamely.

But Karamjit did not belittle her concerns, nor did he chide her. Instead, his eyes grew even darker, and he nodded. "Come inside, where it is warm," he said, "I wish you to tell me more."

He sat her down at the kitchen table, and gravely and respectfully asked Maya to serve them both tea. He took his with neither sugar nor cream, but saw to it that Nan's was heavily sweetened and at least half milk. "Now," he said, after she had warmed herself with the first sip, "Tell me all."

Nan related everything that had happened from the time he came to take both of them to the parlor to when she had left Sarah to find him. He nodded from time to time, as he drank tea and unwound himself from his mufflers and coat.

"I believe this," he said when she had finished. "I believe that Mem'sab is a wise, good, and brave woman. I also believe that *she* does not think that helping her friend will mean any real danger. But the wise, the good, and the brave often do not think as the mean, the bad, and the cowardly do—the jackals that feed on the pain of others will turn to devour those who threaten their meal. And a man can die from the bite of a jackal as easily as that of a tiger."

"So you think my bad feelin' was right?" Nan's relief was total; not that she didn't trust Mem'sab, but—Mem'sab didn't know the kind of creatures that Nan did.

"Indeed I do—but I believe that it would do no good to try to persuade Mem'sab that she should not try to help her friend." Karamjit smiled slightly, the barest lifting of the corners of his mouth. "Nevertheless, Sahib will know how best to protect her without insulting her great courage." He placed one of his long, brown hands on Nan's shoulder. "You may leave it in our hands, Missy Nan—though we may ask a thing or two of you, that we can do our duty with no harm to Mem'sab's own plans. For now, though, you may simply rely upon us."

"Thenkee, Karamjit," Nan sighed. He patted her shoulder, then unfolded his long legs and rose from his chair with a slight bow to Maya. Then he left the kitchen, allowing Nan to finish her tea and run back up to the nursery, to give Sarah and Grey the welcome news that they would not be the only ones concerned with the protection of Mem'sab from the consequences of her own generous nature.

Sahib took both Nan and Sarah aside just before bedtime, after Karamjit and Selim had been closeted with him for half an hour. "Can I ask you two to come to my study with me for a bit?" he asked quietly. He was often thought to be older than Mem'sab, by those who were deceived by the streaks of grey at each temple, the stiff way that he walked, and the odd expression in his eyes, which seemed to Nan to be the eyes of a man who had seen so much that nothing surprised him anymore. Nan had trusted him the moment that she set eyes on him, although she couldn't have said why.

"So long as Nadra don't fuss," Nan replied for both of them. Sahib smiled, his eyes crinkling at the corners.

"I have already made it right with Nadra," he promised. "Karamjit, Selim, and Mem'sab are waiting for us."

Nan felt better immediately, for she really hadn't wanted to go sneaking around behind Mem'sab's back. From the look that Sarah gave her, Nan reckoned that she felt the same.

"Thank you, sir," Sarah said politely. "We will do just as you say."

Very few of the children had ever been inside the sacred precincts of Sahib's office; the first thing that struck Nan was that it did *not* smell of tobacco, but of sandalwood and cinnamon. That surprised her; most of the men she knew smoked although their womenfolk disapproved of the habit, but evidently Sahib did not, not even in his own private space.

There was a tiger-skin on the carpet in front of the fire, the glass eyes in its head glinting cruelly in a manner unnerving and lifelike. Nan shuddered, and thought of Shere Khan, with his taste for man-cub. Had this been another terrible killer of the jungle? Did tigers leave vengeful ghosts?

Heavy, dark drapes of some indeterminate color shut out the cold night. Hanging on the walls, which had been papered with faded gold arabesque upon a ground of light brown, was a jumble of mementos from Sahib's life in India: crossed spears, curious daggers and swords, embroidered tapestries of strange characters twined with exotic flowers and birds, carved plaques of some heavy, dark wood inlaid with brass, bizarre masks that resembled nothing less than brightly painted demons. On the desk and adorning the shelves between the books were statues of half- and fully-naked gods and goddesses, more bits of carving in wood, stone, and ivory. Bookshelves built floor-to-ceiling held more books than Nan had known existed. Sahib took his place behind his desk, while Mem'sab perched boldly on the edge of it. Selim and Karamjit stood beside the fire like a pair of guardian statues themselves, and Sahib gestured to the children to take their places on the over-stuffed chairs on either side of the fireplace. Nan waited tensely, wondering if

Mem'sab was going to be angry because they went to others with their concerns. Although it had not fallen out so here, she was far more used to being in trouble over something she had done than in being encouraged for it, and the reflexes were still in place.

"Karamjit tells me that you four share some concern over my planned excursion to the medium, Nan," Mem'sab said, with a smile that told Nan she was *not* in trouble for her meddling, as she had feared. "They went first to Sahib, but as we never keep secrets from one another, he came to me. And I commend all four of you for your concern and caution, for after some discussion, I was forced to agree with it."

"And I would like to commend both of you, Nan, Sarah, for having the wisdom to go to an adult with your concerns," added Sahib, with a kindly nod to both of them that Nan had not expected in the least. "That shows great good sense, and please, continue to do so in the future."

"I thought—I was afeared—" Nan began, then blurted out all that she'd held in check. "Mem'sab is 'bout the smartest, goodest lady there is, but she don't *know* bad people! Me, I know! I seed 'em, an' I figgered that they weren't gonna lay down an' lose their fat mark without a fight!"

"And very wise you were to remind us of that," Sahib said gravely. "I pointed out to Mem'sab that we have no way of knowing *where* this medium is from, and she is just as likely to be a criminal as a lady—more so, in fact. Just because she speaks, acts, and dresses like a lady, and seeks her clients from among the gentry, means nothing; she could easily have a crew of thugs as her accomplices."

"As you say, Sahib," Karamjit said gravely. "For, as it is said, it is a short step from a deception to a lie, from a lie to a cheat, from a cheat to a theft, and from a theft to a murder."

Mem'sab blushed. "I will admit that I was very angry

with you at first, but when my anger cooled, it was clear that your reasoning was sound. And after all, am I some Gothic heroine to go wide-eyed into the villains' lair, never suspecting trouble? So, we are here to plan what we *all* shall do to free Katherine of her dangerous obsession."

"Me, I needta know what this see-ants is gonna be like, Mem'sab," Nan put in, sitting on the edge of the chair tensely. "What sorta things happens?"

"Generally, the participants are brought into a room that has a round table with chairs circling it." Mem'sab spoke directly to Nan as if to an adult, which gave Nan a rather pleasant, if shivery, feeling. "The table often has objects upon it that the spirits will supposedly move; often a bell, a tambourine and a megaphone are among them, though why spirits would feel the need to play upon a tambourine when they never had that urge in life is quite beyond me!"

She laughed, as did Sahib; the girls giggled nervously.

"At any rate, the participants are asked to sit down and hold hands. Often the medium is tied to the chair; her hands are secured to the arms, and her feet to the legs." Nan noticed that Mem'sab used the word "legs" rather than the mannerly "limbs," and thought the better of her for that. "The lights are brought down, and the seance begins. Most often objects are moved, including the table, the tambourine is played, the bell is rung, all as a sign that the spirits have arrived. The spirits most often speak by means of raps on the table, but Katherine tells me that the spirit of her little boy spoke directly, through the floating megaphone. Sometimes a spirit will actually appear; in this case, it was just a glowing face of Katherine's son."

Nan thought that over for a moment. "Be simple 'nuff t' tilt the chair an' get yer legs free by slippin the rope down over the chair-feet," she observed, "An' all ye hev t' do is have chair-arms as isn't glued t' *their* pegs, an' ye got yer arms free too. Be easy enough to make all kind uv things dance about when ye got arms free. Be easy 'nuff t' make th' table lift if's light enough, an' rap on it, too."

Sahib stared at her in astonishment. "I do believe that you are the most valuable addition to our household in a long time, young lady!" he said with delight that made Nan blush. "I would never have thought of any of that."

"I dunno how ye'd make summat glow, though," Nan admitted.

"Oh, *I* know that," Sarah said casually. "There's stuff that grows in rotten wood that makes a glow; some of the magic-men use it to frighten people at night. It grows in swamps, so it probably grows in England, too."

Karamjit grinned, his teeth very white in his dark face, and Selim nodded with pride. "What is it that the Black Robe's Book says, Sahib? Out of the mouths of babes comes wisdom?"

Mem'sab nodded. "I should have told you more, earlier," she said ruefully. "Well, that's mended in time. Now we all know what to look for."

Grey clicked her beak several times, then exclaimed, "Ouch!"

"Grey is going to try to bite whatever comes near her," Sarah explained.

"I don't want her venturing off your arm," Mem'sab cautioned. "I won't chance her getting hurt." She turned to Sahib. "The chances are, the room we will be in will have very heavy curtains to prevent light from entering or escaping, so if you and our warriors are outside, you won't know what room we are in."

"Then I'd like one of you girls to exercise childish curiosity and go *immediately* to a window and look out," Sahib told them. "At least one of us will be where we can see both the front and the back of the house. Then if there is trouble, one of you signal us and we'll come to the rescue."

"Just like the shining knights you are, all three of you," Mem'sab said warmly, laying her hand over the one Sahib had on the desk. "I think that is as much of a plan as we can lay, since we really don't know what we will find in that house."

"It's enough, I suspect," Sahib replied. "It allows two of us to break into the house if necessary, while one goes for the police." He stroked his chin thoughtfully with his free hand. "Or better yet, I'll take a whistle; that will summon help in no time." He glanced up at Mem'sab. "What time did you say the invitation specified?"

"Seven," she replied promptly. "Well after dark, although Katherine tells me that *her* sessions are usually later, nearer midnight."

"The medium may anticipate some trouble from sleepy children," Sahib speculated. "But that's just a guess." He stood up, still holding his wife's hand, and she slid off her perch on the desk and turned to face them. "Ladies, gentlemen, I think we are as prepared as we can be for trouble. So let us get a good night's sleep, and hope that we will not find any."

Then Sahib did a surprising thing; he came around his desk, limping stiffly, and bent over Nan and took her hand. "Perhaps only I of all of us can realize how brave you were to confide your worry to an adult you have only just come to trust, Nan," he said, very softly, then grinned at her so impishly that she saw the little boy he must have been in the eyes of the mature man. "Ain't no doubt 'uv thet, missy. Yer a cunnin' moit, an' 'ad more blows then pats, Oi reckon," he continued in street cant, shocking the breath out of her. "I came up the same way you are now, dear, thanks to a very kind man with no son of his own. I want you to remember that to us here at this school, there is no such thing as a stupid question, nor will we dismiss *any* worry you have as trivial. Never fear to bring either to an adult."

He straightened up, as Mem'sab came to his side, nodding. "Now both of you try and get some sleep, for every warrior knows that sleep is more important than anything else before a battle."

Ha, Nan thought, as she and Sarah followed Karamjit out of the study. *There's gonna be trouble; I kin feel it, an' so can* he. *He didn' get that tiger by not havin' a nose fer trouble. But—I reckon the trouble's gonna have its hands full with him.*

The medium lived in a modest house just off one of the squares in the part of London that housed those clerks and the like with pretensions to a loftier address than their purses would allow, an area totally unfamiliar to Nan. The house itself had seen better days, though, as had most of the other homes on that dead-end street, and Nan suspected that it was rented. The houses had that peculiarly faded look that came when the owners of a house did not actually live there, and those who did had no reason to care for the property themselves, assuming that was the duty of the landlord.

Mem'sab had chosen her gown carefully, after discarding a walking-suit, a mourning-gown and veil, and a peculiar draped garment she called a *sari*, a souvenir of her time in India. The first, she thought, made her look untrusting, sharp, and suspicious, the second would not be believed had the medium done any research on the backgrounds of these new sitters, and the third smacked of mockery. She chose instead one of the plain, simple gowns she preferred, in the mode called "Artistic Reform"; not particularly stylish, but Nan thought it was a good choice. For one thing, she could move in it; it was looser than the highest mode, and did not require tight corseting. If Mem'sab needed to run, kick, or dodge, she could.

The girls followed her quietly, dressed in their starched pinafores and dark dresses, showing the best possible manners, with Grey tucked under Sarah's coat to stay warm until they got within doors.

It was quite dark as they mounted the steps to the

house and rang the bell. It was answered by a sour-faced woman in a plain black dress, who ushered them into a sitting room and took their coats, with a startled glance at Grey as he popped her head out of the front of Sarah's jacket. She said nothing, however, and neither did Grey as she climbed to Sarah's shoulder.

The woman returned a moment later, but not before Nan had heard the faint sounds of surreptitious steps on the floor above them. She knew it had not been the sour woman, for she had clearly heard *those* steps going off to a closet and returning. If the seance-room was on this floor, then, there was someone else above.

The sitting-room had been decorated in a very odd style. The paintings on the wall were all either religious in nature, or extremely morbid, at least so far as Nan was concerned. There were pictures of women weeping over graves, of angels lifting away the soul of a dead child, of a woman throwing herself to her death over a cliff, of the spirits of three children hovering about a man and woman mourning over pictures held in their listless hands. There was even a picture of a girl crying over a dead bird lying in her hand.

Crystal globes on stands decorated the tables, along with bouquets of funereal lilies whose heavy, sweet scent dominated the chill room. The tables were all draped in fringed cloths of a deep scarlet. The hard, severe furniture was either of wood or upholstered in prickly horsehair. The two lamps had been lit before they entered the room, but their light, hampered as it was by heavy brocade lamp shades, cast more shadows than illumination.

They didn't have to wait long in that uncomfortable room, for the sour servant departed for a moment, then returned, and conducted them into the next room.

This, evidently, was only an antechamber to the room of mysteries; heavy draperies swathed all the walls, and there were straight-backed chairs set against them on all four walls. The lily-scent pervaded this room as well, mixed with another, that Nan recognized as the Hindu incense that Nadra often burned in her own devotions.

There was a single picture in this room, on the wall opposite the door, with a candle placed on a small table beneath it so as to illuminate it properly. This was a portrait in oils of a plump woman swathed in pale draperies, her hands clasped melodramatically before her breast, her eyes cast upwards. Smoke, presumably that of incense, swirled around her, with the suggestion of faces in it. Nan was no judge of art, but Mem'sab walked up to it and examined it with a critical eye.

"Neither good nor bad," she said, measuringly. "I would say it is either the work of an unknown professional or a talented amateur."

"A talented amateur," said the lady that Mem'sab had called "Katherine," as she too was ushered into the chamber. "My dear friend Lady Harrington painted it; it was she who introduced me to Madame Varonsky." Mem'sab turned to meet her, and Katherine glided across the floor to take her hand in greeting. "It is said to be a very speaking likeness," she continued. "I certainly find it so."

Nan studied the woman further, but saw nothing to change her original estimation. Katherine wore yet another mourning gown of expensive silk and mohair, embellished with jet beadwork and fringes that shivered with the slightest movement. A black hat with a full veil perched on her carefully coiffed curls, fair hair too dark to be called golden, but not precisely brown either. Her full lips trembled, even as they uttered words of polite conversation, her eyes threatened to fill at every moment, and Nan thought that her weak chin reflected an overly sentimental and vapid personality. It was an assessment that was confirmed by her conversation with Mem'sab, conversation that Nan ignored in favor of listening for other sounds. Over their heads, the floor creaked softly as someone moved to and fro, trying very hard to be quiet. There were also some odd scratching sounds that didn't sound like mice, and once, a dull thud, as of something heavy being set down a little too hard.

Something was going on up there, and the person doing it didn't want them to notice.

At length the incense-smell grew stronger, and the drapery on the wall to the right of the portrait parted, revealing a door, which opened as if by itself.

Taking that as their invitation, Katherine broke off her small talk to hurry eagerly into the sacred precincts; Mem'sab gestured to the girls to precede her, and followed on their heels. By previous arrangement, Nan and Sarah, rather than moving towards the circular table at which Madame Varonsky waited, went to the two walls likeliest to hold windows behind their heavy draperies before anyone could stop them.

It was Nan's luck to find a corner window overlooking the street, and she made sure that some light from the room within flashed to the watcher on the opposite side before she dropped the drapery.

"Come away from the windows, children," Mem'sab said in a voice that gently chided. Nan and Sarah immediately turned back to the room, and Nan assessed the foe.

Madame Varonsky's portraitist had flattered her; she was decidedly paler than she had been painted, with a complexion unpleasantly like wax. She wore similar draperies, garments which could have concealed anything. The smile on her thin lips did not reach her eyes, and she regarded the parrot on Sarah's shoulder with distinct unease.

"You did not warn me about the bird, Katherine," the woman said, her voice rather reedy.

"The bird will be no trouble, Madame Varonsky," Mem'sab soothed. "It is better behaved than a good many of my pupils."

"Your pupils—I am not altogether clear on why they were brought," Madame Varonsky replied, turning her sharp black eyes on Nan and Sarah.

"Nan is an orphan, and wants to learn what she can of her parents, since she never knew them," Mem'sab said smoothly. "And Sarah lost a little brother to an African fever."

"Ah." Madame Varonsky's suspicions diminished, and she gestured to the chairs around the table. "Please, all of you, do take your seats, and we can begin at once."

As with the antechamber, this room had walls swathed in draperies, which Nan decided could conceal an entire army if Madame Varonsky were so inclined. The only furnishings besides the seance table and chairs were a sinuous statue of a female completely enveloped in draperies on a draped table, with incense burning before it in a small charcoal brazier of brass and cast iron.

The table at which Nan took her place was very much as Mem'sab had described. A surreptitious bump as Nan took her seat on Mem'sab's left hand proved that it was quite light and easy to move; it would be possible to lift it with one hand with no difficulty at all. On the draped surface were some of the objects Mem'sab had described; a tambourine, a megaphone, a little hand-bell. There were three lit candles in a brass candlestick in the middle of the table, and some objects Nan had not expected—a fiddle and bow, a rattle, and a pair of handkerchiefs.

This is where we're supposed to look, Nan realized, as Sarah took her place on Mem'sab's right, next to Madame Varonsky, and Katherine on Nan's left, flanking the medium on the other side. She wished she could look *up*, as Grey was unashamedly doing, her head over to one side as one eye peered upwards at the ceiling above them.

"If you would follow dear Katherine's example, child," said Madame, as Katherine took one of the hand-kerchiefs and used it to tie the medium's wrist to the arm of her chair. She smiled crookedly. "This is to assure you that I am not employing any trickery." Sarah, behaving with absolute docility, did the same on the other side, but cast Nan a knowing look as she finished. Nan knew what that meant; Sarah had tried the arm of the chair and found it loose.

"Now, if you all will hold hands, we will beseech the spirits to attend on us." The medium turned her attention to Mem'sab as Katherine and Sarah stretched their arms across the table to touch hands, and the rest reached for the hands of their partners. "Pray do not be alarmed when the candles are extinguished; the spirits are shy of light, for they are so delicate that it can destroy them. They will put out the candles themselves."

For several long moments they sat in complete silence, as the incense smoke thickened and curled around. Then although there wasn't a single breath of moving air in the room, the candle-flames began to dim, one by one, and go out!

Nan felt the hair on the back of her neck rising, for this was a phenomena she could not account for—to distract herself, she looked up quickly at the ceiling just in time to see a faint line of light in the form of a square vanish.

She felt better immediately. However the medium had extinguished the candles, it had to be a trick. If she had any real powers, she wouldn't need a trapdoor in the ceiling of her seance-room. As she looked back down, she realized that the objects on the table were all glowing with a dim, greenish light.

"Spirits, are you with us?" Madame Varonsky called. Nan immediately felt the table begin to lift.

Katherine gasped; Mem'sab gave Nan's hand a squeeze; understanding immediately what she wanted, Nan let go of it. Now Mem'sab was free to act as she needed.

"The spirits are strong tonight," Madame murmured, as the table settled again. "Perhaps they will give us a further demonstration of their powers."

Exactly on cue, the tambourine rose into the air, shaking uncertainly; first the megaphone joined it, then the rattle, then the hand-bell, all floating in mid-air, or seeming to. But Nan was looking *up,* not at the objects, and saw a very dim square, too dim to be called *light,* above the table. A deeper shadow moved back and forth over that area, and Nan's lip curled with contempt. She had no difficulty in imagining how the objects were "levitating"; one by one, they'd been pulled up by wires or black strings, probably hooked by means of a fishing-rod from the room above.

Now rapping began on the table, to further distract their attention. Madame began to ask questions.

"Is there a spirit here for Helen Harton?" she asked. One rap—that was a *no;* not surprising, since the medium probably wouldn't want to chance making a mistake with an adult. "Is there a spirit here for Katherine Boughmont?" Two raps—yes. "Is this the spirit of a child?" Two raps, and already Katherine had begun to weep softly. "Is it the spirit of her son, Edward?" Two raps plus the bell rang and the rattle and tambourine played, and Nan found herself feeling very sorry for the poor, silly woman.

"Are there other spirits here tonight?" Two raps. "Is there a spirit for the child Nan?" Two raps. "Is it her father?" One rap. "Her mother?" Two raps, and Nan had to control her temper, which flared at that moment. She knew very well that her mother was still alive, though at the rate she was going, she probably wouldn't be for long, what with the gin and the opium and the rest of her miserable life. But if she had been a young orphan, her parents dead in some foreign land like one or two of the other pupils, what would she not have given for the barest word from them, however illusory? Would she not have been willing to believe anything that sounded warm and kind?

There appeared to be no spirit for Sarah, which was just as well. Madame Varonsky was ready to pull out the next of her tricks, for the floating objects settled to the table again.

"My spirit-guide was known in life as the great Paganini, the master violinist," Madame Varonsky announced. "As music is the food of the soul, he will employ the same sweet music he made in life to bridge the gap between our world and the next. Listen, and he will play this instrument before us!"

Fiddle music appeared to come from the instrument on the table, although the bow did not actually move across the strings. Katherine gasped.

"Release the child's hand a moment and touch the violin, dear Katherine," the medium said, in a kind, but distant voice. Katherine evidently let go of Sarah's hand, since she still had hold of Nan's, and the shadow of her fingers rested for a moment on the neck of the fiddle.

"The strings!" she cried. "Helen, the strings are vibrating as they are played!"

If this was supposed to be some great, long-dead music-master, Nan didn't think much of his ability. If she wasn't mistaken, the tune he was playing was the child's chant of "London Bridge Is Falling Down," but played very, very slowly, turning it into a solemn dirge.

"Touch the strings, Helen!" Katherine urged. "See for yourself!"

Nan felt Mem'sab lean forward, and another hand-shadow fell over the strings. "They are vibrating. . . ." she said, her voice suddenly uncertain.

The music ground to a halt before she took her hand away—and until this moment, Grey had been as silent as a stuffed bird on a lady's hat. Now she did something.

She began to sing. It was a very clever imitation of a fiddle, playing a jig-tune that a street-musician often played at the gate of the School, for the pennies the pupils would throw to him.

She quit almost immediately, but not before Mem'sab took her hand away from the strings, and Nan sensed that somehow Grey had given her the clue she needed to solve that particular trick.

But the medium must have thought that her special spirit was responsible for that scrap of jig-tune, for she didn't say or do anything.

Nan sensed that all of this was building to the main turn, and so it was.

Remembering belatedly that she should be keeping an eye on that suspicious square above. She glanced up just in time to see it disappear. As the medium began to moan and sigh, calling on Paganini, Nan kept her eye on the ceiling. Sure enough, the dim line of light appeared again, forming a greyish square. Then the lines of the square thickened, and Nan guessed that a square platform was being lowered from above.

Pungent incense smoke thickened about them, filling Nan's nose and stinging her eyes so that they watered, and she smothered a sneeze. It was hard to breathe, and there was something strangely, disquietingly familiar about the scent.

The medium's words, spoken in a harsh, accented voice, cut through the smoke. "I, the great Paganini, am here among you!"

Once again, Katherine gasped.

"Harken and be still! Lo, the spirits gather!"

Nan's eyes burned, and for a moment, she felt very dizzy; she thought that the soft glow in front of her was due to nothing more than eyestrain, but the glow strengthened, and she blinked in shock as two vague shapes took form amid the writhing smoke.

For a new brazier, belching forth such thick smoke that the coals were invisible, had "appeared" in the center of the table, just behind the candlestick. It was above this brazier that the glowing shapes hovered, and slowly took on an identifiable form. Nan felt dizzier, sick; the room seemed to turn slowly around her.

The faces of a young woman and a little boy looked vaguely out over Nan's head from the cloud of smoke. Katherine began to weep—presumably she thought she recognized the child as her own. But the fact that the young woman looked *nothing* like Nan's mother (and in fact, looked quite a bit like the sketch in an advertisement for Bovril in the *Times*) woke Nan out of her mental haze.

And so did Grey.

She heard the flapping of wings as Grey plummeted to the floor. She sneezed urgently, and shouted aloud, "Bad air! Bad air!"

And *that* was the moment when she knew what it was that was so familiar in the incense smoke, and why she felt as tipsy as a sailor on shore leave.

"*Hashish!*" she choked, trying to shout, and not managing very well. She knew this scent; on the rare occasions when her mother could afford it—and before she'd turned to opium—she'd smoked it in preference to drinking. Nan could only think of one thing; that she *must* get fresh air in here before they all passed out!

She shoved her chair back and staggered up and out of it; it fell behind her with a clatter that seemed muffled in the smoke. She groped for the brazier as the two faces continued to stare, unmoved and unmoving, from the thick billows. Her hands felt like a pair of lead-filled mittens; she had to fight to stay upright as she swayed like a drunk. She didn't find it, but her hands closed on the cool, smooth surface of the crystal ball.

That was good enough; before the medium could stop her, she heaved up the heavy ball with a grunt of effort, and staggered to the window. She half-spun and flung the ball at the draperies hiding the unseen window; it hit the drapes and carried them into the glass, crashing through it, taking the drapery with it.

A gush of cold air, as fresh as air in London ever got, streamed in through the broken panes, as bedlam erupted in the room behind Nan.

She dropped to the floor, ignoring everything around her for the moment, as she breathed in the air tainted only with smog, waiting for her head to clear. Grey ran to her and huddled with her rather than joining her beloved mistress in the poisonous smoke.

Katherine shrieked in hysteria, there was a man as well as the medium shouting, and Mem'sab cursed all of them in some strange language. Grey gave a terrible shriek and half-ran, half flew away. Nan fought her dizziness and disorientation; looked up to see that Mem'sab was struggling in the grip of a stringy fellow she didn't recognize. Katherine had been backed up into one corner by the medium, and Sarah and Grey were pummeling the medium with small fists and wings. Mem'sab kicked at her captor's shins and stamped on his feet with great effect, as his grunts of pain demonstrated.

Nan struggled to her feet, guessing that *she* must have been the one worst affected by the hashish fumes. She wanted to run to Mem'sab's rescue, but she couldn't get her legs to work. In a moment the sour-faced woman would surely break into the room, turning the balance in favor of the enemy—

The door *did* crash open behind her just as she thought that, and she tried to turn to face the new foe—

But it was not the foe.

Sahib charged through the broken door, pushing past Nan to belabor the man holding Mem'sab with his cane; within three blows the man was on the floor, moaning. Before Nan fell, Karamjit caught her and steadied her. More men flooded into the room, and Nan let Karamjit steer her out of the way, concentrating on those steadying breaths of air. She thought perhaps that she passed out of consciousness for a while, for when she next noticed anything, she was sitting bent over in a chair, with Karamjit hovering over her, frowning. At some point the brazier had been extinguished, and a policeman was collecting the ashes and the remains of the drug-laced incense.

Finally her head cleared; by then, the struggle was over. The medium and her fellow tricksters were in the custody of the police, who had come with Sahib when Nan threw the crystal ball through the window. Sahib was talking to a policeman with a sergeant's badge, and Nan guessed that he was explaining what Mem'sab and Katherine were doing here. Katherine wept in a corner, comforted by Mem'sab. The police had brought lamps into the seance-room from the sitting-room, showing all too clearly how the medium had achieved her work; a hatch in the ceiling to the room above, through which things could be lowered; a magic-lantern behind the drapes, which had cast its image of a woman and boy onto the thick brazier smoke. That, and the disorienting effect of the hashish had made it easy to trick the clients.

Finally the bobbies took their captives away, and Katherine stopped crying. Nan and Sarah sat on the chairs Karamjit had set up, watching the adults, Grey on her usual perch on Sarah's shoulder. A cushion stuffed in the broken window cut off most of the cold air from outside.

"I can't believe I was so foolish!" Katherine moaned. "But—I wanted to see Edward so very much—"

"I hardly think that falling for a clever deception backed by drugs makes you foolish, ma'am," Sahib said gravely. "But you are to count yourself fortunate in the loyalty of your friends, who were willing to place themselves in danger for you. I do not think that these people would have been willing to stop at mere fraud, and neither do the police."

His last words made no impression on Katherine, at least none that Nan saw—but she did turn to Mem'sab and clasp her hand fervently. "I thought so ill of you, that you would not believe in Madame," she said tearfully. "Can you forgive me?"

Mem'sab smiled. "Always, my dear," she said, in the voice she used to soothe a frightened child. "Since your motive was to enlighten me, not to harm me—and your motive in seeking your poor child's spirit—"

A chill passed over Nan at that moment that had

nothing to do with the outside air. She looked sharply at Sarah, and saw a very curious thing.

There was a very vague and shimmery shape standing in front of Sarah's chair; Sarah looked at it with an intense and thoughtful gaze, as if she was listening to it. More than that, Grey was doing the same. Nan got the distinct impression that it was asking her friend for a favor.

Grey and Sarah exchanged a glance, and the parrot nodded once, as grave and sober as a parson, then spread her wings as if sheltering Sarah like a chick.

The shimmering form melted into Sarah; her features took on a mischievous expression that Nan had never seen her wear before, and she got up and went directly to Katherine.

The woman looked up at her, startled at the intrusion of a child into an adult discussion, then paled at something she saw in Sarah's face.

"Oh, Mummy, you don't have to be so sad," Sarah said in a curiously hollow, piping soprano. "I'm all right, really, and it wasn't your fault anyway, it was that horrid Lord Babbington that made you and Papa send me to Overton. But you *must* stop crying, please! Laurie is already scared of being left, and you're scaring her more."

Now, Nan knew very well that Mem'sab had not said anything about a Lord Babbington, nor did she and Sarah know what school the poor little boy had been sent to. Yet, she wasn't frightened; in fact, the protective but calm look in Grey's eye made her feel rather good, as if something inside her told her that everything was going wonderfully well.

The effect on Katherine was not what Nan had expected, either.

She reached out tentatively, as if to touch Sarah's face, but stopped short. "This *is* you, isn't it, darling?" she asked in a whisper.

Sarah nodded—or was it Edward who nodded? "Now,

I've *got* to go, Mummy, and I can't come back. So don't look for me, and don't cry anymore."

The shimmering withdrew, forming into a brilliant ball of light at about Sarah's heart, then shot off, so fast that Nan couldn't follow it. Grey pulled in her wings, and Sarah shook her head a little, then regarded Katherine with a particularly measuring expression before coming back to her chair and sitting down.

"Out of the mouths of babes, Katherine," Mem'sab said quietly, then looked up at Karamjit. "I think you and Selim should take the girls home now; they've had more than enough excitement for one night."

Karamjit bowed silently, and Grey added her own vote. "Wan' go back," she said in a decidedly firm tone. When Selim brought their coats and helped them to put them on, Grey climbed right back inside Sarah's, and didn't even put her head back out again.

They didn't have to go home in a cab, either; Katherine sent them back to the school in her own carriage, which was quite a treat for Nan, who'd had no notion that a private carriage would come equipped with such comforts as heated bricks for the feet and fur robes to bundle in. Nan didn't say anything to Sarah about the aftermath of the seance until they were alone together in their shared dormitory room.

Only then, as Grey took her accustomed perch on the headboard of Sarah's bed, did Nan look at her friend and ask—

"That last—was that—?"

Sarah nodded. "I could see him, clear as clear, too." She smiled a little. "He must've been a horrid brat at times, but he really wasn't bad, just spoiled enough to be a bit selfish, and he's been—learning better manners, since."

All that Nan could think of to say was—"Ah."

"Still; I think it was a *bit* rude of him to have been so impatient with his Mother," she continued, a little irritated.

"I 'spose that magic-man friend of yours is right," Nan replied, finally. "About what you c'n do, I mean."

"Oh! You're right!" Sarah exclaimed. "But you know, I don't think I could have done it if Grey hadn't been there. I thought if I ever saw a spirit I'd be too scared to do anything, but I wasn't afraid, since she wasn't."

The parrot took a little piece of Sarah's hair in her beak and preened it.

"*Wise* bird," replied Grey.